Ready for the Defense

WhoooDoo Mysteries
A division of
Treble Heart Books
1284 Overlook Dr.
Sierra Vista, AZ 85635-5512
http://www.trebleheartbooks.com

Printed and Published in the U.S.A.

ISBN: 978-1-932695-70-0

Thank you for choosing
a
WhoooDoo Mysteries
Dramatic Suspense

Ready for the Defense

Mike Langan

WhoooDoo Mysteries

a Division of

Treble Heart Books

Dedication

For my three girls.

T he last case I'll ever try ended in a whopping judgment. Against me.

Things had started off innocently enough. I was in Small Claims Court, representing the firm's cleaning woman, Marita, in a suit against her lying abusive brother, Jorge. She wanted back the five grand she'd scraped together and lent him for a "coyote" to smuggle his wife and kids up from Nuevo Loredo. I was doing this pro bono, which meant Marita was getting what she paid for. The gallery was packed with DC's unemployed and unemployable, waiting for their day in court, their chance to nail the ex-landlord who'd kept their security deposit, the auto mechanic who'd charged them for repairs he hadn't made, or the dry cleaner who'd lost their best velvet sweatsuit. None of them had a lawyer, except Marita.

What's more, she had evidence. So far I'd introduced four exhibits: a letter from Jorge in San Antonio to Marita in DC begging for the loan, a Western Union receipt recording the transfer, a second letter from Jorge promising to pay Marita back as soon as he moved to DC, and a third letter from Jorge's wife in Mexico to Marita asking where in the world Jorge was. Then I'd pulled out the last exhibit, a stack of credit card statements, and I asked Jorge where he'd gotten the money for all the stuff.

"What stuff?" Jorge said.

"Let's see," I said. "An emerald necklace your wife never received, a membership to a 'gym' convicted of being a front for selling steroids, and an apartment full of expensive exercise equipment. Tread mill, stair climber, home gym. There's also the boxing gear: heavy bag, speed bag, double-end bag. I could go on."

Jorge just ducked and jabbed. "You think I write these?" he said, waving the letters.

"Are you denying it?"

"You *mamom*."

"Excuse me?"

"How you say, a sucker."

"Your defense is I'm mistaken?"

"For believing my sister. *La puta*."

Marita gasped. Although I didn't speak Spanish, I had a pretty idea what the word meant.

"Objection," I said, "nonresponsive."

The judge's head was down, his fingertips supporting his forehead, his hand shielding eyes which were, no doubt, closed. He was pushing mandatory retirement and had missed his noon nap.

"He no listening," Jorge said.

I raised my voice. "Motion to strike."

Jorge laughed. "Who you gonna strike? You skinny arms."

There was some laughter from the peanut gallery.

"Motion for sanctions," I said to the judge.

"I sanction you," Jorge said. "Pop, right in the nose."

He rammed his fist into a flattened palm. More laughter.

A string of drool dripped from the corner of the judge's mouth. The scales of justice were going to need a nudge.

I smiled at Jorge and leaned closer to him, lowering my voice. "From what I hear, you couldn't punch a hole in a donut."

"What you say?"

"That you talk a big game out of the ring, but when you step through the ropes you go down like a *puta*."

The laughter stopped. Jorge was on his feet now, starting to climb out of the witness box. I stood my ground, not believing he would do it.

But he did it, all right.

He crossed the room to counsel's table, and I went down under a torrent of fists. A fairly impressive show of skill on his part, I have to admit. Although I was waiting for him, I didn't even see the first blow. It took three court security officers to pry him off me.

I picked up my glasses, popped a lense back in, and took a good look at Jorge. He was writhing on the ground, face red, sputtering Spanish at me. *Leguleyo! Bastardo! Muerto!* I licked my bloody lip and turned to the interpreter, the cute single one I'd been glad to draw from the roster, until now.

"What did he say?" I said.

"He doesn't care for lawyers so much."

"Did he threaten to kill me?"

"When he's through with you, if you're lucky."

"Don't act so worried."

"I'm trying not to make a scene." She was filing a fingernail.

"How do I look?" I said.

"Skinny."

"Want to buy me dinner?"

I'd decided things couldn't get any worse, but before I could add rejection to the day's accomplishments my cell phone rang, rousing the judge. He cracked his gavel.

"No telephones in my courtroom. How many times do I have to tell you people? Bailiff, cuff the culprit."

The officers, who were sitting on Jorge, looked back at me.

"You heard the judge," I said. "Cuff the culprit."

I shouldered my way through the gallery, stepped into the hall, and took out my phone. It was my boss, Mac.

"Hammerin' Hank," he said with more than a trace of sarcasm. "How's your first trial?"

"Better than expected, actually," I said, "and it's not my first."

"The first one I'm not holding your hand through. Is it over already?"

"I guess you could say we're on a break."

"You gonna win?"

"Does our malpractice insurance cover fines?"

He chuckled. "When you get out of jail, and you're done threatening to appeal to the Supreme Court, hustle back to the Bat Cave. Commissioner Gordon called."

—*Chapter 2*

"Have I got a girl for you," my mother said, when I got back to my desk.

"What's wrong with this one?" I said, scrolling through the Federal Election Campaign Act online. The statute was long and nearly incomprehensible, which made it like almost every other statute I'd ever read.

"Why does there have to be something wrong with her?"

"Let's briefly review your last three referrals."

"Don't talk like a lawyer, Hank."

"Bachelorette number one, a cute legislative assistant to an Ohio congressman. Exceptionally fashionable and well-dressed, then I find out why. Open *Roll Call* one morning and see she's pled guilty to stealing her roommate's credit card and going on a ten-grand shopping spree."

"Everyone makes mistakes."

"Bachelorette number two, a tortured poet. Writes me a love sonnet after the second date then joins the Peace Corps before the third."

"She'll be back in two years."

"Bachelorette number three, a lesbian psychology student who was trying out men as an experiment. Only problem was she didn't tell her girlfriend."

"There's nothing wrong with being gay. Miriam Feldmeyer's son Chaz is going to have his own show on Fox, *Closet Queen.* It's about helping brave men come to terms with their true selves. Such a nice boy, Chaz, and a snazzy dresser. New York's not too far from DC, you know."

"Mom?"

"Yes?"

"I'm not gay."

"What a relief. I was worried I would have to paint your room some exotic color, like fuchsia or chartreuse. We'd have to replace the rugs upstairs, and then redo the wallpaper in the hall, and then the drapes in the living room, and then there goes the house's resale value. We'd never afford a place in West Palm."

"You sound stressed," I said. "I mean, even more than usual."

"It's my migraines. A lonely son and a herniated disc I've learned to live with, but I draw the line at having white hot pokers stuck in my eye. They're killing me."

"Is there anything I can do?"

"You can stop being a burden. You can stop making me worry."

"I don't know if anyone can do that."

"Don't be disrespectful."

"I'm going to be fine."

"Do you go to synagogue? Church even?"

"Sometimes."

"Your father's congregation is praying for you."

I squeezed my eyes shut and groaned. "The whole congregation?"

"They have a candle in your honor, out in the vestibule, beside the box for the Rwandan relief fund."

"Please stop."

"I won't rest until you find a nice girl."

"You used to deny you cared."

"I confess, I want my only child to be happy."

"The prospect of grandchildren has never crossed your mind."

"I'd settle for one, preferably a girl, but I know you can't control such things, unless you adopt, which is getting harder and harder lately, what with all those rules the Chinese have started imposing. Are you still taking that antidepressant? I know it's unfair, but they don't like that."

"Would you stop? I'm only thirty-two."

"Your father and I had your brother by twenty-two."

I tried to ignore this reference to Grady, telling myself it was an innocent statement of fact. Like the fact I was a failed teacher who had strayed from God's wisdom and light, and was living alone in the center of betrayal and corruption, helping common criminals go free. I broke the pregnant silence by saying, "You want to know why I don't have a steady girlfriend?"

"You actually know the answer?"

"You ever try telling a union president who's about to be indicted that you didn't have time to read the box of files seized from union headquarters last night because you were waiting in line for a table at Pizza Paridiso before catching the late show of some stupid chick flick at the Uptown Theater?"

"You're talking gibberish again, dear."

"Like right now, I'm supposed to be on my way to the Mall in shorts and a T-shirt so I can play softball and meet my buddy's sister. She's looking for a frustrated writer who shares her love of reality TV and her fear of people in Halloween costumes."

"Your soul mate."

"Except I have to do some rush research before a big meeting with a new client."

"Can't you tell him you have plans?"

"It's a her, and I can't tell her 'I have plans.' She's a senator."

"Which one? What did she do? Is it Hillary?"

"I have to go."

It was a line I used a lot with my mom, but this time it was true. Mac was standing in my doorway.

"Nice face, Fisher," he said, grinning at my swollen lip and black eye. "So help me, your knuckles better be bloody."

Chapter 3

I admit, I'm no superhero. But Mac was another story.

Six foot five, on the wrong side of three hundred pounds, John Paul MacPherson could carry a keg of Guinness on his shoulders, two when he was sober. To strangers, he was the grumpy green giant who parked his can on two bar stools at The Dubliner from dawn 'til dark every St. Patrick's Day, rising only to pick a fight or hit the head. To his parents and his priest, he was John Paul. To his seven brothers and sisters, he was JP. To me and the other lawyers in DC, he was Big Mac.

Mac saved my life at the end of my first year of law school when I was twenty-seven years old, already a hundred grand in debt from grad school in English, and still clueless about what I wanted to do when I grew up. It seemed high-powered law firms weren't in the market for average law students who had spent three years teaching teenagers what the green light means in *The Great Gatsby*. The day after Mac had lectured my class on appellate arguments, I was sitting in his office, my résumé shaking in my hand. The following Monday I was his law clerk, and three years later, as I sat across from him in a limo for the very last time, I was his associate.

But I was still his student.

"There are three rules of practicing criminal defense," Mac told me as he fanned out a stack of hundreds. "Get paid up front, never give the money back, and if someone has to go to jail don't let it be you."

I rolled my eyes. Our new client, Senator Victoria Serling, had sent over a new black Lincoln Town Car limousine and an unmarked envelope, two things that always put Mac in an advice-giving mood.

"Can you believe they pay us to do this shit?" he said. He lit a cigar. "Look at these vents. They suck the smoke right up. What's that scent? Pine?"

"We haven't done anything yet. That's our retainer."

"Relax, Fisher. Have some peanuts."

"Those are cashews."

"Some wine then."

"That's Dom Perignon."

"Who? Hey, remember that Christmas bonus I owe you?" He counted out ten bills.

"I can't take that. What about taxes?"

"Why do you think I asked for cash?"

I tried to give him the disapproving look my father used to give me on Sunday mornings back in Cleveland when I would march into the sacristy in my acolyte's robe and give my two weeks' notice.

The limo slowed for a light at the corner of 9th and Pennsylvania Ave. On one side of the street loomed the J. Edgar Hoover Building, guarded by a row of fluttering flags. On the other side sat a black woman wearing a torn wool coat, her back against a utility box. Between her legs sat a little girl holding a sign that read *GOT MONEY?*

Mac lowered his window and said, "Hey, lady."

The woman looked over her shoulder then stood up, tugging the girl's hand.

"You drink?" Mac said. "Do drugs?"

She stepped back and raised her hand. "I don't want any."

"I'm not offering."

She blinked. "I've been clean a year."

"No shit. Congrats."

"Her father beat me."

"Sounds like an asshole. No offense, kid."

The girl looked up at him coolly.

"You got any family, you know, who'll take you in?" Mac said to the woman.

"Got a brother in San Diego. He's in the Navy."

Mac held the ten bills out the window. "I'm a lawyer. I tell people what to do when they're in trouble. My advice to you, buy two plane tickets. This city's no place to be if you're poor *and* without family. The people here suck."

Pedestrians schlepping home from work turned their heads toward the homeless woman being offered cash from a limo.

"Go on," Mac said, "it's from Uncle Sam."

The woman folded the bills and picked up her daughter as we pulled away.

"Happy, Robin Hood?" Mac said.

"I thought you're in a thirty percent tax bracket," I said.

"What're you, my fucking accountant? I got three mouths to feed, not including yours."

I liked to think I pulled my weight around the office, but I let that one go, seeing as Friday was payday. We turned southeast on Pennsylvania Avenue, and over Mac's shoulder rose the white dome of the Capitol Building. Familiar but faded, like the backdrop of last semester's school play. Mac's pocket beeped and he pulled out a cell phone.

"Hey, Pen," he said. "Milk, eggs, peanut butter, got it. Don't wait for me. Just leave it on the stove. No potatoes."

He glanced at his stomach.

Convinced he should still be able to fit into his high school boxing trunks, Mac was always on a diet. Atkins, Zone, South Beach, Sugar Busters. He'd tried them all. His newest kick was something called the *Russian Air Force Diet*, which consisted of nothing but rations from a Cold War Siberian survival pack: coffee, saltine crackers, Spam, sardines. The only thing he'd lost so far on it was his temper. In addition to horrible breath, it gave him a blood-sugar level so low he tripped over it...when he wasn't shouting at me. I thought he was going to pop the vein in his temple a few days before, when he'd caught me pouring sugar into his Sweet 'N Low packets.

"Who?" he said to Penny, "Hank? Yeah, he's here, wearing a shit-eating grin. You think he'd never been in a fancy car before. And no, I'm sure I didn't ruin his evening. Kid would still be back at the office with his nose in a book if I hadn't invited him along. You do, huh?" He lowered the phone. "Penny wants to fix you up with our new babysitter. Just got her masters in child psychology. Smart. And sweet." He pinched the phone between his cheek and shoulder and cupped his hands in front of his chest. According to this juvenile gesture, either the girl wore a Double D cup or her day job was in a side show at the fair.

I shook my head and turned on the mini-TV, trying to act my age.

Penny had recently decided I needed a wife. One night, over pizza and three-too-many beers, she'd cogently presented the advantages of marriage. Companionship, comfort, and stability. Then, the next morning, she'd started desperately throwing at me every unmarried female she could find. Her little sister Fran, her daughter Clare's first-grade teacher, the sales clerk from the local Barnes & Noble. No waitress in the greater-DC area was safe. I gave each of the matches the old college try, but for some reason none of the women liked me having to cancel our dates at the last moment.

Mac asked for his son Tommy, who had just lost a little league baseball game. As a consolation prize Mac promised to take him to the big tournament in a few weeks, the NCAA Division I men's lacrosse championship at the University of Maryland. I pictured them at the game, Tommy stuffing his face with nachos, Mac sneaking him sips of Bud Light and teaching him to cuss at the refs. I had to admit, the wife-and-family thing didn't seem half bad.

On the limo's TV appeared a copper-skinned woman wearing a white bandanna over her mouth and holding the shrouded body of a child. Across the bottom of the screen flashed the words *Mystery Virus*. I turned up the volume.

"A seven-year-old girl is dead today in India's northwestern city of Chandigarh. She was admitted to the Post Graduate Institute of Medical Education last night with a high fever, severe chest pains, and muscle fatigue. Even though doctors gave her antiviral medicine, her condition rapidly worsened. She is the hundredth victim of the virus, which was first observed a week ago in the Pakistani town of Harappa. Pakistani authorities have identified the virus as a possible biowarfare agent, after discovering vials and syringes in an evacuated terrorist training camp near Harappa. They are working with the American military to try to track down the terrorists. Meanwhile, Indian authorities have dispatched a team from the National Institute of Communicable Diseases to assist Pakistani authorities in investigating the progression of the virus, which is believed to be transmitted through casual contact. Employees of the World Health Organization have started calling the virus Harappa."

Harappa.

"Ought to do wonders for the Pakistani-Indian conflict," Mac said, snapping his phone shut. "Makes the bird flu look like a head cold. Where do they come up with that shit?"

"I think scientific names usually come from Greek and Latin prefixes, suffixes, and roots. Nicknames usually come from the place of discovery, the name of the discoverer, or the type of symptoms."

He looked at me with sardonic amusement, like the time I'd fixed my glasses with a Band-Aid. "Not the name, professor, the disease. I mean, how does stuff like that get created?"

I didn't answer, not wanting to appear any geekier than usual. I turned off the TV. "How come you never invite me to lacrosse games?"

"I don't let you crawl into bed with me during thunderstorms either. Want me to wipe Desitin on your fanny and read you a story?"

I was sorry I raised the subject. "Speaking of fiction, here's the Senate Ethics Manual you asked for."

Mac snubbed out his cigar. "Fucking thing took up a ream of paper."

"Why did she bump up our meeting, anyway?"

He popped the lock on his briefcase. "She's in committee all day tomorrow. Only reason she can do it tonight is she got out of some benefit dinner, only had to go to the cocktail party."

"She tell you anything else about this tax problem?"

"She didn't want to talk about it over a cell phone. Said she was worried about"—he looked over his shoulder at the chauffeur, who sat behind a pane of glass— "about someone intercepting the signal."

"Because of a tax code violation?"

"What're you laughing at, Fisher? She's nervous. Said she was being framed. Political espionage or something."

"Doesn't that only happen in movies?"

"Then it should be right up your alley. A real whodunit."

"What's that supposed to mean?"

"It means you practice law more like Sherlock Holmes than Oliver Wendell Holmes."

What was he talking about? I had just battled Jorge in court, literally. But setting aside skirmishes against unrepresented litigants in Small Claims Court, I guess I knew what Mac meant. During the recent bribery prosecution of our client, Vincent Bustamonte, I'd learned a key Department of Labor witness had bought a new home computer. So I bought his old computer off eBay, hired an expert to restore the backup memory on its hard drive and uncovered a *deleted* e-mail message. The e-mail enabled Mac to elicit, on cross-exam, an admission that the bribery allegation had been a politically motivated ruse to destroy our client's union presidency. Okay, so I didn't make an impassioned closing argument that pulled the twelfth juror from the brink of conviction. But hey, an acquittal is an acquittal, right?

Still, I found myself avoiding Mac's eyes, staring instead at groomed lawns and flowering dogwoods. At the top of Capitol Hill, we stopped at a light. To the right, half-way down the block, lay the steps to Supreme Court, where I'd watched Mac argue, and win, a pro bono case the year before. I recalled him standing there matching wits with the big guys. At the time, I'd been surprised he'd had it in him. Now, nothing he did surprised me. As I contemplated whether I'd ever be half the lawyer Mac was, the chauffeur turned left onto First Street, towards Union Station. On our right stood the Dirksen Senate Office Building, a city block in length and masked in marble. The chauffeur pulled over at the corner of First Street and C Street, short of another light.

Up ahead, C Street looked like an Army checkpoint, a half-dozen concrete-potted plants forming a one-lane entrance and a one-lane exit, with a guard booth in between. Beyond the booth's right parking gate arm stood a massive bronze door, the visitor's entrance to Dirksen. The booth's left arm lifted, letting out a silver Lexus, its driver lifting an ivory hand.

"Sorry for busting your balls," Mac said. "Pre-game nerves. Just do me a favor."

"You got it, boss."

"Don't pull any private eye crap this time. This once, just be a lawyer. No offense, kid."

Who would take offense at the implication that the previous five years of one's life had been a giant waste of time? "No sweat."

Mac got out of the limo and buttoned his gray double-breasted suit. As I did the same, a man called to Mac from across C Street. He wore a charcoal suit and had slick silver hair, a long sharp nose, a square cleft chin and a clenched-toothed grin. A genteel Kirk Douglas. He extended his hand, a gold Cartier on his wrist, glinting in the waning sun.

"Lawrence Marshall," he said, "Vicky's better half."

Mac introduced us, even though *I* was the one who'd told *him* about Dr. Marshall back at the office, how he'd founded a small but wildly successful pharmaceutical company. Behind him appeared Senator Serling, just as she looked on TV. She wore a slim blue suit and had short blonde hair, soft high cheekbones and smart brown eyes. She was indeed, as one pundit had once quipped, a corporate version of Jessica Lange. She flashed Mac a hydrogen-peroxide smile.

"Sorry to tear you away from the gym. This must be Mr. Fisher. For someone so clever, he certainly is handsome. Even with a black eye."

I took her hand by the fingertips, resisting the impulse to bow. "I'm handsome...I mean, Hank."

"And nervous. How charming."

Dr. Marshall reached up and clapped Mac on the shoulder. "Recognized you from the news. Great job getting Bustamonte off."

"It's easy when they're innocent."

"Innocent, right." Dr. Marshall jerked his thumb toward Senator Serling. "That's why I told her to hire you. You're a true believer."

Mac looked back at the limo, which still sat at the corner, waiting for the light to turn green. "I'd give you a finder's fee, but it doesn't look like you're missing any meals."

"You never know. My other car's a Chevy."

Mac didn't laugh; he drove a Blazer.

Senator Serling glanced over her shoulder down First Street, two perfect worry lines appearing on her forehead. "We probably shouldn't stand here."

Mac craned his neck. "Don't tell me you're that worried about eavesdroppers."

The senator continued to stare over her shoulder.

Dr. Marshall put an arm around her. "Darling, you're imagining things. No one would attack a senator on Capitol Hill."

"Hold on," Mac said. "*Attack*? I thought this was about a tax violation."

"That's why I wanted to talk to you," the senator said. "It's a little more complicated than I first thought."

"How much more complicated?" he said, and I knew he was thinking of increasing her retainer.

As she started to explain, Mac listened intently, knitting his eyebrows and cocking his head. Then his face lit up, and he shoved his briefcase into Dr. Marshall's chest, sending him flying off his feet. At first I thought he was reacting to something the man had done. Then I heard Mac cry, "Car!" and I saw him lunge at the senator, whose head was turned away from the impending blow.

Over my shoulder an engine roared. I whirled around just in time to see an SUV bearing down on us: headlights dead, vertical grill slats looking like teeth. The passenger-side mirror clipped my shoulder, spinning me round. Before I hit the ground, I caught a glimpse of Mac flying over the SUV, his briefcase bouncing off the hood.

The pages of the Senate Ethics Manual sprang into the air.

Sheets of paper settled over Senator Serling, who lay on the other side of C Street. Next to her, Dr. Marshall reached for his hip and groaned. In the middle of the street lay Mac, one arm by his side and the other bent over his head. I opened my mouth but couldn't draw any air. I rolled to my side and caught a better look at the SUV, which had twisted to a stop between a potted plant and the limo.

It was a Grand Cherokee, fire-engine red, Virginia plates. The driver was olive-skinned, mid-fifties, with a black cap, black sunglasses and black gloves. The sleeves of his windbreaker reached only his forearms. Something dark and small clung to the underside of his arm. The Cherokee's gears clanked and its wheels spun, pulling it back towards Mac.

A security guard appeared and drew his pistol. "Stop!"

The Cherokee screeched to a halt, its engine growling.

The guard leveled his pistol at the cracked windshield. "Engine off and hands on the wheel!"

A sheet of paper skittered across the ground and the guard's eyes dropped to Senator Serling. The Cherokee lurched forward, tires squealing. The guard stepped into the street, spread his legs and fired the pistol. Pops filled the air. Glass shattered behind the Cherokee, which sped away down First Street, smoke from its tires mingling with smoke from the pistol.

Mac lay there, his socks a shade darker than his pants. Between us, one of his Italian dress shoes stood upright in the street, laces tied.

"Get an ambulance!" I shouted at the guard.

"On its way. Stay still."

Stay still? A halo of blood spread out around Mac's head. I reached out to stop it, but there was nothing I could do. I stood up and staggered into the intersection. Through the smoke, I could see down First Street. The Cherokee was passing cars stopped at a red light. It turned left onto Constitution Ave., where it disappeared. I couldn't believe it. A man had just run down Mac and no one was going to stop him.

I ran to the limo and flung open the door. I grabbed the lapels of the chauffeur and rocked back on my heels, using every ounce of my hundred-and-seventy pounds as leverage. The chauffeur stumbled out of the car. I slid behind the wheel, threw the engine into gear and tried a U-turn. A cab approached the intersection from the opposite direction, its driver rubbernecking at the scene outside his window. I foolishly calculated I could complete the U-turn and jump ahead of him before he passed me. Long story short, always fasten your seat before you decide to play Magnum, PI.

When the limo came to a stop, I stared at the new white spider web covering the limo's windshield and touched my forehead, which was wet with blood. That's when things on Capitol Hill really started to spin.

* * *

When I was eight, on summer vacation with my family in Vermont, I went swimming in a bend of the Mad River, which didn't seem so mad to me. As I gaped at the mountains above, something tugged at my feet and suddenly I was under water. I couldn't find the surface. No matter which way I turned, there was nothing but darkness. My lungs started to burn and water filled my nose. I was on my way to a watery doom when I felt something fumble around my head. It was a hand, it turned out, belonging to my older brother Grady. He grabbed my hair pulled me up into the light.

This is what I was thinking when I regained my senses. Someone flashed a light in my eyes. There was a voice and the crinkle of plastic. I squinted in its direction. A face appeared, behind which hung a white curtain. The face had smooth bronze skin, large brown eyes, and pink pouting lips. The woman's long dark hair rested on the shoulders of a white coat. Over the coat's breast pocket, in red cursive letters, were stitched the words "Dr. Amelia Fuentes." I tried to lift my head.

"Lie still, Mr. Fisher," she said. "That thing on your neck is a splint, in case you've suffered any trauma. That thing on your arm is another splint to protect the IV so we have a fluid route in case you go into shock." She waited then said, "This is when you're supposed to ask what happened."

"ZBK six one one three," I said.

She stuck a scope in my ear. "Are we hallucinating again?"

I repeated the license plate number.

A man popped his head over her shoulder. "State, make and model?"

The man was about fifty, with short gray hair and coffee-colored skin, and he held a tiny pen and notepad. I told him, and he ripped off a sheet of paper and swept open the curtains. A uniformed police officer, who had been leaning against a wall with his thumbs under his utility belt, straightened up.

Dr. Fuentes shined the penlight in my eyes again. "Guess I don't have to ask you what year it is."

"Where's Mac?"

She clicked off the light then held out a finger, which I followed with my eyes. "Down the hall. Critical condition but stable."

I tried to sit up, propping myself up on my elbow. "I have to see him."

"The only thing you have to do right now is lie still. There's nothing you can do for him we're not already doing."

I tried to push her arm away.

"I don't care what kind of heroics you pulled back there. You're no match for a sleep-deprived intern hopped up on Powerbars and caffeine."

She was right. I fell back onto the gurney.

"Guess I don't have to ask if you can wiggle your toes either." She took the splint off my neck.

"What happened to him?"

"Broke six ribs." She rolled up the sleeve of my free arm, folding over the blood-stained cuff. "One of them caused a tension pneumo."

"English."

"A tension pneumothorax. A hole in the lung, making it collapse. Paramedics inserted a plastic hose between his ribs and rushed him here."

"Which is where?"

"GW."

"Wasn't Howard closer?"

Dr. Fuentes gave me a look which I couldn't quite read. It was a cross between *How dare you?* and *Don't you know?* "The senator's husband insisted on GW. Her niece is a doctor here."

"I didn't know EMTs took requests from victims," I said.

"We happen to have some of the best cardiac doctors in the country."

"I know. This is where Reagan was rushed after the Hinkley thing."

"You can second guess it, but it was the right call, bringing your friend here. In the trauma room, while Dr. Singh was examining him, your friend went into cardiac arrest. The collision had bruised his heart. Dr. Singh saved his life."

"So he's going to be okay?"

"I told you, he's in good hands."

I'd heard that before, at the Cleveland Clinic, right after Grady and I had been pried out of my mother's Vista Cruiser. I pictured Mac down the hall, on a table surrounded by strangers, his shirt ripped open, an exit hatch for his soul. How could this have happened so fast? Why wasn't it me lying there? Dr. Fuentes wrapped a blood pressure cuff around my arm, fastening it with Velcro.

"Don't you have nurses do this stuff?"

She squeezed the rubber bulb until my fingers tingled. "We're a little short staffed right now. Every hypochondriac in the city suddenly thinks he's contracted a super virus."

The man with the notepad returned. He wore a blue blazer that strained against his broad shoulders. Plain white shirt, solid red tie, crisp ironed khakis. "Mr. Fisher," he said, "do you remember anything about the driver?"

"Don't MPD detectives introduce themselves anymore?"

"It's Lieutenant Detective, actually."

"You guys still got those cool badges with the Capitol on them?"

The man took out his wallet. His name was Calvin Mills, and his shield was legit. Gold plated and shaped like an eagle on top, with sides that curved out then came to a point at the bottom. On its face was the image of the Capitol Building, above which were the words *Metropolitan Police* and *DC*, and below which was his badge number, 704.

"Now about that driver—"

"I'm flattered, Lieutenant. There must be, what, three or four sergeant detectives you could've sent. You're from the First District, right?"

When I was in law school, I'd helped Mac represent a teenager who was suing a cop for brutality. I'd learned the First District covered a huge chunk of DC: from L Street to the north, to 17th Street to the west, to Massachusetts Ave. to the east, down to the intersection of the Potomac and Anacostia Rivers to the south. Most important, it covered the area surrounding the Capitol Complex. Mills stared at me with brown eyes magnified by a pair of steel-rimmed reading glasses.

"The reason I ask is I'm wondering where the Capitol Police are. Don't they have primary jurisdiction?"

"If you must know, the Capitol Police conceded jurisdiction."

"So quickly?"

"A member of the Senate's Select Committee on Terrorism was run down during an international terrorist attack."

"You mean that Harappa thing? How do you know it was part of a terrorist attack?"

"Don't you listen to the news? They found a bunch of equipment in an abandoned training camp in Pakistan. Microscopes, flasks, vials. All made in France. Name one good thing that country has ever done for us."

"France?" I said. I didn't understand how Harappa was the French's fault, but I was glad the guy was loosening up. "Other than save us during the Revolution, it gave us the Statue of Liberty and some pretty good stories, Jules Verne and Alexandre Dumas. Not to mention Camus and Sartre."

"Those existentialist guys? Thanks for nothing."

"What about Descartes?"

"I think therefore I am? Guy smoked too much cannabis. Me, I prefer Wittgenstein. Not that *Tractatus Logico-Philosophicus* garbage. I like the later stuff, when he stopped trying to relate words to the world and realized words relate only to other words, and when he said that most arguments result from disagreements about terms. What did he say? 'Philosophical problems arise when language goes on holiday.'"

"Shit happens when you're on vacation."

"Don't think I'm dumb just because I'm a cop."

"So, Detective, other than the fact there was a terrorist attack happening on the other side of the globe, what makes you think the hit-and-run was intentional?"

"You mean besides the fact the driver swerved into an oncoming lane to hit you, didn't brake hard enough to leave skid marks and sped off at gunpoint?"

"He could've sped off because he freaked. That's why they call it 'hit and run.' You got any more than that?"

"Look, who's doing the interview here? Stick to chasing ambulances and leave the detective work to the pros."

"Where'd you hear I was a lawyer?"

"I've done this three times now," Dr. Fuentes said, looking at the blood pressure gauge, "and I get a different reading each time. One of you is going to have to give."

I'd gotten about as far as I could, so I told Mills everything I remembered, starting with the arrival of the limo and ending with my loss of consciousness, but skipping over the purpose of our visit to the senator. When he stopped scribbling, he chewed on his pen cap.

"The driver look, you know, middle-eastern?"

Dr. Fuentes unwrapped the cuff and blood rushed into my hand, making it prickle.

"What do I look like, an anthropologist? I told you, he wore sunglasses and a baseball cap. Orioles, I think. I saw him only for a second."

"Fair enough." He put his notepad and pen in his pocket. "Oh, one more thing. Do you know why Mac had nine grand in cash on him?"

"Now my head is really starting to pound," I said. "Imitations of Columbo do that to me."

I had to admit, he had me. Telling him about the money meant telling him we represented Senator Serling, which was the same as telling him she'd committed a crime, once he figured out what sort of law Mac practiced. I shuddered at the thought. Mac would kill me. Telling Mills I couldn't answer because of my duty of confidentiality to the senator was the same as telling him we represented her. I knew I could've just lied, but I'd worked too hard for my license to practice to risk having it taken away. I covered my eyes with my hand and let out an audible sigh.

"Here." Dr. Fuentes offered me two Tylenol and cup of water.

"Isn't this what you give kids who fall off their skateboards?" She tapped out another pill.

"Thanks, this should definitely stop the blinding pain."

"Just be grateful you didn't get clocked as hard as the senator."

"What happened to her?"

"Intracranial hypertension."

"Again, Doc, English."

Mills exhaled sharply. Dr. Fuentes ignored him.

"High blood pressure in the skull. When the brain is injured, fluids accumulate, causing it to swell. If the pressure isn't relieved it can impair circulation, and push the brain against the bony edges of the skull. Either way it can kill tissue, causing permanent damage."

I wasn't looking for a primer on brain injuries, but I preferred Dr. Fuentes's medical-garble to Mills' questions. Besides, I found myself feeling more than a twinge of concern for the new client who thought I was clever, handsome and charming.

"What're you going to do?"

"We have a variety of options. Hyperventilation for one."

"Breathing into a bag?"

"Not exactly the medical procedure we follow but basically yes. Deeper and faster breathing helps keep carbon dioxide pressure in the blood below normal. If that doesn't work we use drugs to reduce swelling. Diuretics, steroids, osmotherapy."

I didn't want to know what osmotherapy was, but we were on a roll. Mills was shifting his weight from foot to foot, impatiently. "If drugs don't work?" I said.

"Then we operate. Drain excess fluids from the skull, but hopefully it won't come to that."

"How's her husband?"

"Bruised hip, otherwise back to his old crotchety self."

I looked at her, wondering how she knew him. Mills cleared his throat, like we'd cut in front of him in line at Dunkin' Donuts.

"I believe I've got a question pending, Mr. Fisher. Was the cash related to your visit to the senator? And while we're on the subject, why were you visiting the senator?"

I wanted to call a time out. I could punt and suggest Mills talk to Dr. Marshall, but I didn't want to subject the senator's husband to a similar sort of interrogation. I could fake a hand-off and say our visit was social, but as I said lying wasn't my specialty. Or I could fall on the ball and answer the purpose was confidential, but I figured the senator had enough trouble with intracranial whatever; she didn't need to arouse the suspicion of the police too. I laid my head back and turned to Dr. Fuentes.

"All this thinking. Can you please tell the lieutenant detective I'm too dizzy to talk right now?"

Mills stepped closer. "The lieutenant detective suggests you suck it up."

I looked up at Dr. Fuentes plaintively. She turned to Mills.

"I'm going to have to agree with him, Detective. I'm worried he may have a subdural hematoma."

"A pocket of blood in his brain? Give me a break, Doc. He doesn't even have any stitches. I've got a senator in critical condition and Mohammed Andretti tearing up Capitol Hill at the height of Cherry Blossom season. A tourist is gonna get killed."

"Sorry, Detective. I'm going to order an emergency MRI."

"You win, Doc." Mills turned to me. "We'll continue this interview after your head shrinks."

"I'll bring my résumé. Oh, and Detective?"

Mills stopped.

"Dr. Marshall is too dizzy to talk to you also."

"So he's your client too, huh?"

Technically he was right. Mac and I represented only the senator, but surely Dr. Marshall wouldn't talk to Mills if Mac and I didn't want him too. Besides I was too angry to admit the bluff. I kept my mouth shut and waited for Mills' footsteps to fade down the hall. Then I said, "Thanks, Doc."

"I'm taking this IV out. Hold this gauze here for a minute so you won't get a bruise. We try to accommodate the police to the extent the patients can bear it, especially in criminal investigations. But sometimes things get out of hand."

I flicked my fingers carelessly, as if brushing away a crumb. "He's just doing his job."

She lowered the side rail on the gurney and stepped back. "Well."

"No subdural hematoma?"

"You just have a mild concussion. Don't drag race any limos for a while."

"Don't you have to observe me or something?"

"We took a CAT scan while you were out. Came back negative. I'm supposed to get you a wheelchair, but from the way you fought to get out of bed I don't think you'd use it. You'll have to fill out some forms before you're discharged."

I nodded slowly, suddenly feeling guilty my injury wasn't worse. "Did someone call Penny?"

"Mrs. MacPherson?" said a nurse who had suddenly appeared. "She's in the waiting room. She asked for you. Her husband's gone into cardiogenic shock."

Dr. Fuentes turned to me. "That happens when the heart fails to propel enough blood to the body's vital tissues. Dr. Singh will use a cardiac drug to support heart function."

"Which way?" I said.

The nurse pointed, and I eased my legs over the side of the gurney, my feet feeling as heavy as ski boots. With Dr. Fuentes holding my elbow, I limped down a mauve-colored hall, my head thumping with each step. Along the way I passed two men with wires running from behind their ears to under their suit coats. Penny stood in the middle of an empty waiting room, a barrette holding back her long auburn hair, redness rimming her large dark eyes, and mascara streaking her cheeks.

"Oh, Hank."

I stepped back from her desperate embrace and led her to a gray couch.

"What did they tell you?" I said.

"That there was some sort of accident and he went into shock. What happened?"

When I finished telling her, she sat staring at the wall.

"Where're the kids?" I said.

"Fran took them."

"He's strong, you know."

She looked at me.

"He saved our lives," I said.

"The man cried at the end of *Moulin Rouge!*"

We shared a laugh.

A man wearing a lab coat came in, and Penny and I stood up.

"Mrs. MacPherson, I'm Dr. Singh."

Penny waited.

The young doctor held a clipboard to his chest like it was a life preserver. Behind him appeared a man wearing a black suit, a Roman collar and a grave expression. Leave it to the Catholics to spoil a good laugh.

P enny stared at the back of Dr. Singh's clipboard as he explained that Mac had died. We listened, stunned. Finally the priest stepped forward.

"I'm Father Miguel Rodriguez, from Chaplain Services."

After a moment Penny said, "I'd like to see him."

"Of course. Is this gentleman a relative?"

"Yes."

I ignored the lie and followed Father Rodriguez down the hall. In the recovery room, Mac lay near the window, a clean green sheet covering him from neck to ankle, his size-thirteen feet dangling over the edge of the bed. His hands lay at his sides, half-open and turned up, like he was waiting to give blood. I wanted to go over and nudge him awake. I couldn't believe he was dead.

Penny was too quiet. I put an arm around her and guided her to the side of the bed. Father Rodriguez took his post at the other side. As Penny stared speechless at her husband, the priest removed from his suit jacket a long purple stole, which he draped around Mac's neck. Then he bowed his head and waited, giving her a moment. Outside, the lavender sky grew dark.

Next came the praying. Father Rodriguez prayed for the happy repose of Mac's soul. He prayed for the comfort, support and strength of Mac's family. He even led us in the Lord's Prayer. I took Penny's hand and placed it on Mac's shoulder, and mid-way through the Hail Mary that followed she joined us. When we finished, Father Rodriguez made the sign of the cross over Mac's body.

"Grant eternal rest unto John, Oh Lord, and let perpetual light shine upon him."

I took one more look at Mac, his closed eyes, his pale skin, the short pink scar on his cheek. I remembered the day he'd gotten it, the January before.

We had just won a two-week jury trial in US District Court and had gone to the Irish Times to celebrate, which to Mac meant getting leave-your-credit-card-at-the-bar, drop-your-beer-on-the-floor, forget-where-you-parked-your-car drunk. The bender had ended when we'd slipped on a patch of ice while hailing a cab. I don't know why I'd come away from the fall uninjured and Mac had needed stitches. I guess he'd had farther to fall.

When we reached Penny's home in Chevy Chase, Tommy and Clare were waiting in the driveway in pajamas and bare feet. Behind them stood Fran.

"I tried to keep them inside," she said.

Penny picked up Clare with some effort. Dr. Singh had given her enough sedatives to bring down a horse. I picked up Tommy, who would soon be too big to carry. In the kitchen, the phone was off the hook.

"The reporters are vicious," Fran said, pulling back a chair for her sister. "They want to know if Senator Serling had gotten any death threats from terrorists. They want to know if Mac had any enemies. They want to know the names of his kids."

"They're just doing their jobs," said Penny, who used to work for *The Boston Globe*. She sat down, letting Clare slide into her lap. I put down Tommy, who rested his head against his mom's shoulder.

"Is Daddy really dead?" Clare said.

The MacPhersons' dog, a chocolate brown lab named Buster, came in through a hole in the kitchen door, stopped at Penny's feet and licked Clare's face.

"Yes," Penny said.

"Am I going to be a pawbearer?" Tommy said.

"Pallbearer. If you want."

"Can I see him?" Clare said.

"In a few days."

"After the autopsy?" Tommy said.

"Where did you hear that?"

"He stays up past his bedtime to watch reruns of *Law and Order*," Clare said.

"They show coroner's exams?"

"He's had a crush on Angie Harmon ever since *Agent Cody Banks*."

"Do not," Tommy said, shoving Clare.

"Do to," Clare said, shoving back.

The two fell silent, surprised their mom hadn't stopped them.

"Mom?" said Clare.

"Yes."

"Do we have to go to school tomorrow?"

"No."

Clare yawned. Penny started to stand, letting Clare wrap her arms around her mom's neck. Seeing that he was too much for his mom to carry, Tommy led her upstairs. Fran and I watched as

Penny tucked in the kids, then Fran took the bed in the guest room. I was left with the pull-out couch in the family room.

I lay awake, staring at the moonlight creeping across the room and listening to the sounds a house makes. The running toilet, the whirling dishwasher. Upstairs a door creaked, and the hallway floor moaned. I got up. From the bottom of the stairs I heard another door open. Tommy followed his sister into Penny's room. When he saw me he lifted his chin.

"My mom needs me."

"You're a good man," I said.

Early the next morning, Penny's father arrived from Boston. A widower, he seemed to know just what to do to comfort his little girl. I stuck around to help him plan the funeral, then I caught a ride to the Metro.

Back at the office, as I flipped through the pile of mail on my desk, I dialed my voicemailbox, which was full. Clients asking questions, friends offering condolences, reporters requesting interviews. I pushed *Delete, Delete, Delete.* The last message was from Detective Mills.

"Mr. Fisher, I was hoping—"

Delete. All hoping was temporarily stayed, by order of the court of last resort, pending the final appeal of Mac's soul. I called my parents and told them they could use my apartment while I stayed with the MacPhersons for a few days. *Are you all right?* my mother said. *You sound awful.* I was awful. I found Mac's life insurance policy and pension documents. Then I got some empty boxes from storage.

I started with his bookshelf. *Donnie Brasco: My Undercover Life in the Mafia. The Boys from New Jersey: How the Mob Beat the Feds. Busting the Mob: United States v. Cosa Nostra.*

Mac had been obsessed with wise guys like Lucky Luciano, Carlo Gambino, and Vito Genovese. He had every episode of *The Sopranos* on DVD, and had seen *The Godfather* twenty-nine times.

Reminders of him filled the rest of the office. Diplomas from Holy Cross and NYU. A photo of him as an Assistant US Attorney in the Southern District of New York when he still had a full head of hair, standing beside US Attorney General Aaron Weissman. A beat-up bowling pin from the DC Law Firm Bowling League, a gag prize for the highest handicap. It was white with gray nicks on its trunk, a red crown on its head and the words *Brunswick Flyer* across its chest. Over its heart lay a blue ribbon bearing the words *Budweiser & Gutterball LLP*.

I couldn't believe Mac and I would never embarrass ourselves in a bowling alley again. I couldn't believe some asshole had killed him. What's more, I couldn't believe the guy thought he could get away with it. I left the boxes on Mac's desk and got in my old Volkswagen, listening to the engine cough to life, trying to remember the route the chauffeur had taken.

Between a parking meter and a sawhorse hung a strand of yellow tape that read *CRIME SCENE—DO NOT CROSS*. The police were probably wrapping up interviews, having finished taking photos, drawing diagrams and collecting physical evidence. Just to be safe, I took out my sunglasses and put on my Indians cap. A uniformed officer chatted with a guard as I passed by.

Near Union Station I did a U-turn, this time without knocking myself out. I re-approached C Street from the other direction and pulled over. In front of the visitors' entrance to Dirksen stood a man talking to an attractive young woman with a government-ID around her neck. The man wore a brush cut, a white dress shirt whose neck size was too big, and a blue blazer whose sleeves covered his knuckles.

Mills' other sergeant detectives were probably at Union Station talking to cabbies. I didn't want to get out of my car and invite another interview. I rolled down my window and looked around, trying to find something out of the ordinary. Chalk silhouettes on the ground, check. Enormous potted plants in front of the guard booth, check. Tiny shards of glass in the middle of the street, check. The only thing that seemed unusual was the ground in front of my car, which was empty of debris. No candy wrappers, no chewing gum, not even a cigarette butt. Fascinating, except I wasn't sure what it meant.

I considered Mills' theory the hit-and-run was connected to the terrorist attack in Asia. It presented too many questions. How would the terrorists have known that Senator Serling would have been outside Dirksen at that particular moment? And how could you reconcile the disparity between the two means of attack, one of which was out of a TV melodrama and the other out of a science fiction novel? A better theory was the attack on the senator was connected to the tax violation. That was why she hired Mac to represent her, but that theory wasn't without problems. Who would try to frame her for a tax violation, and why would they want to kill her?

This raised a more pressing question: should I investigate the crime with or without Mills' help? Sharing information with Mills meant that I would benefit from the resources of the MPD, but it also meant that I would become a criminal defense lawyer who couldn't keep a secret, in other words, an out-of-work criminal defense lawyer. Currently I still represented the senator, since she had hired the Law Office of John P. MacPherson, a firm of which I was the sole remaining employee. If I could somehow continue to represent her in the tax matter, maybe I could find the motive for Mac's murder. Of course, that meant I would be defending a senator in a high-profile federal investigation all by myself, not exactly up my alley.

I wondered why I'd even come up here. Did I honestly expect to learn something from a crime scene that had already been cleaned up? I hadn't collected a single clue. Across the street, the police officer frowned at me. I noticed that to my right stood a street sign prohibiting parking without a permit. From the sign's staff fluttered a broken strand of yellow tape. It was odd the tape had extended across the street from where the limo had been. Unless...

As the officer crossed First Street toward me, I rolled up my window, frantically started my engine, then drove past him, struck by my own stupidity.

There was a clue.

T he door to the MacPhersons' back deck slid open, and into the family room stepped Dr. Fuentes, wearing a black dress and one of those large broad-rimmed hats.

"Doctor, you didn't have to come."

"It's Amelia, and I hope that wasn't your family you just left to come greet me."

I walked Amelia to the kitchen and introduced her to Mac's parents and my parents. As they chatted, I noticed that, at some point during the previous two years, my father had started to get old, wearing tortoise-shell bifocals instead of his oval gold-rimmed glasses, and a washed-out gray reverend's collar instead of a shiny white one. My mother hadn't changed, except for a little more makeup to hide a few wrinkles only she noticed. Seeing them wearing black, standing in the middle of a tearful crowd, was giving me flashbacks to an even darker time, so I volunteered to get people drinks. When I returned, Amelia slipped her arm through mine, and subtly guided me back into the living room.

"You look tired," she said.

"I don't know how they can do it," I said.

"You mean look at that album?"

"Mini-Mac crying in a pumpkin patch in his Batman costume. Middleweight Mac shadowboxing at the YMCA, where the black kids dubbed him the 'Thrilla in Vanilla.' Missed-me Mac mugging in front of his apartment building whose lobby had been shot up during his prosecution of Tony 'Two Fingers' Torelli."

"Sounds like quite a guy."

I managed a smile, not wanting to bring down the party. Out back, under a tent the size of a basketball court, Mac's cousins were all crowding around the open bar, ignoring the buffet table. It made me wish I was Irish.

"Sorry I missed calling hours," she said. "That was sweet, what you said about him at the church."

I shrugged. "I listened to my father do enough eulogies, growing up."

"Mac's parents must be grateful to have him to talk to."

"My parents lost a son when I was a kid."

I'm not exactly sure why I chose this particular moment to volunteer the most intimate of facts, but there it was.

"I'm sorry," she said.

So was I. Time to change the subject.

She stepped closer, reaching to touch my cheek. "Mind if I look how you're doing?" She peeled the bandage away from my forehead with careful fingers.

Suddenly I was back in middle school. "Umm, how's the senator?" I said.

"They couldn't lower the swelling in her brain, so they've put her into a coma."

"On purpose?"

"A barb coma. Barbiturates slow the metabolism in the brain. Once the blood vessels narrow, the swelling decreases."

"So she'll be okay?"

"There's a slight risk of brain damage. We won't know until she wakes up."

"Which will be when?"

"Five or six weeks."

"Weeks?"

She stepped back. "I try to think of it as an extended vacation. She'll come back a new person."

"What about Dr. Marshall?"

Amelia looked through the bay window to the front yard. Dr. Marshall, who was hobbling to a forest-green Bentley at the bottom of the driveway, brushed off his chauffeur's helping hand.

"He'll live," she said.

"Do you know him?"

"I thought so."

As the chauffeur opened the door, Detective Mills appeared and put a hand on it, blocking Dr. Marshall's entrance. That was my cue. I excused myself, then I bolted out the front door and down the driveway.

All three men turned to me in surprise, the chauffeur actually flinching. I guessed I'd made quite an impression a few days before. He seemed relieved when Dr. Marshall told him to get behind the wheel. Dr. Marshall placed the butt of his cane on the ground and pivoted toward me.

"Just came to pay my respects," he said. "Mac probably saved my life, you know."

I nodded, although there was no probably about it. I turned to Mills.

"Please don't tell me you're interrogating a witness at a funeral."

"This is just the reception, the part when all the micks get bombed. Actually, that could be any part."

"Since you like to question so much, maybe you won't mind answering some. What did you find when you ran that plate?"

Mills laughed. "Yeah, right," he said.

Dr. Marshall pivoted back and raised an eyebrow.

Mills sighed then said, "The plate was stolen from a Cadillac parked at Tyson's Corner a few hours before the accident. Belonged to a little old lady with blue hair. Lives at Eden Gardens, in the city. The Cadillac was clean. No witnesses, no prints. The Cherokee hasn't been recovered yet."

"The lady didn't happen to have a Senate parking permit, did she?"

"Now that's just the sort of question that tells me you revisited the crime scene."

"I'll take that as a no."

"Maybe I should make something clear to you, Mr. Fisher. This is the Detective Mills Show. Here's how it goes. I look for who killed Mr. MacPherson and you cooperate. If you don't, well, I'd hate to see a skinny white boy like you have to spend the night in a DC jail."

"Is that a threat?"

"Now there you go again, making this hard for me."

"That's my job, Detective. I hold up the constitutional hoops and you jump through them."

"This isn't a circus."

"Then why are you such a clown?"

That did it, settling a blanket of silence over the three of us.

Mills took off his glasses and pointed them at me. "I know you lost a friend. You have my sympathy, but watch yourself, kiddo."

"Look, call Dr. Marshall on Monday. He'll set something up with you then."

Dr. Marshall waited for Mills to get in a Chevy Impala across the street. Then he said, "I appreciate your help, but I can take care of myself."

"It's not you I'm trying to protect."

"Vicky doesn't need your help either. I'm going to find someone with some more experience."

"I guess that's your choice." Actually his authority to make that decision for the senator depended on whether she had granted him a rather broad power of attorney, including the power to conduct litigation. But it wasn't a stretch of the imagination to assume she had. Besides I didn't want to argue anymore.

"I'd also like Mac's firm to return the retainer she gave him," he said. "It was, after all, my money."

This was another matter. I didn't know what to say. I thought of Mac's second rule of practicing criminal defense.

Dr. Marshall grinned down at me, arching his shoulders. I put him in his early sixties, around my father's age.

"Look, Lawrence, can I give you some free advice?"

He guffawed. "Sure, Hank, now that we're on a first-name basis."

"Mills thinks there's a link between the hit-and-run and your wife's service on the Select Committee on Terrorism. To prove it he's going to examine her affairs. Interviews, subpoenas, the whole thing. Eventually he's going to find out about the tax violation. When that happens, things are going to get ugly. The FBI, the press, her political opponents. They're not going to stop digging up dirt just because she's in a coma. You need to find the man who was 'framing' her for the violation."

"What makes you think the tax set-up is connected to the hit-and-run?"

"We were meeting about the tax set-up, and the killer was waiting for us in an area of the street on which parking is prohibited without a permit."

"A ticket is hardly a concern for a man willing to murder."

"It's not the ticket that would've concerned him but being noticed by the Capitol Police as he waited for us to arrive. Either he had a parking permit or he knew the exact time of the meeting.

And since the Cherokee didn't have a parking permit, that leaves one conclusion."

"There's a leak in my wife's office?"

"Or outside her office." I glanced down at the chauffeur, who was still eying me fearfully.

"So the murderer could've learned of the meeting from you or Mac," Dr. Marshall said.

"We don't breach our clients' confidences," I said with some irritation. Then I remembered there was no *we* anymore. "Look," I said, "it's your call. I'm just saying your lawyer needs to do some digging."

"And I think that lawyer should be Hank," Amelia said, appearing by Dr. Marshall's side. "Aunt Vicky would want him to stay on the case."

Aunt Vicky?

"She was impressed with what he did for Bustamonte," she said.

"I didn't realize you two knew each other," Dr. Marshall said.

"Mr. Fisher put on quite a show the other day in the hospital. Mills seems to have met his match."

"There are more than enough lawyers in this town who can give Mills a run for his money."

"Each one you hire will be another person who knows about all of this. If he's a member of a firm, you can count on his secretary and associates knowing too. And if they know then their spouses will probably know. Hank, on the other hand, is a one-man show. No associates, no secretary, no wife."

No wife? No *life*. She was right. The question was, how did she know that?

Dr. Marshall mulled the issue over, then turned to me. "Okay, I'll keep your firm on to represent Vicky, but only to keep this Mills fellow from discovering the violation. After that, I'm dropping you and hiring a real lawyer. Don't forget that, until Vicky wakes up, I stand in her shoes. So, for all intents and purposes, *I'm* your client. You take orders from *me*, got it? I'm staying at Amelia's place in Georgetown. Meet me there on Monday morning at ten. Oh, and in case it's not clear to you. You're on the Lawrence Marshall Show now."

As he got in the car, Amelia squeezed my arm. "He likes you."

Then she slid in beside him, pulled the door shut and rode away.

When I got home that night, my front door was open and the doorjamb was cracked. Last time I checked, DC detectives didn't search Virginia apartments, especially without a warrant. I considered knocking on Mrs. Baumgartner's door and asking if I could use her phone or maybe crawl behind her couch. I decided against it. If there was nobody in my apartment, what good would calling the police do, other than give Mills a reason to poke around my life? I nudged the door open and felt for the light switch on the wall. What I found pissed me off more than any burglary.

Somebody had thrown a party in my apartment. Empty beer bottles ringed the surface of my coffee table, globs of chocolate ice-cream stained my couch, trays of half-eaten frozen pizzas stunk up my kitchen, and an open refrigerator door was spoiling my milk and orange juice. Ants had already made trails to various of the messes from an open window. Next to the window the liquor cabinet was bare. I found my vodka bottle and my tequila bottle standing empty on either side of my fish tank, at the top of which was floating little Nemo. I scooped him up and brought him to the bathroom, where I found another present...a toilet clogged with tissue paper.

Did the man have no shame?

After cleaning up and using a hammer and nails to repair the front door, I changed into my pajamas, turned off the lights and crawled under the covers. In the morning I would call Marita and see if Jorge had paid her a little visit too. For now I would try to inject some normality back into my life. I reached for a mystery novel on my night stand, *The Long Goodbye* by Raymond Chandler. I'd read some of his others: *Farewell, My Lovely*, *The Lady in the Lake*, *The Big Sleep*. For some reason I'd never read this one, and so far I liked it the best. Every night for a week, I'd looked forward to bed just so I could find out how Philip Marlowe was going to get himself out of this one. Tonight I was going to reach the end, and nothing was going to deprive me of that little pleasure, not even Jorge. But when I got to the last chapter, I couldn't believe it.

The jackass had ripped it out.

————————————————————————— *Chapter 7*

In the morning, I called Marita. Jorge had, indeed, visited her too, and unfortunately she had been home. I told her I had a meeting but would stop by afterward to bring her down to the police station. She was going to file a complaint and request a temporary protection order. She agreed without hesitating.

Dr. Marshall answered the front door of Amelia's townhouse wearing an apron that read *Chef of Staff*. Without a cane he led me down a long hall, favoring his good hip. We stopped at a large kitchen with skylights, hardwood floors, an island stove and a sectional couch. On a marble counter sat a pot of coffee and two trays of croissants. Beside them sat a spiral-cut ham and a pile of shaved Swiss cheese on wax paper.

Amelia finished washing her hands at the sink and turned around. "I'm packing some meals to give my mom relief from hospital food."

I was hoping her apron read *Kiss the Cook*, but instead it read *If You Don't Like My Cooking, Lower Your Standards.*

She wiped her hands on a dish towel and said, "Come here, let's have another look."

She lifted the bandage on my forehead. Her emerald eyes showed tiny flecks of gold. I could get used to these examinations. "Your doctor does good work."

"Looks like she can cook too."

"Eat at your own risk. Lawrence tells me my croissants are in the experimental phase."

Dr. Marshall motioned toward the croissants. "Not bad, given the ingredients. Twenty years of vaccinations and I can't eat squat. Peanuts, milk, eggs."

"At least it's nothing that tastes good," I said, assuming he was talking about vaccinations against diseases he was trying to cure. Harmless things like anthrax, plague and tularemia.

"I've lost half my sense of smell anyway. Not to mention the oils in my skin. Have to rub ointment on my face three times a day. Hell, my hair color returned only a few months ago. Bleached by that peroxide they spray in the air."

"As a disinfectant?"

"Don't encourage him," Amelia said. She poured me a cup of coffee and fixed me a plate, complete with raspberry jam. Despite the synthetic ingredients, the croissants were warm and flaky. A drop of what I hoped was margarine ran down my finger.

"How's your aunt?"

"Stable."

"And your mother?"

"She got here Thursday. She hasn't left my aunt's side."

"I'm sorry."

"At least I'm used to waiting for people to get better."

Dr. Marshall washed his hands. "Should we get started? Her shift begins in an hour, and I want to go in with her."

Amelia sat in the middle of the couch. I looked at Dr. Marshall. He looked at Amelia.

"Oh, I'm not leaving," she said. "Aunt Vicky told me everything before the accident."

Dr. Marshall's expression softened. "I'm afraid it wasn't an accident, dear."

"All the more reason you need me. Maybe I can give you some insight into all of this."

Dr. Marshall seemed to struggle for the right words. Then he turned to me. I decided to throw in my two cents.

"Just for the record, Amelia, my only concern is not whether you'd willingly divulge anything he and I would say, just that anything we say wouldn't be privileged if you were here. If a prosecutor were to ask either your uncle or you what your uncle or I said here today, your aunt couldn't invoke the attorney-client privilege to protect it from disclosure."

"Don't give me your legal mumbo jumbo. This little meeting you're having is about an attack that nearly killed my aunt. Is she blood to either of you?"

I had to admit, she had a point.

Dr. Marshall shook his head and sat on the other end of the couch. "I'd object, but it wouldn't do any good. Stubbornness runs in her family. Besides, this case better not get to a point where a prosecutor is asking me questions or your ass is grass."

Nothing like getting off on the right foot.

"When Mac and I ran into you and the senator," I said, "you were returning from a benefit?"

"At the Willard, for the IDAA. The Infectious Disease Association of America. I'm on the board. Vicky agreed to say a few words about the nation's biodefense efforts."

"Did she say anything controversial?"

"Everything about biodefense is controversial. Should we develop vaccinations that target specific pathogens or multiple pathogens, or should we develop immunotherapy techniques that stimulate the body's immune system? How many doses of anthrax vaccine and smallpox vaccine should we keep stored and where? Do our first-responders have the right training and equipment? Is our milk supply safe from bioterrorists after that exposé by the National Academy of Sciences?"

"Did anything unusual happen?"

"Like someone threatening to run her over?"

"How about during the drive back to Dirksen? Anyone follow you or try to cut you off?"

"Now that you mention it, an olive-skinned man in a red Cherokee. He pulled up beside us at a light, lowered his window, and said he was going to take us out when we reached Dirksen. I forgot to tell you. Was that important?"

I kept my voice even. "Apparently you think the attack had to do with something else. What was it, the tax violation she was being framed for?"

"That wasn't a tax violation so much as a campaign finance violation. Vicky insisted on calling it a 'tax matter' in case someone overheard her."

I leaned back and folded my arms. "Anything else you haven't told me?"

"Since you asked, Vicky wasn't just being framed. She was being blackmailed."

I felt myself growing angry. Mac and I had walked into a trap. "Maybe you should start from the beginning."

Dr. Marshall sighed. "Even though she was in her first term, Vicky had landed on an important committee, the Select Committee on Terrorism."

"I heard," I said. "Because of her background as an intelligence officer, right?"

Dr. Marshall nodded. "Among the Committee's activities is tracking the proliferation of biowarfare agents, one of which has recently been in the news."

"Harappa?" I didn't like where this was going. Maybe Mills was onto something.

"The *Post* had an article about it this morning," Amelia said. "Said it has spread to Bangladesh. The World Health Organization has tried a cocktail of antiviral medicines. They haven't done any good. They said it could turn into a pandemic."

"From what I'm reading," Dr. Marshall said, "it could be the most virulent filovirus ever created."

"Filovirus?"

"There are four types of diseases that can be weaponized: rickettsiae, fungi, bacteria and viruses. Bacteria and viruses are the most common. Bacteria include things like anthrax and plague. They're not communicable from person to person and are generally treatable with antibiotics. Viruses are much smaller than bacteria and include things like smallpox and encephalitis. They *are* communicable from person to person and are generally treated only with antiviral medicines, if at all."

"A filovirus is a sort of virus?"

"A new family of viruses. Up until now its only members were Marburg and Ebola. We don't know much about them, except they can spread from person to person without any physical contact. Once they devour a cell, they shoot out tiny threads bent at the top, like fish hooks, to invade another cell. Eventually they liquefy a person's organs. Mortality rate of fifty to ninety percent within a few weeks of contact. Immune to any known antiviral medicines. Looks like Harappa is even more virulent than Marburg and Ebola. A hundred percent death rate within three days of contact. Too short a time period for the disease to evolve naturally. Viruses like to prolong their hosts' demise, so they can spread to other hosts. Harappa is intended solely to kill. It's a remarkable advancement of science, really."

"Listen to yourself," Amelia said.

"Armies have been using biowarfare for centuries, dear. In ancient times, Scythian archers dipped their arrowheads in manure, and Romans poisoned the wells of their enemies. In the Middle

Ages, Tatars catapulted plague-infected carcasses over castle walls. In World War I—"

"I know, the Germans spread glanders to the horses of enemy cavalries. Thank you for the history lesson, Dr. Death."

Dr. Marshall's face turned pink.

"How could anyone turn that into a science?" I said.

"Easy," Dr. Marshall said, "when there's a war on. Of course we had a policy of creating only diseases to which we had a cure. The Russians weren't burdened with such ethics. When the Soviet Union collapsed, although most of their diseases were destroyed, some were sold on the black market. Since then, rogue nations have been fiddling with them, trying to concoct new strains. Evidently some of them have gotten quite good at it."

"How do you know Harappa was created by a rogue nation?"

"No civilized nation would make such a thing. Too many treaties, too many weapons inspectors."

"That's not what Aunt Vicky thought," Amelia said.

"A few months ago," Dr. Marshall said, "Vicky heard a rumor Harappa had been made by a biopharm company."

"Was it true?" I said.

"She thought it was."

"She have any evidence?"

"No. In fact, the evidence was to the contrary. The virus isn't on file with the ATCC. The American Type Culture Collection in Rockville, Maryland. A sort of global germ bank. They have cultures of more than two thousand viruses. They're the ones who sold the University of Baghdad anthrax, botulinum toxin and brucella before the first Gulf War."

Nice, I thought.

"Scientists need samples of diseases to research cures," he said.

"So do sociopaths to create biowarfare programs," Amelia said.

"So the senator thought Harappa had been made by a company in secret?" I said. "Where did she hear the rumor from?"

"She wouldn't say," Dr. Marshall said.

"Even to you?"

"Said it was a matter of national security. Didn't want to put me at risk. I told her I probably still had a higher security clearance than she did, but she never listens to me."

"You mentioned a campaign finance violation. What happened?"

"She unknowingly received an illegal contribution from PEACE. People for the Education of something or other."

"Arabic Children Everywhere," Amelia said.

"The civil rights organization?" I said. "The one founded after 9/11?"

"Nothing but a front for middle-eastern terrorists," said Dr. Marshall.

"Says Senator McCarthy," said Amelia.

"What do the other Committee members think?" I said.

"She hadn't yet told them," Dr. Marshall said. "She didn't have any evidence and didn't want to lose her credibility. Her relationships with them have been strained lately, what with the liberal hogwash she's been spouting about civil rights. She was going to look into the matter on her own and then try to launch a Senate investigation."

"What could the Senate do?"

"Persuade the president and the secretary of state to lean on other countries to inspect their biopharm companies. After the anthrax scare in the fall of 2001, the Centers for Disease Control inspected the ninety-one American labs that had worked with anthrax."

"Did she do anything else?"

"You mean look into it on her own? Not that I know about and not that her chief of staff knows about."

"Which is who?"

"Marni Bardoni. Spoke to her an hour ago. She's expecting

your call. Here's her number and Vicky's appointment book. Lots of meetings with staff, lobbyists and constituents. No mention of PEACE."

"I don't get it," I said. "What does a rumor about Harappa have to do with the senator being framed?"

"Do I have to spell everything out for you?" Dr. Marshall said. "Someone's turning up the heat to drive Vicky out of the kitchen."

"'Turning up the heat' is a nice way to put it," Amelia said. "I can't believe it," I said. "Someone actually threatened a member of the Select Committee on Terrorism?"

"A couple weeks ago," Dr. Marshall said. "A man called our home in Middleburg. Told her to stop asking questions about Harappa. When she asked who it was, he told her to check her campaign accounts. Next day she found a fifty grand contribution from PEACE. It was from three months ago, right before she voted against the immigration bill."

"The one that didn't pass by a vote?" That ought to raise a few eyebrows. In addition to a federal statute prohibiting politicians from accepting contributions from non-profits like PEACE, there was a federal bribery statute, the one that congressman from Louisiana was charged with violating. The idea of piles of cash stuffed in the senator's freezer sent a shiver down my spine.

"Marni will show you the documents," said Dr. Marshall.

I nodded, wondering what I'd gotten myself into. "Her campaign finance director hadn't noticed the contribution?"

"Riley Conway," said Dr. Marshall. "Says he was totally in the dark. Supposedly his assistant, Sam, left the contribution off Vicky's FEC report."

"They submitted a false report to the FEC?"

"Conway signed it without reading it."

Still, it was a violation of FEC Act, and maybe the False Statement Act. "What was Conway's assistant doing filling out FEC reports anyway?"

"He doubled as the campaign finance accountant."

"Isn't that a conflict of interest?"

"Real life. Budgets are tight, people wear two hats."

Since when did the trophy wives of biotech tycoons have tight budgets?

"Didn't Conway read the report?" I said.

"You'll understand when you meet him. He's a hell of a fund-raiser, but details aren't his strong suit."

"Translation," Amelia said, "he's a bullshitting salesman."

"His assistant's explanation?" I said.

"He's missing," Dr. Marshall said.

"Missing as in dead or missing as in vamoose?"

"I wish he were dead."

"When did this happen?"

He told me.

"Have you looked for him?" I said.

"We didn't know he did anything wrong until Vicky got the phone call. That was around the beginning of the month."

"Who else works in her campaign office?"

"Just Conway and his assistant. She trimmed her fund-raising staff after the campaign."

"No one outside the office discovered the contribution? Don't political opponents watch for that sort of thing?"

"Vicky's next election's five years away. No one was paying attention yet."

"She didn't notice an extra fifty grand coming and going?"

"She's got other things to do than balance her books. She relies on Conway for that sort of thing."

Just like Conway relied on his assistant. This passing-the-buck defense wasn't going to work.

"She sent PEACE a check for the full amount," Amelia said. "Doesn't that count for something? Before that thing with her campaign finance director, Hillary avoided a scandal by returning twenty thousand dollars from some crook. A Miami drug lord or something."

"But she hadn't spent it," I said. "Besides, this contribution was illegal, not just unethical. What's more, it was arguably tied to the performance of an official act. The government is going to want more than a refund."

"Like what?"

I shrugged. "A few years ago, an electronics company pled guilty to violating the FEC Act. Although it'd made only ten grand in illegal contributions, it was fined a hundred and fifty grand." I turned back to Dr. Marshall. "What did PEACE say about all this?"

"They were thrilled to get the money back, seeing as they had no idea where it'd come from. The person responsible for sending it in has disappeared too. Hired the same week as Conway's assistant, quit the same day."

A conspiracy? What was going on here? I said, "Did the senator have any idea who called her?"

"She didn't recognize the man's voice."

"Do you have an unlisted number?"

"Ever since she ran for Senate. The only people who know it are staff members and close friends."

"Do you have caller-ID?"

"The number came up as unavailable. I know we could have put a trap down, but we would have had to file a complaint with the police first, and Vicky didn't want to risk the publicity. Have her sworn statement pop up on some website. Smoking gun dot com."

I was beginning to think he was worried about more than the senator's next re-election campaign. "Is there something else you're not telling me?"

Dr. Marshall exchanged a look with Amelia, then shrugged. "She's on the short list for director of the CIA. She has her PhD in politics, was an agent for twenty years, and speaks fluent Farsi."

Wow.

"It'll never happen if her campaign violation hits the press," he said.

"So who do you think might be behind it?"

"I don't know. A biopharm company, maybe a political enemy."

"Isn't it kind of early in her career to have political enemies?"

"In the past year Vicky has done a terrible thing for a new politician, she's grown a conscience. I suppose it's the ACLU's fault. Told her too many horror stories about racial profiling, invasions of privacy, uncharged detentions. Got her to propose a bill limiting the power of federal agents to do their jobs."

"In other words," Amelia said, "she was trying to protect our civil liberties."

"Which conservatives don't like her?" I said.

"Oh," said Dr. Marshall, "fringe organizations like the Republican National Committee, the Department of Defense, and the FBI."

"Any smaller, more probable suspects?"

"Right-wing non-profits."

"For example?"

"ARM," said Dr. Marshall. "Americans for the Restraint of Muslims. A group of hawks."

"Hawks?" Amelia said. "They're lunatics. They want to deport all non-citizens of Arabic descent. Even some citizens. They've hated Aunt Vicky ever since she trounced their president on *The O'Reilly Factor*."

I remembered the debate. Warren Shifflett had tried to play the sympathy card, having lost his wife and daughter on 9/11, but his personal loss couldn't justify his extreme political views. Senator Serling had also lost a spouse to terrorism: her first husband, Congressman Harrison Serling. He'd been killed in Central America about ten years ago.

"Do you think there's any connection between the attack on the senator a few days ago and the murder of her first husband?"

"I thought about that," Amelia said. "My uncle was killed by a car bomb outside the Presidential Palace in Guatemala, and he was killed because he was overseeing an investigation."

I remembered. "An American nun had been murdered."

"But the three individuals responsible were a splinter group of the Revolutionary Organization of the People in Arms. They were captured, tried and executed. And ARM wasn't even around back then."

"What about biopharm companies?"

"There are probably two dozen companies in the world that could've made Harappa," Dr. Marshall said. "As for which one it was, your guess is as good as mine. I never heard of a super-virus when I was at Panacea."

"What about that guy you sold it to?" Amelia said. "He might've heard something."

"Robert White? Haven't talked to him since the sale. He's a rookie in the industry. Probably just as much in the dark as we are."

"Can you send me a list of those companies?" I said.

"Whatever you need to keep this thing from the press. Just send me the bill."

My five favorite words. "The retainer you sent should tide me over for a few weeks."

"We don't have a few weeks."

The phone beeped and Dr. Marshall crossed the room. "Hello, Governor."

I stood up automatically, like a state's chief executive had just walked into the room. Amelia scratched at some dried flour on her apron.

Dr. Marshall covered the transmitter. "Keep me notified of every development." Then he strode out of the kitchen, leaving me alone with Amelia.

"Do you get that a lot?" I asked.

"Comes with the territory."

The same territory on which Senator Serling was standing when she'd been run over. Not to mention Mac. We picked up our plates and took them to the sink.

"Now that I've made you breakfast," she said, "how about you buy me lunch some time?"

I felt my knees grow weak. "You mean a date?"

I don't know why I said it. Honestly, sometimes I say the stupidest things.

"More like an update," she said. "You can keep me up notified of every development too. In return, I can answer any questions you have. Help find the creep who did this."

It was a deal. Amelia and I made plans to meet for lunch in Georgetown in two days. Our first update.

Chapter 9

I drove Marita down to the MPD, where I helped her request a temporary protection order against Jorge. The officer in the Domestic Violence Intake Center said the Department would serve the petition on Jorge free of charge, and that the DC Superior Court would notify us of the hearing date in a few days, after they had made personal service. Luckily we got out of there without running into Mills, who would have probably had some questions about Marita's and my matching black eyes.

A little while later, Marni Bardoni showed up at the Senator's campaign finance office. She wore a low-cut blouse, a tight skirt, dark red lipstick and rectangular glasses. Over her shoulder she carried a big brown leather bag, which swung in front of her as she leaned over to unlock the front door to the senator's campaign office.

"My LAs call this thing my emotional baggage," she said, pushing the door open. "The brats."

The office consisted of one room, with no windows.

"Here it is," she said, "where all the magic happens. Couple of desks, couple of filing cabinets, second-hand copier, second-hand couch, puke-green coffee table and matching ratty chair. Over there a mini-fridge, coffee maker and toaster."

She dropped the keys in her bag. "Politicians keep their campaign offices apart from their political offices to avoid the 'appearance of impropriety.' Some senators use space at the RSCC, the Republican Senatorial Campaign Committee. Others keep small offices here downtown. When there's no campaign, there's no need for a lot of space."

Posters and buttons from the senator's previous campaign covered the walls. *Vicky Victorious! Sterling Serling!*

She must have seen me wince.

"Luckily, you don't need to be clever to win," she said, heaving her bag onto the leather chair. "Just the bucks."

"And being a Republican in Virginia doesn't hurt," I said.

"First you have to win the nomination. Thank God her opponent in the primary was Ashton Sweet."

"The seventy-year-old incumbent who'd just been caught in a coat room with a teenage intern."

"The guy didn't stand a chance." Marni walked over to the file cabinets. "What do you want to see first? I'm not sure what's in here—"

I caught her hand in mid-air. "It's probably best if we don't touch anything."

"What, you think there are still prints? Look over there, at the bottle of window cleaner and the empty roll of paper tolls."

It was true. All the surfaces in the room still glimmered. Even the trashcans were empty. I let go of Marni's hand.

She adjusted her diamond ring so the stone was facing out again. "Looks like I'm not the only one who's had too much coffee."

She checked the vintage gentleman's watch on her wrist, sat on the edge of the leather chair and tapped her foot on the floor.

"Let's get on with this. I've got deck chairs to re-arrange on the Titanic."

I sat on the couch. "Before we begin, you should understand that I represent the senator, not you. So don't tell me you mailed that anthrax a few years ago, expecting me to keep that secret. It's true anything you tell me is privileged because you're the employee of my client, Senator Serling, and we're talking about a potential legal claim against her arising from the performance of her duties as a senator. But it's the senator who holds the privilege, and only her."

"I was in my second year of law school when the senator recruited me."

"You quit for her?"

"I prefer to think of it as her rescuing me."

"Have you spoken to anyone about our meeting?"

"No."

"Not even your husband?"

She glanced at the ring on her left hand. "Oh, he's just my fiancé. Sorry if I don't take this thing more seriously. I've gotten these before. Never amount to anything. Anyway, no one in the office knows we're meeting. Just Dr. Marshall and Riley Conway."

"Conway is coming when?"

"Any minute. He had a 'situation' at his PR firm."

"He works here only part-time?"

"So did Sam, his assistant. His other job was at the National Association of Public Accountants."

Lucky day. NAPA's office was next door to mine.

"What sort of background check do the staff go through before being hired?"

"Other than fund-raising staff? They fill out an application. Name, address, Social Security number. If anything looks funny, I check it out."

"Personally?"

"I call their references."

"What sort of background check do you do on the fund-raising staff?"

"I make Riley check their references, to keep the offices separate."

"Did he check Sam's references?"

"Assume so. Have to ask him."

"What's Riley like?"

She eyed me.

"Professionally," I said.

"Professionally, he's a muckety muck. Georgetown Law School, youngest chief of staff in Congress, youngest partner in his PR firm, member of both Congressional and Avenel. Your typical DC power tool."

I didn't ask the next question.

"And non-professionally?" She glanced at the door. "He's an arrogant, sexist asshole, with wandering eyes and hands that follow. But, hey, he brings in the bucks."

"What was Sam like?"

"Didn't really know him."

"What kind of car did he drive?"

"Took the Metro."

"Did he have any friends?"

She shrugged.

"How about what he looked like?"

She thought about it and said, "He reminded me of mayonnaise."

"Meaning?"

"If you have to ask..." She looked me up and down.

"Forget it."

She unlocked a drawer in the bigger desk and took out two folders. "One's Riley's personnel file. Other one's Sam's."

"Are they originals?"

"That's the first thing I looked for," Marni said. "The ink on Conway's file is blue. The ink on Sam's file is black."

"Are there any other copies?"

"We don't keep a copy on the Hill. And, before you ask, no one else has a key besides Conway and the senator."

I ran my eyes over Sam's employment application. It had a lot of blanks. No home address or phone number. But there was a copy of his Social Security card and DC driver's license.

"Did anyone check out this address?"

"That's what you're for, I guess."

I returned my focus to his license. I saw what she meant about mayonnaise. Samuel F. Doyle. Thirty-five years old. Five foot ten, hundred and fifty pounds, blond hair, blue eyes, fair skin, toothless smile.

"Looks just like you except for the hair," she said.

Thanks a lot, I thought. "Is this it? What about administrative documents? Health insurance, life insurance, pension plan? I was hoping for something showing his next of kin or maybe the address of a doctor."

"The senator doesn't offer benefits to her campaign staff. Besides, he said he had health insurance from his other job."

"Do you have a copy of any personal charges? Long-distance telephone calls, copying, postage?"

"Zilch."

"Did he get paid by direct deposit?"

"By check. I think he said he'd just closed his bank account in Kansas, where he was from, and he hadn't opened one here yet."

"What bank cashed his paychecks?"

She told me. Then she said, "I called it. The branch manager said he never cashed them."

"You never noticed that before?"

She slid her glasses down her nose. I rubbed my eyes. Whoever was financing Doyle had thought things through. I looked at the phones on the desks.

"Were you able to get his voicemail passcode?"

"No messages. He even deleted his greeting."

"Is that stored on magnetic tape or something?"

"Overwritten every week."

Doyle left more than a month ago. It couldn't be a coincidence. Before Marni had arrived, I'd talked to the building's security guard. The security video tapes were reused every two weeks. It was as if whoever made that threatening call to the senator had intentionally waited two weeks for the security tapes and the voicemail tapes to be overwritten. I looked at the computers.

"Did you find any documents?"

She pulled a folder from her leather bag. "This is everything."

The folder held a stack of documents. On top was a letter.

March 15

Riley,

I can't do this anymore. I did what you asked. Now I'm taking my money and going home.

Don't try to find me or I'll go to the authorities.

"Underneath are letters from Sam to contributors," she said, "and spreadsheets describing contributions from the past six months by amounts, sources, and dates. That tab there is an e-mail from Sam to a guy named Abdul Hassan at PEACE, thanking the president there, Dr. Mukhtar, for the contribution. The next tab is a spreadsheet recording the fifty thousand dollar contribution from PEACE a few days before the e-mail." Marni slid closer and looked over my shoulder, so I could feel her breath on my neck. "At the bottom there's a surprise. Sam tried to delete it but a shadow file existed."

A personal letter with Sam's home address.

"Good catch. Any more like this?"

"That's the one and lonely."

"Did you find any of the websites Doyle visited?" I knew web browsers keep a record of visited sites on the hard drive, before they're overwritten.

"That was another funny thing. The slackers at the office surf the web all day. Sam only visited two the whole time he was here: one for the FEC and the other for our 'partner in crime.'"

"PEACE?"

"Guess you have your work cut out for you. Mind if I ask you a question?"

I turned to face her. We were inches apart now. She didn't lean back.

"Is it true what they say?" she said. "You tried to chase the guy who ran down the senator?"

"The guy who killed Mac, yes."

"What would you have done if you'd caught him?"

"I honestly don't know."

She shook her head and brushed the hair away from my bandage with soft cool fingers. This was too close for a man who hadn't had a date in months to be sitting next to a woman on her second or third fiancé, but I didn't stand up.

"I'm just curious," she said. "I mean, you seem like a nice guy. A little uptight but, you know, nice. You sure you know what you're getting into?"

For a second, I wondered if she was talking about something other than the investigation. Before I could answer, the door opened. In walked a gentleman wearing a tan cashmere sports coat, a pale-blue oxford shirt and a lime-green tie.

"Hello, sweetheart," the man said to Marni. "Hope I'm interrupting."

Chapter 10

E. Riley Conway shook my hand then held out an arm toward Marni. "Mags, how long has it been? You don't write, you don't call."

"Didn't you get my message?" she said.

"You didn't leave me a message."

"That was the message. And don't call me Mags." She turned to me. "I've got a political career to save, thanks to the fine work of our campaign office."

I gave her my card in case she thought of anything else.

Conway watched her leave, then slapped me on the back. "I wouldn't mind financing her campaign."

I gave him my spiel about privilege.

"I know the drill, Counselor. I was editor of the *Law Review*, and my firm specializes in crisis management, saving the asses of CEOs in hot water. Product recalls, oil spills, class-action lawsuits. Securities fraud, insider trading, hostile takeovers. Labor strikes, cyber-terrorism, mass identity thefts. God help me, I love it all."

He fell back into the couch, put his feet up on the coffee table and spread out his arms. "Fire when ready."

"How'd you meet Sam Doyle?"

"Showed up at my office about six months ago, just after my last assistant had given notice."

"Who was your last assistant?"

He pulled out his address book. I asked him if I could make a copy.

"Now is that really necessary, Counselor?"

"I'd like to know what's in it before the FBI seizes it."

As I ran the copier, I said, "You just gave Doyle a job, there on the spot?"

"I was lucky to find a CPA."

"You keep a copy of his résumé?"

"It's missing. From his personnel file in that desk drawer there. The one with the lock." I asked him the same questions I'd asked Marni, and I got the same answers. I gave him back his address book. "So tell me what you do here."

"Raise money, what else? Through dinners and lunches mostly, sometimes just through phone calls. Our cash on hand is a quarter million. Half of it comes from large individual contributions, large' meaning more than two hundred bucks. A quarter of it comes from small individual contributions, and the other quarter comes from PACs. Half of them are labor PACs, a quarter of them are business PACs, and the other quarter ideological PACs, ones pushing a single issue."

"Like PEACE?"

"I told Lawrence, I never saw a contribution from them. Would've raised a red flag in my mind. I don't know, maybe the kid kept two sets of books."

What was I missing?

"You're going to wear out the rug pacing like that, Counselor."

"What's in these file cabinets?"

"Cabinet to the left is pre-election, cabinet to the right is post-election. Top drawers contain bank account statements, accounting ledgers, and FEC campaign finance reports. Middle drawers contain letters to and from contributors. Bottom drawers contain call sheets, records of telephone solicitations of potential contributors."

I opened the drawers. The financial documents, letters and call sheets were arranged chronologically. "What are these yellow stickies?"

"The results of the senator's panic attack. Happened the day after she got that phone call."

He drummed his fingers on the couch as I read the flagged documents. One of them was a call sheet recording PEACE's pledge of fifty grand. Another was a bank account statement recording the deposit of the contribution. Another was an accounting ledger page recording the expenditure of the contribution. All photocopies. So much for Doyle's fingerprints.

"Can I get copies of these too?"

"Help yourself," he said.

When I was done, I said, "This call sheet refers to a conversation between you and Dr. Ahmad Mukhtar shortly before the contribution."

"That's Doyle's handwriting. I've never spoken to Mukhtar."

"Do people ever make mistakes when they fill out call sheets?"

"Not unless you want the FEC sniffing around."

"Any idea why Doyle would do this to the senator?"

"This is politics."

"You spend much time here with him?"

"I work out of my office down the street. Doyle had his run of the joint when he wasn't at his other job."

"NAPA?"

"Nerds-R-Us."

"Did he have a cell phone?"

"Kept promising to get one."

I gave him my card.

He stood up, smoothed out his tie and buttoned his coat. "I know, call you if I remember anything."

"And don't talk to anyone about this."

"About what?" he said, a little too convincingly.

Chapter 11

"Can you do some digging?" I said to Roger Lynch over my cell phone.

Roger was an ex-cop who had been forced into early retirement because he liked to resolve domestic disputes with a baseball bat. Now he worked at Capitol Crimes, Inc. Mac and I had used him to track down reluctant witnesses, serve subpoenas and do background checks. Roger had access to the computer databases of the National Criminal Information Center, the three major credit reporting agencies and all fifty departments of motor vehicles. I gave Roger the information I had on Conway and Doyle. Then on a hunch I threw in the name on the letter Marni had found, Tariq Shaheen.

"Got it," he said. "Get back to you soon as I can. Captain has me on a tight leash this week."

Marcus O'Neil, a retired Maryland police captain, was the owner and founder of Capitol Crimes. He rode his team of investigators hard, when he wasn't giving himself four-foot putts for par at Rock Creek Golf Course.

The address on Doyle's license belonged to a brownstone near Washington Circle. The front door was locked and Doyle's name was not listed by the intercom. I waited until a young woman rushed down the steps, book bag slung over shoulder and apple in mouth. Then I ran up and caught the door.

Doyle's apartment was on the bottom floor. Loud music came from inside. Blink 182, if my time in the law library hadn't put me completely out of touch with modern rock. I knocked on the door.

There was no response.

I pounded, rattling the hinges. The music stopped. A young man opened the door, holding a bag of Doritos. He wore an untucked black T-shirt that read *Matchbox Twenty* and showed a photo of a chubby naked guy bearing a disturbing resemblance to Henry Kissinger. I caught a whiff of a Phish concert.

"Tariq?"

"Do I, like, know you?"

"No." I handed him a copy of Doyle's license. "But do you know this guy?"

"You mean Deadbeat?"

"He break your sublease?"

Tariq's eyes widened.

I stopped the door with my foot. "Relax, I won't tell your landlord."

"Who are you? A cop?" Tariq glanced over my shoulder. "Shit, was he dealing?" He let go of the door and raised his hands, the Dorito bag falling to the ground. "I don't know anything."

"I just want to find the guy."

Tariq's lowered his arms. "Few weeks ago, I came by to get my mail and all his stuff was gone."

"Mind if I look around?"

He eyed me.

"I promise I won't look in the closet for your little indoor garden."

He stepped aside. "For your information, it's a hydroponic water-culture system with dual-mode solar lamps."

A wide-screen plasma TV dominated the apartment's living room. It displayed the frozen image of a monster shattering to bloody bits. Wires from the TV snaked across the room to a Sony PlayStation, which sat beside a bottle of Red Dog beer on a glass coffee table. Behind the coffee table sat a black leather sectional with a matching La-Z-Boy recliner. A pair of high-end speakers sat perched on wall mountings. I wondered what kind of rent tenants were charging subtenants these days.

"No class today?" I said.

"I scheduled my classes so I could have four-day weekends."

In the corner of the room stood a skateboard. On the wall hung a poster of a man floating upside down, one hand holding a snowboard, the other hand free. Beside it hung a poster of a stock car crash, one car with its tail high in the air, its frame flying apart, above two cars passing through a cloud of smoke.

Tariq stepped beside me. "That's Ross Powers doing a switch McTwist at the Olympics. Other one's Tony Stewart going airborne at Daytona."

Below the posters stood a glass cabinet containing CDs, DVDs and video games. The games had names like *Grand Theft Auto*, *Road Rage* and *Motor Mayhem*. Not exactly the kind Mac had bought for Tommy.

"You like car crashes?" I said.

"Who doesn't?"

"Been in any lately?"

"Only on TV."

On top of the cabinet stood a photo of Tariq in his high school graduation robe beside an older man in a gray suit. Behind them sat a black car with blue-and-white plates.

"Your dad a diplomat?"

"Used to be. Now he's just a teacher."

I turned Shaheen's name over in my mind. "Former assistant secretary of state for South Asian affairs, right? Didn't he just write that biography about bin Laden?"

"He's all bitter it made the bestseller list. Says it'll, like, detract from its scholarly value."

"You want to go into foreign service?"

"I'm too addicted to electricity and clean water."

I peeked into the bedroom.

"King-size water bed," I said. "Thin-screen computer. All this stuff yours?"

"Just got it out of storage. Moved in with my lady six months ago. She kicked me out three days ago. She dumped me for the manager of the Writing Center. The *Writing Center*, dude. I was like, can there be a bigger dork in the whole school? She goes, you don't have any motivation. Me! You believe that shit?"

The pause-feature on the video game expired, filling the TV screen with snow.

"Did Doyle leave anything behind?"

"Just cleaning stuff."

"Where'd you meet him?"

"Answered a flier I put up at school."

"You ever hang out with him?"

"Naw."

"Ever see anything unusual?"

"Like what?"

"Visitors, parties, trouble?"

"Dude was a loner."

I asked the usual questions about what Doyle looked like, whether he had a cell phone, etc., and I got the same answers as from Marni and Conway.

"How did he pay?"

"Cash."

"Through the mail?"

"In person."

"How much was the rent?"

"Fifteen hundred."

"That's a lot of cash."

"Said he just moved here and hadn't opened a bank account yet. I was just psyched to find someone who wouldn't piss off the neighbors. Geezer across the hall has, like, bionic hearing."

"He sign up for his own phone service?"

"Used mine. I'd pay it and he'd paid me back."

"You have an answering machine?"

"Voicemail."

"Were there any messages to Doyle in your mailbox when he left?"

"He deleted everything."

From the piles of textbooks and clothes on the floor, I guessed he didn't keep copies of his old phone bills. "Do me a favor," I said. "Call your phone company and ask for a list of all your calls for the past six months." I took out my card and put it on top of a fifty dollar bill. "Have them fax the list to this number."

Tariq took the fifty by either end and pulled it apart with a snap. "Hello, Mr. Franklin."

As he picked up his phone, I looked around the apartment. Living room, bedroom, kitchen. As they did at the campaign office, all the surfaces sparkled and shone. Doyle was thorough, I had to give him that. Even the inside of the fridge was spotless.

Tariq returned. "Said it'd take about an hour. You hungry or something?"

I was ready to call it a day when I spotted something wedged between the counter and the fridge. "That yours?"

"What, that piece of paper? Do I, like, get another fifty if it's a clue?"

Chapter 12

After Tariq helped me shove the fridge aside, I fashioned a hook from a coat hanger and fished out the paper. It was a piece of business stationery, bearing the return address of guess what? Senator Serling's campaign office. The rest of it looked blank. I held it up to the light. An impression appeared. I asked Tariq for a pencil and began shading.

"Cool," Tariq said when the phone number appeared.

"Just a dumb trick," I said. "Can I use your phone?"

I punched the numbers.

"ARM," said a husky voice, "before it's too late."

I hung up. Americans for the Restraint of Muslims. Why wasn't I surprised? I checked my messages so Tariq couldn't hit *Redial* and reach ARM. No use getting him any more involved. I gave him another fifty.

"Buy yourself a lava lamp," I said.

"My first real job," he said. "I'm, like, a paid informant."

No one else was in the building except the "geezer with bionic hearing" across the hall. He wore pajama bottoms, an inside-out undershirt and a baseball cap that read *WordPerfect*. One hand held a stack of papers, the other a red pen. A black cat curled around his ankle and Mozart played behind him.

"I know a fellow teacher when I see one," I said.

"You from the university?"

"I'm just looking for someone."

"You look like one of those assholes from the administration." I described Doyle.

"You mean that kid who used to live across the hall?" the man said.

"You remember him?"

"Was he a friend of yours?"

"I just want to ask him some questions."

"Kid never said boo to me."

"You remember anything about him?"

"No, that's what I liked about him. No loud music, no seedy guests, no funny smells."

"How about when he moved out?"

"One morning I step out to get the paper and I find the mystery kid's gone and Shaheen's pot-head son is back."

"I'm looking for your director of member services," I said to a thin young man with blond highlights, who was sitting behind the front desk at NAPA.

"That would be Tamika," the young man said. "She's out to lunch. Can I help? I'm the assistant director of administration and information systems. Don't look so impressed, I'm really just a glorified receptionist. I'm just doing this 'til I get my MFA in poetry. Then the dough will really start rolling in."

"Barry," came a voice from in back, "are you scaring the members again?"

"That's Simon, my boss. He likes to keep the talk straight, if you know what I mean. Ahem, how may I be of service to you, sir?"

I introduced myself, and he said he thought he'd seen me around. We chatted for a moment about the other businesses in the neighborhood, the lack of parking and the crime in the city. Then Barry frowned.

"You're the one whose friend was killed," he said. "Everyone here is so sorry. He seemed like a nice guy, kind of grouchy sometimes, though once I saw him give a sandwich to that homeless guy on the corner."

I told him that was one of Mac's diets. The Seven Day Juice Fast, followed by the Cabbage Soup Diet, followed by the Chunky Soup Diet, followed by the pizza-and-ice-cream eating binge. Barry told me he'd tried the first one and all the apple juice had given him gas. It was time to change the subject. I told him why I was there. He studied Doyle's license, spun around in his chair, tapped his keyboard and shook his head.

"We have over ten thousand members, but no one by that name."

"Can you tell if he's ever worked here?"

He made a face. "I've been here two years, nine months and thirteen days. Like a prison sentence, except the guards wear short-sleeve dress shirts and calculator watches. I've never seen him before, not even at our annual conventions, and I never forget a face. This one's not half bad, if you don't mind my saying. He's got nice cheekbones, like you."

I decided to invite Barry along to dinner the next time my parents came to town, just to push my mother over the edge.

"Can you check with the rest of the staff?" I said. "It's important."

Barry took the license from my hand and disappeared in back. As I listened to some lowered voices, I turned his computer screen toward me, found the mouse and scrolled down through the names to the *H*s. There was no *Hassan, Abdul*, but I did find a name that made me gasp audibly. *Huffington, Carl*. The name of ARM's Recruitment Officer. His address was in Manassas.

"Hey," Barry said, returning. "That's private information. You trying to get me fired?" Then he smiled. "Please, God, please get me fired."

"Sorry."

He reported the verdict of the office staff: no one had ever seen the man before.

I thanked him and gave him my card. "No home number?" he said.

Back at the office, a fax had come through from Verizon. Tariq's last six phone bills. I leaned back in my chair. No long-distance charges. Evidently Doyle had used a cell phone.

I logged onto the internet and typed variations of *Samuel F. Doyle* into a couple web browsers. I got hits in Pennsylvania, New York, Massachusetts and Ireland. No one said Doyle had spoken with an Irish brogue, and I couldn't tell anything about the other Doyles without their Social Security numbers.

I logged onto Lexis/Nexis, a collection of legal and news databases Mac and I had used to find legal decisions and newspaper articles. I searched for Samuel F. Doyle in the person locator database, coming up with even more names. I punched the *Print* button and scanned the list. I crossed off any Sam Doyles who didn't have the middle name Franklin. Then I crossed off the Sam Doyles who were younger than twenty-five or older than forty.

That left...no one.

I logged back onto Lexis and searched for Samuel F. Doyle in the news database and the state public records database. If he'd been mentioned in any newspaper or magazine articles, or if he'd owned a house or car, I'd get a hit. No luck. As a last-ditch effort I searched the case database to see if Samuel F. Doyle had ever been involved in litigation. A long shot. My search retrieved a single case. The phone beeped.

"Tariq Shaheen was charged with possession last year," Roger said. "No conviction. Otherwise clean."

"What about Conway?"

"A few speeding tickets. Doyle's another matter. You're not going to believe this."

"Don't tell me. He's in a maximum-security prison in New York State."

"Sing Sing Correctional in Ossining. How'd you know?"

"I'm looking at the 1990 decision dismissing his civil rights action. He alleged he was deprived of a kosher diet."

"Doyle, kosher? Besides, he killed a New York State trooper in 1982. He's lucky they didn't deprive him of an oxygen diet. New York had the death penalty back then, didn't they?"

"He must be fifty years old."

"Fifty-two."

"I'm looking for a guy between twenty-five and forty who's been free for the past six months."

"Same Social Security number though. Maybe this kid you're looking for borrowed his identity."

"That would explain why no INS flags were raised on his I-Nine Form. What about his driver's license?"

"Hell, I could make one of those."

"Let's hope it never comes to that, Roger."

"My job's just one step short of a life of crime."

"Doesn't seem like such a bad life."

"For you? You're way too honest. You won't even let me go through that Department of Labor guy's garbage. You're probably the most honest lawyer in America. They should bury you next to Abe fucking Lincoln."

Static crackled over the line.

"Hey," Roger said, "sorry I couldn't make it to Mac's funeral. Captain sent me down to Richmond on a job."

"Penny told me to thank you for the flowers."

"Anything I can do?"

"Put today on my tab, and keep this under your hat."

"It's getting crowded under there."

While I'd been on the phone, I'd gotten more voicemail messages.

The first was from Holly Hickey at Channel One News. I punched the *Delete* button half-way through it. The second one was from an angry Detective Mills. I started to dial his number then I put down the handset. The more I talked to him, the more likely it was he would learn why Mac and I had met with the senator. Before I called him I needed to find at least a clue leading to Mac's killer.

I went to Mac's office. A cup of coffee sat molding on his desk. A car passed by, shining headlights onto a bare wall. A bad feeling came over me. I was up to my neck in student loan debt, I'd just fired all of my clients except one, and I was picking a fight with a police detective and a cold-blooded murderer. I went to my office, turned off the light and lay on my couch.

The phone woke me.

"Been trying you at home," Roger said. "You might want to turn on the news."

It was 11:00 p.m. I went to the conference room and turned to Channel One. An elderly black woman with short gray hair stood outside a modest brick home beside a reporter. The woman's name, which was printed on the bottom of the screen, rang a bell. Eugenia Carver.

"He's the one who gave me the money," she was saying in a raspy voice.

"Ten thousand dollars?" the reporter said.

"Half was before the verdict and half was after."

"Did it influence your acquittal of the defendant?"

"I needed the money. My granddaughter was sick."

The reporter faced the camera. "A rich defendant, an ambitious attorney and a vulnerable juror. The recipe for a bribe? This is Holly Hickey for Action News."

The camera cut back to the anchorman. "The attorney accused of tampering with the jury is John MacPherson, recently killed in a hit-and-run accident. His co-counsel in that trial, Henry Fisher, has been unable to be reached for comment."

Crap.

"Who's grandma?" Roger said.

Chapter 13

"The fuck you do?" shouted Vincent Bustamonte the next morning. "Fuck with the fucking jury? You fucked me!"

When he got angry, Vincent made Mac look like a Boy Scout. *Fuck* could become a verb, a noun, an adverb, an adjective, a gerund and an interjection...all in the same sentence. I held the phone a safe distance from my ear, then assured him the allegation by the foreperson of the jury his trial was a lie. I hadn't bribed anyone and I'd never known Mac to do anything unethical except maybe use some creative fee arrangements for tax purposes. I explained how I'd spent the night rereading the firm's files from his case, and pouring over the firm's bank account records and Mac's personal bank account records. Not a hint of wrongdoing. No unexplained withdrawals or deposits during the months before, during or after the trial. The only mention of Ms. Carver was a handwritten note of mine from Mac's voir dire during jury selection. The note read *Carver: retired postal worker, widow, no kids*.

"So the fuck what?"

"No kids, Vincent. Didn't you see the news?"

"I got this problem. My eyes stop working when my heart stops beating. Which reminds me, some cop called."

"Mills?"

"Wanted to know where I was time a Mac's death."

I didn't want to know where Vincent was at the time of Mac's death.

"This is crazy. Me whack Mac? What do I look like? A fucking mobster?"

I decided to treat that as a rhetorical question.

"I'll find out why she's lying," I said.

"You better, Fisher, and fast. Or you're going to have worse problems than getting your ticket pulled."

The line went dead. Who said anything about being disbarred? When I checked my voicemail, I found out what he meant. There was a message from the Office of Bar Counsel.

"Mr. Fisher, I'm extending you the professional courtesy of notifying you that earlier this morning my office received a phone call from a Vincent Bustamonte. Mr. Bustamonte insisted he didn't have anything to do with any jury tampering in his recent trial and if such tampering occurred you and Mac were acting on your own. We reminded Mr. Bustamonte about the attorney-client privilege, and told him he has to file a written complaint to initiate an investigation, but we felt it appropriate to inform you the OBC would, of course, treat any such complaint seriously."

Suddenly I knew what my clients felt like. I washed my face and replaced my bandage with a Band-Aid. Then I got a clean pair of underwear and socks from my office closet. It was going to be a long day. I looked up the number for Channel One News.

"Figured you'd be calling," Holly Hickey said. "You have any idea how many messages I've left with you in the past week?"

"You and every other reporter."

"So you ready to talk?"

"I'll answer one of your questions if you answer one of mine."

"Is that how investigative reporting works?"

"That's the deal, take it or leave it."

"What's your question?"

"Do you believe her?"

"Who?"

"Ms. Carver."

"You're joking, right?"

"Well?"

"Yeah, sure."

"Doesn't sound like a ringing endorsement of her veracity."

"Why are you asking?"

"Because Mac would never bribe a juror, and I know I didn't do it."

"Why am I not surprised you'd say that?"

"If you don't believe me, look into whether Ms. Carver and her late husband had any children."

"What do you mean?"

"She was trying to help her sick granddaughter, remember? Did you see any family photos on the walls? Any drawings on the refrigerator? Any toys lying around? She even give you a name?"

Holly Hickey paused. "Okay, now my question."

"Shoot."

"Do you know why Senator Serling was attacked?"

"Yes."

"Well?"

"Was the deal one question or two?"

"My mom told me never trust lawyers."

"You really want to know?"

"Hello, I'm a reporter."

"Senator Serling was attacked because she ignored the warning of a mysterious man not to launch a secret Senate investigation of the creator of the world's most lethal biowarfare virus."

Holly let out her breath. "If you're not going to tell me, just say so. I'm too busy for this shit."

She hung up. The only reporter in the DC area who didn't want to talk to me.

Chapter 14

I logged back on the internet, punched in A-R-M, and scanned a dozen miss-hits: bank pages on adjustable rate mortgages, medical pages on human anatomy, even the website of something called the *Anti-Robot Militia*, which pledged to free the world of machines. Finally I found what I was looking for, the terrible image of American Airlines Flight 175 slamming into the South Tower of the World Trade Center, black smoke billowing from the North Tower. Imposed over the image was the following text:

Americans for the Restraint of Muslims

Mission:	*To deport all unnaturalized Muslims from America*
Weapons:	*Truth, Justice and the American Way*
Headquarters:	*Manassas, Virginia, USA*
Command:	*Commander-in-Chief, Warren Shifflett*

	Recruitment Officer, Carl Huffington
	Public Affairs Officer, Ray Pole
Brigade:	*2,000 Americans and counting*
Yearly Donation:	*$50 (cash preferred)*

I did some quick math and figured that the salaries of the staff plus office, lobbying and marketing expenses probably amounted to more than a hundred grand per year. So unless someone had robbed a bank, ARM probably couldn't have come up with the cash for the setup. The contribution alone was fifty grand, and Doyle's and Hassan's hush money must have been at least fifty grand. Six months' lost income, plus six months' living expenses, plus a premium for the risk involved. I called Roger and gave him the men's names.

"Focus on stuff like bribery, extortion, embezzlement and fraud," I said.

"The crimes that pay," he said.

I returned to ARM's main page and clicked on the button reading *Battle Plan*. ARM's tactics were to flood the internet with data about the *Muslim menace*, to lobby politicians in favor of stricter immigration laws, and to conduct mass-mailings to recruit new members.

I clicked on *Service Records* and got a biography of Shifflett. Born in New Hampshire, he was an altar boy in grade school, an Eagle Scout in middle school and an All-American pitcher in high school. He received an athletic scholarship to a small Catholic college in central New York, where he met his wife. After college they moved to Virginia, and he got a job as a sales rep with Applied Chemical Sciences, Inc. Then, one Monday in September he went to New York City on business, bringing his wife and daughter. The next morning, as he was meeting a client downtown, his wife and daughter went sightseeing, starting with breakfast at Windows on the World. That was the day the sky turned black. After waiting six months for their bodies to be recovered, he quit his job and founded ARM. I was still surfing the web for more info on him when Roger called back.

"Tell me about the staff of one of America's worst hate groups," I said.

"Pretty boring stuff, actually. Nothing on the public affairs officer, although the recruitment officer was arrested once for picketing, back when he was chief organizer for a labor union."

"And Shifflett?"

"Nothing but an arrest for unlawful assembly, disturbing the peace and assault."

"Assault?"

"A dozen skinheads were marching in front of a mosque in Manassas, carrying signs. 'Muslims Are Hoodlums!' 'Drop Dead, Towel Head!' You know, get-to-know-your-neighbor stuff. They were having a good ol' time until the members of the mosque showed up. Shifflett held his ground and exchanged broken noses with a retired Army colonel. A couple days later, both sides dropped their charges, too proud to admit injury."

"Nothing other than that?"

"Otherwise average citizens."

"That's scary. Can you do something else?"

"Born to serve."

"Check out ARM's assets. I'm looking for the receipt or expenditure of a chunk of change in the past six months."

"How big a chunk?"

I told him.

"I'm not going to even ask if this is connected to what we were investigating yesterday," he said.

"Then I won't have to tell you."

My watch said 9:00 a.m., about when Mac usually strolled in, a bag of Krispy Kreme donuts in hand, another diet out the window. I put on my coat and grabbed my car keys. I wasn't ready yet to sink into a swamp of self-pity.

Manassas was thirty miles southwest of DC. Small old town, strip malls, middle class.

Many people knew it as the site of two huge Civil War battles in July of 1861 and August of 1862, the First and Second Battles of Bull Run. One of its more-recent claims to fame, however, was as the former home of Lorena and John Wayne Bobbitt. Back in 1993, she had used a kitchen knife to cut off a portion of his manhood and then had thrown it out her car window because he had allegedly abused her. Later police found it and surgeons reattached it. She got off on temporary insanity, and had to spend forty-five days in a psychiatric hospital. He was acquitted of the charge of marital sexual assault. The whole sordid affair had given the town a black eye, earning it the nicknames *Manasshole* and *Manasty* among feminists. John had gone on to a brief but successful career as a porn star, making such cinematic gems as *John Wayne Bobbitt...Uncut* and *Frankenpenis*. Later he became a host/bartender/limo driver at the Moonlight Bunny Ranch, a cathouse in Carson City, Nevada. Mac once told me that what was scarier than Bobbitt's professional career was the fact that I knew about it. As you have probably already guessed by now, I do love the internet.

Anyway, this was what I thought about as I approached the old frame building that bore the address of ARM's office. I parked across the street and put some quarters in a meter. In ARM's parking lot sat a half dozen cars. On one side of the lot were a green Saturn coupe and a tan Ford Taurus. On the other side, against the wall of the building, were a white Chevy pickup, an old dark-blue Dodge Diplomat and...I stopped. Parked beyond the Dodge, tucked away in the shadows, sat a fire-engine red Jeep Grand Cherokee. I grabbed a pen and paper, and crossed the street.

No one was coming out of the building, so I slipped between the Dodge and Cherokee and got a good look. Although the

Cherokee's hood bore a shallow dent, its front fender was clean and its windshield was free of cracks. In fact it was spotless, not a speck of dirt on it. In the upper right hand corner, I saw a tiny transparent sticker. I leaned in close. It read *OLD GLORY WINDSHIELD*. I wrote down the license plate number, went back to my car and took out my cell phone. I dialed 411 for directory assistance.

"Operator," a man said.

"Every time I call a certain number I get a message saying 'all lines are busy.' I think something's wrong. Could you try it please?"

"What's the number?"

I read the number from the piece of paper.

"Hold, please."

I guessed ARM had caller-ID since ARM was high-tech enough to have a website...and since Shifflett appeared to be a deranged paranoid lunatic. The phone rang and the operator hung up.

"ARM," said the same husky voice as before, "before it's too late."

"Warren Shifflett?"

There was a muffled sound, then another voice came on the line. "Yo."

"Warren," I said. "It's me, Sam."

"Who?"

"Sam Doyle."

"You have the wrong number, son. I don't know any Doyles."

"I work for Senator Serling."

"Vicky Serling? That traitor?"

"It's about your contribution."

"Contribution? Boy, why in the hell would I give that bitch my money?"

"Is this Warren *Schiff* of Fairfax?"

"No, it ain't, but when you find him, tell him he's a traitor too."

He hung up.

It was a credible show of cluelessness on his part, but I needed something more. I left the safety of my VW again and climbed the rickety steps to the building's entrance. I walked down a long dim hallway, passing an insurance agency, a real estate appraiser and something called *Madam LeFleur's Fortunes*. I stopped at the door on which were painted the words *A.R.M.— BEFORE IT'S TOO LATE*.

I drew a deep breath and turned the knob. The office consisted of a single room holding a couple desks, a couple filing cabinets and a refrigerator. On the walls hung picket signs from rallies and a dartboard bearing the image of Osama bin Laden. Next to the dartboard hung a glass encased knife collection. Warm and fuzzy stuff.

In the back of the room, three men hunched over a copier-fax machine. Two of them wore jeans and T-shirts, one bearing a picture of the American flag, and the other reading *ARMY OF ONE* with the first three letters colored red. The third man wore khakis and a golf shirt. He straightened up and slapped his forehead.

"Samsung? No wonder it's broke. Who bought this piece of crap? You, Ray? Maybe you can get one of them Japs to crawl in there and fix it."

As the other men laughed, I began to question whether these guys even knew what caller-ID was.

The man in the golf shirt turned around, his deeply set eyes hidden in shadow. "Can I help you?"

"Mr. Shifflett?"

"Christ," he said. "Not another one."

"I'm just here to support the cause." I fished a fifty out of my wallet, handing it to him. I hoped it would do the trick; I was running out of those things. The bigger of the two men behind Shifflett hiked up his pants. "No shit. That's what I'm talking about."

Shifflett handed me an application. "Might as well enlist while you're at it."

One page, few questions. Not many criteria for being a racist vigilante. I wondered how fast they would throw my ass down the stairs if I told them I was half-Jewish.

I caught the pen he tossed me. "These the other commanding officers?"

He turned and waived behind him. "Big ugly fella there is Carl, our recruiter."

"Howdy," said Carl.

I raised a hand as if trying to stop traffic. No need to mosey over, big fella.

"Tall mute one there is Ray, our lobbyist."

Ray lifted his chin.

Shifflett said, "Politicians can hardly get a word in edgewise."

Shifflett had pasty white skin and tattoo-free arms. Carl had a mustache, a double chin and a pot belly. Ray had glasses, a pencil-thin neck and bad posture. None of them looked like the man in the Cherokee.

"You got a name?" said Shifflett.

My heart jumped up my throat. I hadn't planned on that question. "Henry Fisher," I finally said. Habits of honesty die hard.

Shifflett's grip was firm and cold. I resisted the impulse to wipe my hand on my pants.

"Fisher, huh? It's ringin' a bell." My stomach tightened. "How'd you hear about us?" he said.

"Word of mouth."

"Whose mouth?"

"Just a guy I work with at a bank in the city."

"Just a guy, huh? Is everyone at that bank as mysterious as you, Mr. Fisher?"

"We like to keep a low profile. Our clients like it that way. Which reminds me," I said, looking at my watch, "I have an appointment. Have to fill this out later. Good to meet you, and good luck with that copier." I tossed the pen back to him and walked out.

My heart was still pounding when I got in my car and locked my doors. What made me think I was savvy enough to do undercover work? Luckily, no one followed me, and I made it out of there in one piece. On my way back to DC, I called Roger and gave him what I had about the Grand Cherokee, Old Glory Windshield and Shifflett.

"You've been a busy little beaver."

"Can you look into it? Like where Shifflett was at the time of the hit-and-run, and whether he recently filed a claim with his insurer. I'd do it but—"

"It might involve bending the law?"

I was going to say, *I have no balls,* but his reason worked too.

"I'm on it," he said.

When I got off the phone with Roger, Marni called.

"Where have you been? All I've been getting is your voicemail."

"I turned my phone off. What's wrong?"

"A cop just came by, asking questions about the senator and, boy, was he pissed."

Chapter 15

"Let me guess," I said. "Detective Mills."

"Guy wouldn't let up," Marni said. "Finally I told him if he wanted to talk to us he had to go through you."

"Good job."

"What're we going to do?"

Usually I liked to postpone witness interviews. Mac had taught me that every day your client wasn't indicted was a victory, and that postponing government interviews of witnesses often meant postponing an indictment, if not avoiding it altogether. Of course it also opened the door to surprise visits at your client's place of business.

"Can you get everyone together in an hour?" I said.

"We're pretty busy." She waited for me to back down, then said, "I'll see what I can do."

I called Dr. Marshall.

"You're calling from your cell phone?" he said, his voice tense.

I assured him my cell phone was digital. Roger had once told me regular cell phones transmit low-frequency radio waves that can be intercepted, but digital phones are fairly secure from eavesdropping. Then again, who knew what the NSA was listening to? I gave him an update of my investigation, ending with Detective Mills' interest in the senator's staff.

"For Chrissake," he said, "don't let them tell him anything."

"I don't think they know anything."

"Keep it that way."

I called Detective Mills.

"Don't tell me," he said, "you represent the senator's staff too."

"I hadn't heard from you all afternoon. I was beginning to think you'd met someone else."

"You going to let me talk to them or you too busy fixing juries?"

Nice. "How about tomorrow?"

"How about right now?"

"What's the hurry?"

"I'm tired of getting the run-around from a kid."

"You're lucky the kid is letting you talk to his client's staff without a subpoena."

"I'm working on it."

"I'll have it quashed."

Both threats were equally unlikely. We settled on late afternoon. Hopefully that way he wouldn't have much time to conduct the interviews. Trouble was I wouldn't have much time to prepare for them.

Twenty people waited for me in the senator's conference room. Her chief of staff, Marni, her legislative director, a woman named Gale Fowler—who supervised the legislative assistants and advised the senator on terrorism issues—five legislative assistants, five legislative correspondents, the press secretary, the deputy press secretary, the office manager and five staff assistants.

I was used to speaking to groups from my prior life as a teacher, but sleepy kids were different from annoyed Hill staffers. I hadn't faced such a hostile audience since a mock jury trial in a trial advocacy class in law school two years before, which I'd lost after only about ten seconds of deliberation. I cleared my throat. "Thanks for coming."

Mrs. Fowler slammed shut her appointment book. "As if we had a choice. Why were the police here?"

"Routine investigation of a crime."

"You mean attack."

"They do believe it was intentional."

"Are we in danger?"

"I don't think so," I said truthfully.

"Was it terrorists who ran down the senator?"

"That's one theory. Another is the attack was personal."

"Are any of us suspects?"

"No. The gentleman from the MPD who was here earlier, Detective Mills, thinks you might have information that could lead to finding the assailant. He's just being thorough."

"Then why are you here?"

"Because you have other information, sensitive information, that the senator obtained from her seat on various Senate committees. I want to minimize Mills' questions about that information, and your disclosure of it."

"Are you implying one of us would betray the senator's confidences?"

"Gale," Marni said.

"It's all right," I said. "You don't know how Detective Mills' mind works, and he doesn't know how your office works. You might misinterpret his questions or he might misinterpret your answers."

"How can you clear up any misunderstandings if you don't know how our office works?"

"What I don't know you're going to tell me when I interview each of you."

The group let out a collective groan.

"It'll take only fifteen minutes per person. We'll hold the meetings here after this meeting. Ms. Bardoni made up a schedule. You can pick up a copy on your way out the door."

People started to stand.

"One more thing," I said, remembering what it felt like to keep a class after the bell. "Mills likes to show up unannounced. One of these days he might show up with a few friends. Next to the pile of schedules is a pile of memos about some rules to follow when served with a search warrant. Let me know if you have any questions."

The staff left and in a few minutes started returning, one by one.

Each of the meetings was pretty much the same. Give my spiel about privilege, cover the staff member's duties, including any contact with the campaign office, and ask my Joe Friday questions. Did anything unusual happen before the crime? Where were you at the time? Do you know why someone would want to hurt the senator? This last question invariably led to a discussion of the senator's activities on the Select Committee on Terrorism, but no one said anything about Harappa, PEACE or Sam Doyle. A good sign. I ended by explaining that their own lawyer could attend the interview. They all refused, so I gave them some ground rules on being a witness.

Relying on coffee and Life Savers I worked through lunch, finishing all but one of the meetings by mid-afternoon, the meeting Gale Fowler. As she settled into her chair, I studied her. She was a sturdy woman in her late-fifties, with jet-black hair and an unflinching stare. I ran through my script. Privilege, duties, Joe

Friday. She gave me the same answers as everyone else. Her only problem was her attitude. I would have to bring things to a head.

"The senator sits on the Select Committee on Terrorism," I said.

"Are you asking me or telling me?"

"Part of her duties on that committee includes talking to people, lobbyists and public interest groups about biowarfare, right?"

"My, you have acquired a commanding knowledge of what we do here."

"You don't seem to like me."

She recoiled for only a moment. "I don't like getting surprise visits from detectives. I don't like having to meet with lawyers when I'm trying to get my work done, and I don't like a child doing an adult's job. The idea of you protecting the senator. How old are you?"

I stared evenly into her blue-gray eyes. "Who has the senator talked to about biowarfare within the past six months?"

"What does that have to do with the investigation?"

"Among the theories Mills is likely to cover is that the senator was attacked because someone didn't like a position she had recently taken, either because it was too bold or too tame."

"That's ridiculous."

"I agree."

Deep down, we both knew it was neither ridiculous nor something with which I agreed. She grudgingly rattled off a list of individuals and organizations. Among them was PEACE. Not among them was ARM.

She waited for my next question, which would no doubt tell her the point of my questions and my theory of why the senator was attacked. I stared out the window at the waning sunlight, my eyes burning. We were both tired and liable to make a mistake in the careful conversation that would have to follow. I decided some questions were better left unasked.

I stood up and stretched, massaging my shoulder. Then I peeled the bandage from my forehead and pretended to examine the spot of dried blood on it. My badge of honor from the attack that killed my partner. I wasn't above playing the sympathy card.

"You're right," I said, "it's probably a dead end. I appreciate you putting up with me. I know I look young. Hell, I am young, especially for such a big job. I didn't ask for any of this. I'm just trying to find the guy who killed my best friend and who put the senator in the hospital. She hired me and Mac because she trusted us. To be honest, I don't want to let her down too. I hope you can understand."

I offered my hand. She rolled her eyes, then took it.

Marni popped her head in. "Dick Tracy's here."

As I took notes, I quickly realized Mills was tired, lazy or just not paying attention. He interviewed only a handful of staff members. He failed to ask key follow-up questions, he got sidetracked by the answers, and he spent less than half the time with each person that I had. The staff, on the other hand, followed my instructions. They told Mills if they didn't understand his questions, they answered without speculating, and they didn't say anything unexpected. God bless them.

By the time Mills called in Mrs. Fowler, darkness had fallen. He got up to pour himself a cup of coffee. As he checked the credenza for more sugar packets, I yawned loudly and tapped my watch.

"What's the hurry?" he said.

"Been a long day."

"Crime doesn't sleep."

"Taxpayers do."

"You live in Virginia."

"You get paid with federal tax dollars."

"Children," said Mrs. Fowler, "can we get this over with?"

Finally Mills got started, asking her the usual questions. Position, background, what happened the day of the accident, whether she knew why someone would want to hurt the senator. He thought enough to ask the names of people or organizations with whom the senator had recently talked about terrorism, but the question was vague, and luckily Mrs. Fowler, whether because of fatigue or instinct, didn't mention PEACE.

Mills stared at the ceiling and chewed his pen cap. I tilted my chair back against the wall and folded my arms. The day had been a moderate success. I was tracking down leads, crossing off suspects, and no one was in jail. I imagined my bed, the cool sheets, the soft pillows, the down comforter.

Then Mills said, "Was the senator having any sort of legal problems?"

I nearly fell out of my chair. "Time out," I said. "You don't expect her to actually answer that, do you?"

"It's relevant to the perp's motive."

"You're fishing in protected waters."

"I'm entitled to know the general subject-matter of your representation of Senator Serling. Facts like that aren't privileged, only communications."

"In that case, the general subject-matter of our communications was legal advice regarding a potential criminal matter." This much, I figured, he already knew from the fact Mac and I were white collar criminal defense lawyers.

"What are you trying to hide?"

I could see the wheels start to turn in Mrs. Fowler's head. I jerked my thumb toward her. "Can she go? You know I'm not going to let her answer the question, and it looks like that's all you have left."

"No, she can't go."

I turned to Mrs. Fowler. "You can go."

She looked at me and then Mills.

"Pull the door shut on your way out," I said.

I was gambling. She must have been as tired as I was.

Mills watched her leave then shook his head. "That was a mistake. Now I want to interview Marshall."

"The husband of the target of your investigation? Sure, he'd be happy to help you try to put his wife in jail."

"I'm investigating a murder, not Senator Serling."

"Right, that's why you asked if she was having legal problems."

"Knowing why she was meeting with you is the key to knowing the murderer's motive. Maybe if you stopped covering her ass and started helping me, you'd see that."

"I want to find Mac's murderer as much as you do, Detective. I'm just going to do it the right way."

"I don't know, maybe you and Mac weren't so buddy-buddy."

I felt my face redden. "Maybe it's time for you to pull your head out of your ass."

I expected a barrage of return fire, but this time making me lose my cool seemed to please Mills. He finished his coffee, slipped his notes into a Manila folder and stood up. "I was looking forward to working with you to find Mac's killer," he said. "I'm sorry you and the senator have chosen not to cooperate with the department's investigation."

I stood and pretended to pack up my papers. After he left, I sank into my chair, feeling sick. I was such a fool. I should've known. Mills was going after the senator with or without any evidence.

T he next morning I represented Marita in a hearing in DC Superior Court. Jorge didn't show up, despite having been served with her petition. I presented evidence in favor of a protective order: eye-witness testimony of Marita and her children of Jorge's recent assault, digital photos of her black eye and swollen nose taken the morning after he'd broken into her apartment, hospital records of her injuries, and more photos of her broken door and ransacked apartment. Marita cried tears of joy when the judge granted motion. *Don't get too excited,* I wanted to tell her. *It's just a piece of paper.* What I said instead was "It's only as good as our ability to enforce it. Be sure to immediately report any violation."

That afternoon, after I'd dropped off Marita and her kids at home, Amelia arrived at Tony & Joe's in the Georgetown Harbour out of breath. "Don't you look happy," she said.

I was guilty as charged, although I felt bad about it, under the circumstances.

"Saw you on the eleven o'clock news last night," she said. "Those reporters camped outside your apartment building, sticking microphones in your face. It looked like they knocked you down."

"I just tripped on an electrical cord."

"You look like you've recovered. You didn't have to wear a coat and tie."

"You don't look like you just came from the hospital."

She wore a sky-blue silk sweater set and a black slim-fitting knee-length skirt with a girlish ruffle at the bottom. "This old thing?" she said.

The hostess showed us to an outside table under a blue umbrella, where we ordered iced teas. As we waited for them to arrive, we exchanged smiles. Then hers faded. "In the interest of full disclosure," she said, "there is sort of this other guy."

Other guy? Christ. I'd ironed my pants for this woman. "Thanks for the heads up," I said, straining to keep the sarcasm out of my voice.

"I didn't know if I should say something sooner," she said. "I mean, I didn't know if it was relevant."

Relevant? The word struck me as so...scientific. Was I just another patient to this woman?

"Sorry," she said. "I guess I was confused. I guess I wanted ...I wanted to pretend he didn't exist." I stopped fidgeting with the silverware, wanting to dig the wax out of my ears. Hi ho, come again. You wanted to pretend he didn't exist? Could it be? Yes, I believe it could. She liked me. No, she more than liked me. She wanted me. She was digging the ol' Hankster!

"Don't get me wrong," she said. "Brock is a good guy—"

I flipped up my hand. *Time out*, I wanted to say. *Hold the phone. Curb the wagon and post the horses.* "Not Brock Aurelia," I said.

"You know him?"

I stopped our waitress, who was passing by carrying a tray

of Coronas to a table of drunk college girls, and I took one of the bottles. When I was done with half of it, I burped under my breath and said, "From softball. He plays first base." Taking the high road, I didn't add that he *insists* on playing first base, and that he couldn't catch a cold if he were singing Carmen in his birthday suit on an iceberg.

"I've been too busy to come watch," she said.

"That's all right," I said. "He's been too busy to play lately. He's an associate over at Pound & Shields."

Although the firm had its own team, Brock was too obnoxious to be welcome on it. He showed up to games wearing a batting glove and metal cleats, and carrying a titanium bat. He argued with the ump over a call, threw down his helmet when he struck out, and heckled opposing batters. Okay, fine, some losers did that stuff, but this guy actually talked smack to runners while on base. *Your mama is so poor she goes to Kentucky Fried Chicken to lick other people's fingers.* It might be funny if he wasn't serious. One time he actually tried the hidden-ball trick on a girl. She just slapped the ball out of his glove and jogged to second base. After the games, the guys would tell him we were going to a bar on the Hill, and then make a beeline for Adams Morgan. They called him *Brick* because he had such a bad rap with girls. It wasn't just lame, it was lethal. And infectious. If you were standing within ten feet of him, no girls would make eye contact with you. You had to leave the bar and come in again like you were from out of town.

"Are you guys, you know, serious?" I said.

"He keeps asking me to marry him."

When I stopped choking on my beer, I said, "What do you keep answering?"

"Well, no. It's too soon. We've just been out to the movies, dinner a couple times, a baseball game once."

"How long have you been seeing him?"

"A few months, here and there. I've been working so hard. He doesn't care if I can't get together, or if I have to cancel. He just keeps calling."

Christ, I thought, if she marries him, her last name would be Aurelia. *Amelia Aurelia bo belia. Banana fana fo felia. Fe fi fo felia. Amelia!*

"What are you smiling at?" she said.

"Just wondering how you met him."

"I'm getting the feeling you don't like him."

"No, please, I want to hear about him, about you two."

Amelia told me how she'd been set up with him by her aunt, because Brock is the nephew of another senator. I remembered something about that, about how before law school Brock had worked on the Hill, as an intern on the Senate judiciary committee archiving files, attending hearings, making crucial runs to Starbucks. Now he was working as a complex commercial litigation associate at Pound & Shields, raking in the bucks. Reviewing documents, cite-checking briefs, never having tried a case probably, but then again, never slumming it in DC Small Claims Court for a cleaning woman either. Suddenly I remembered he was the chair of the Young Lawyers Section of the DC Bar Association. He recently had his photo on the cover of some bar association journal. *Young Guns* was the title, or something equally cheesy. God, the kid was more like a pea shooter. I smiled and shook my head.

"Really, Hank," Amelia was saying, "if you don't want to hear about it, just say so."

"Who?" I said. "Me? No, I was just listening. 'Brock took me to the Holocaust Museum on our first date. It was really romantic.'"

"You know, it's beneath you to be jealous."

Jealous? "My, don't we have a high opinion of ourselves?"

"Would you stop? What I wanted to tell you, I mean, the whole reason I brought it up—"

"Go on."

"I'm going to break up with him."

Now we were talking. "Any particular reason?"

She gave me her *Come off it* look.

"All right then," I said. "In that case I was jealous."

"I would hope so."

I breathed in the briny air, trying to relax, trying to appreciate just being there with her, trying to remember what it was like to come here before Mac died. Upriver a boat blew its horn under one of the low arches of the Key Bridge. Laughter came from the deck of a yacht tied to a cleat on the boardwalk. The yacht bobbed up and down, its long antennae swaying. A Marine wearing running shoes, red nylon shorts and dog tags wove his way through a pack of camera-toting tourists. He had a small blue tattoo on his shoulder. It looked familiar.

"Penny for your thoughts," Amelia said.

"That's about what they're worth," I said. "How's your aunt?"

"Getting better. The swelling's going down. I'm more worried about my mom. She won't eat, she won't sleep."

As we talked about Mrs. Fuentes, a cloud passed over Amelia's face. When we finished, it was her time to grow quiet. She opened the menu listlessly, her eyes focusing on her lap. Around us people chatted. At the bar a pop song came on the radio. Amelia noticed me watching her.

"I'm glad you picked this place," she said. "I'm starving, and I love seafood."

Just like that, her eyes were twinkling again. Our waiter appeared with our drinks. Amelia ordered a cup of clam chowder and a tuna filet sandwich.

"That's all a starving seafood-lover orders?"

She offered to throw in a shrimp cocktail if I would split it with her. I ordered a crab cake sandwich and French fries. She squeezed a lemon wedge, dropping the rind into her glass.

"So how long have you been my aunt's lawyer?"

"Why do I feel like I'm about to have a physical?"

"I'm not that sort of doctor."

"Not long. Mac was who she hired. Your uncle—"

"Step-uncle."

"He'd heard about Mac from a case he'd recently handled."

"That case against Bustamonte. Didn't you work on it too?"

I sipped my iced tea. "Mmm hmm."

"Then why'd you say Mac handled it?"

"My job was just to make him look good."

"You're not good at lying, are you?"

"I did the easy stuff: investigating the facts, researched the law, writing the briefs. He did the hard stuff: negotiating with prosecutors, trying cases, arguing appeals. He was a natural in court."

Amelia hesitated then said, "I know it's not true what they're saying about him on TV."

"I appreciate that."

"What's the Office of Bar Counsel, anyway?"

"The prosecutorial arm of the DC Board on Professional Responsibility. It investigates the ethics of lawyers' conduct."

"It must be busy."

"Funny."

"What if it finds a lawyer did something wrong?"

"It either admonishes him or petitions the Board for a hearing."

"What happens if there's a hearing?"

"The Hearing Committee drafts a report for the Board, which then hears oral argument and drafts another report for the DC Court of Appeals."

"What if the court decides the lawyer did something wrong?"

"Admonition, censure, suspension, expulsion." *Shame, disgrace, inebriation and a permanent tropical vacation.*

"You don't seem worried," Amelia said.

"Ms. Carver's lying. The truth will come out sooner or later."

Amelia nodded, then said, "How old are you?"

I laughed.

"Sorry," she said, "my friends tell me I put them under a microscope."

"It's okay. Thirty-two."

"You must be good to be able to represent a senator all by yourself in a criminal investigation."

"Some of us have greatness thrust upon us."

"I get the impression," she said, "that you don't like being a lawyer."

I shrugged, pretending this wasn't getting uncomfortable. "I like some of it."

"What parts?"

"Investigating things."

"Like what? Crimes?"

I thought about it. "Well, as a kid, I *was* addicted to mystery novels. Mickey Spillane, Dashiell Hammett, Ed McBain. I even went through a snooty British phase: Arthur Conan Doyle, Agatha Christi, PD James, anything I could get my hands on."

"Huh."

"Said the doctor after making an astute diagnosis."

"So why didn't you become an FBI agent or a private detective?"

Was she serious? "The closest I've ever come to solving a murder was guessing Rusty's wife did it by Chapter Four of *Presumed Innocent*. Besides, guns aren't my thing."

"I don't think guns are the reason. I think it's something else. Fear maybe."

Ouch, I thought. Put away the microscope and take out the scalpel.

"Not physical fear," she said. "More like moral fear."

"You sound like my father."

"What did he want you to be?"

"A girl."

"Seriously."

"A minister."

She laughed.

"Hey, I thought about it," I said, "even majored in religion, but I couldn't pull the trigger. Too many questions, not enough answers."

"Was he disappointed?"

"He doesn't care, as long as I obey at least six of the Ten Commandments."

"Which ones?"

"Any of them. He just figures sixty percent is passing."

She laughed again, a sound I was getting used to. "I don't know," she said, "maybe it's just fear of not being respectable."

"Could be. To my mother, a career tapping people's phones and repossessing cars is one step short of joining the Klan. She's Jewish."

"And your dad's a minister?"

"They were children of the sixties. Met on a commune. They gave up the alfalfa sprouts and tofu when they started paying taxes."

"So what does that make you?"

"Spiritually? Schizophrenic."

"What did she want you to be?"

"A college English professor. You know, with patches on the elbows of his tweed coat, and the next great American novel in his desk drawer."

"Was she disappointed?"

"Inconsolably."

She studied me. "I don't see you as a teacher."

"Neither did the ninth graders I was trying to teach *Catcher in the Rye* to."

"So why'd you switch to law?"

"If I had to work with obnoxious adolescents all day, I figured I might as well get paid something for it."

"What about the great American novel part?"

"I once wrote a really bad novel about a high school English teacher who was struggling to write a really bad novel about a high school English teacher."

"What happened to it?"

"I couldn't figure out how to end it."

"You have a good sense of humor. She must be happy."

"My mother? She'd be happier if I moved back home and enrolled in the PhD program at Case Western."

"Do you have any siblings?"

"No."

"But you had a brother, right?"

I was back to feeling uncomfortable again.

"Sorry," she said.

"Car accident," I said, "sixteen."

"Oh. Do you not want to talk about it?"

"No, it's okay."

She paused, then said, "How old were you?"

"Twelve. I was in the car with him."

That seemed to be enough. "I'm sorry," she said.

I nodded. We were all sorry. Sorry was our middle name. I was a sorry teenager, then I was a sorry teacher, and now I was a sorry lawyer. Luckily the waiter arrived with our shrimp cocktail. As Amelia and I ate, we made some much-welcomed small talk about mindless subjects. The Europeans who frequented the Harbour's bars at night. The best seafood restaurants in DC. Things to do in nearby Annapolis. She described how her Uncle Harry and Aunt Vicky used to take her sailing there sometimes when she was visiting them during the summers at their beach house in Virginia Beach.

I waited until she'd finished her soup before I started my own cross-exam.

"Back at the reception after Mac's funeral, you told your uncle—"

"Step-uncle."

"You told your step-uncle I was—what was it? 'A one-man show. With 'no associates, no secretary, and no wife.'"

"Aren't you?"

"How did you know that?"

"I'm a good listener."

"I guess so. Not much of a talker, though. You didn't tell me at the hospital you're Senator Serling's niece."

"You never asked."

"Or maybe you don't like being the niece of a famous senator."

"My turn to squirm under the microscope? I can take it or leave it. Half the people who find out tell me how much they respect my aunt for going after terrorists while protecting our civil rights. The other half just shake their heads, but you can see the hate in their eyes."

"You don't like politics."

"My patients don't care what I think about racial profiling or illegal immigration. Still, I campaigned for Aunt Vicky in Fairfax County. Big Hispanic population. They seemed to listen to me."

"And you didn't like that feeling being out there?"

"My dad's in politics. *Was,* I should say. He retired last year. He was a judge."

"Elected?"

"Down in Fort Myers. First to the Lee County Court, and then to the Florida Circuit Court. Always hated campaigning. Used to say, 'This yob's for the birds.' He still has a Cuban accent. Emigrated in 1960, after Castro took over."

"So you decided to become a doctor?"

"My," she said. "It really is my turn to squirm. I decided my freshman year of college. That's when my uncle died. I was depressed and threw myself into school."

"Chemistry's a lot more predictable than life." I'd meant the remark sympathetically. I winced inwardly.

"Touché," she said. "I guess that, on some level, I became a doctor because I knew if Guatemala had offered better emergency care..."

Your uncle might have lived. Now I really sympathized with her. I knew what it was like to want to go back in time and save someone's life. Time to change the channel. "Must have been hard on your aunt," I said.

"She had a rough time being alone. She'd been with my uncle since UVA. He went on to law school there, and she went on to get her PhD. Comparative Politics."

"*Comparative* politics?"

"She concentrated in Middle East studies."

"Is that when she joined the CIA?"

"When my uncle went to work at a firm in Richmond, she started posing as an energy analyst for a small consulting firm there."

Like Valerie Plame, I thought.

"When my uncle left the Virginia General Assembly and went to Congress, her firm moved to Georgetown. She would go with him to embassy parties and on trips abroad. No one suspected a thing until he was murdered in Central America. The press started snooping around for a motive, and her cover was blown."

"But she used it to her advantage."

"It's not like it's the first time a widow has taken her husband's Congressional seat. Mary Bono, Lois Capps, Jo Ann Emerson, all winning special elections."

"You know your stuff."

"Politics is all she talks about."

"How did she meet Dr. Marshall?"

"At a biopharm conference in Maryland. He was there on behalf of Panacea. She was speaking on biowarfare."

"And they caught the love bug."

"Ugh. I take back what I said about your sense of humor, but they did have a lot in common. They helped each other with their jobs. She flew up on weekends to visit him in New York. They were married within a year."

"Wow."

"She was lonely."

"He lived in New York?"

"Upstate, small town called Cazenovia, outside Syracuse. Few hours from where he grew up in Westchester."

"Nice."

"How do you think he got the capital to start Panacea? His trust fund was larger than most hospitals' endowments."

"So what did he do about his job when he got married?"

"Tried to get his employees to relocate to Montgomery County, Maryland, ground zero for biotech companies. They wouldn't go for it. Evidently they were addicted to the rain, sleet and snow. So he bought a house in Middleburg and a corporate jet, and commuted. Only took an hour or so."

And hundred gallons of jet fuel. "He and your aunt lived happily ever after?"

"Until she decided to run for the Senate. Lawrence wanted her to retire. He humored her, giving his moral and financial support. I don't think he really expect she'd win."

"Was he upset?"

"You have to understand Lawrence was fifty-seven when they got married. Hadn't dated much. Hadn't even worked with women much. His company was in the business of curing infectious diseases. Few female scientists wanted to work with viruses or bacteria that were known to cause birth defects. Even if he'd been around women more, I doubt he would have known how to act. He'd been the big kahuna at the company for twenty-five years. He was used to having things his way."

"In other words, what he really wanted was a trophy wife, not a power-broker."

"Don't tell me you're afraid of strong women or we might not have another date."

"I thought this was just an update."

She smiled. The waiter appeared with our bill. Amelia politely let me pay but couldn't resist a jibe. "If you're going to write this off as a business expense, don't we have to talk about the case?"

"The cherry blossoms are in bloom."

We walked along the Potomac toward the Jefferson Memorial, passing the Watergate Hotel and the Kennedy Center. I told her about the past two days' events: my investigation of her aunt's campaign office, Sam Doyle, ARM and my attendance at Detective Mills' witness interviews. As expected she had a lot of questions. It wasn't until we reached the Tidal Basin that her curiosity was finally satisfied.

The tourists were out in full force. Cars circling for parking spaces, families posing for photos, kids whining. We squeezed between some baby strollers and found an empty space along the Basin. The water's edge was wreathed in pink-and-white buds exploding in color.

"I read there are thirty-seven hundred of these things," I said.

Amelia yawned. "Sorry," she said.

"When's the last time you slept?"

She looked at her watch. "Umm, Tuesday."

We walked back to the Harbour in silence. She said she'd taken a cab from the hospital and let me drive her home. When we reached my car, she stopped in her tracks. "You do *not* drive a powder-blue Cabriolet."

I'd been so focused on her that I'd forgotten what was coming. "I won it in a raffle," I said.

"Where? At your college sorority?"

"At my father's church."

"People bought tickets to win this?"

"My dad pitched it as a 'mystery dream car,' not 'a dopey chick car.' I tried to return it but the fund-raising director wouldn't accept it. Said it was too funny. She posted a big picture of me driving it in the church bulletin."

"How many miles does it have on it?"

"The odometer stopped working at a hundred and eighty thousand."

"Does the rest of it work?"

"When it's in the mood."

"What's happening with the bumper?"

"I've been meaning to redo that bungee cord."

"Is that a hole in the floorboard?"

"Just slide that piece of plywood over it."

"Do I have to sign a waiver or something before I get in?"

"That's what Mac used to say."

"My God, he must have loved it."

"I think he used to lie awake at night thinking up jokes about it. He was the one who put that bumper sticker there."

"'I brake for kittens.'"

"And that one."

"'My other car is a Miata.'"

"Always got him laughing. I considered it my little gift to him."

"That's the reason you kept it?"

"I promised myself I'd pay off my student loans before I bought a new one. And by 'new one,' I don't mean a VW but a ten-cylinder Ford Mustang or maybe a Dodge Viper."

"You'd actually drive one of those?"

"No."

"Well, it takes a secure man to drive a car like this."

I decided to leave well enough alone, and unlocked her door. The car was ready and willing but not able. The low-oil buzzer went off as I exited the parking lot even though I'd put in a quart of Pennzoil that morning, and the engine stalled three times while climbing the Georgetown hill. In her driveway, the engine rattled nervously. Amelia leaned over and examined the dashboard, whose lights were blinking...the ones that worked.

"You going to be able to get home?" she said.

"Are you kidding? This baby's just warming up." When I thumped the dashboard, the engine belched a cloud of black smoke then quit. "I'll make it to Rosslyn at least. It can still roll down hill."

She opened her car door before I could make it out of mine. We stood in the driveway, looking at each other. Sunlight filtered through the trees above, dappling her golden skin and brown hair, her hazel eyes squinting, just like her aunt's.

"Thanks for the update," she said, putting a hand on my shoulder and offering me her cheek.

I pressed my lips against her soft skin, losing myself in her perfume. By the time I opened my eyes, she was half-way up the steps to her townhouse.

"Can I call you?" I said before I could stop myself.

She smiled down at me. "You sure you want to date the boss's niece?"

Before I could think of a clever answer, she waved and disappeared inside the house.

Chapter 17

D_{r.} Mukhtar had been expecting my call. We set up a time for me to come by the next morning and interview PEACE's employees, whose names I asked for, along with a copy of Hassan's employment file. After a few moments, a fax came through.

Abdul Hassan's *file* consisted of a two-page employment application. Social Security number, home address, telephone number and photocopy of his DC driver's license. I called Roger. "The usual?" he said.

"Focus on Hassan."

"Be a few hours."

"Put it on my tab. By the way, did you find out anything about Shifflett's Cherokee?"

"Apparently it was stolen a few days before the hit-and-run. Showed up on Sunday back in Manassas on the side of the road. Windshield smashed."

"His alibi for the time of the hit-and-run?"

"You're not going to believe this."

"He was doing charity work with his priest."

"He was down at the police station reporting the theft."

"The entire time?"

"That's what the desk sergeant says."

I wondered what it all meant. Another setup? It would fit the killer's MO. I thanked Roger and pulled up PEACE's website.

The association's purpose was to educate children about the tenets of Islam and to support Arabic-Americans who've been subjected to discrimination. It taught children by promoting cultural events, encouraging teachers to ensure an accurate portrayal of Arab history, and offering scholarships to study the Arabic language. It fought discrimination by giving legal and financial support to victims, publishing a monthly newsletter reporting cases of discrimination, and lobbying TV networks and film studios about the fair portrayal of Muslims.

It had about ten thousand members. Yearly dues were fifty dollars per person, additional yearly donations were about a hundred grand, and the endowment was more than a million. I didn't have to do any math to realize PEACE could easily have come up with the hundred-plus grand needed for the setup.

I finished my coffee and grabbed my blazer. The address on Mr. Hassan's employment application belonged to a large, brick, crescent-shaped apartment building on Wisconsin Ave., near the Cathedral. *Eden Gardens*. I tried to remember where I'd heard the name before.

The door was locked, requiring a security code. In front was a bench on which sat a little old lady holding a Tupperware container. I took a *Washington Post* from a trashcan and sat down. Pretty soon a van labeled *Holy Roller* pulled up and discharged an old man, who shuffled up the sidewalk. I waited for him to punch in the security code, then I courteously opened the door for him.

One look around the lobby and I knew the address on Hassan's application was bogus.

Straight ahead was a dimly lighted chapel, and to the right was a sleepy reading room. Against the other wall hung a bulletin board listing the day's rousing activities. *9:00 a.m.—Aqua Aerobics at YMCA. 10:30 a.m.—Trip to Wal-Mart. 11:30 a.m.—2:00 p.m.—Buffet in Main Dining Room. 2:00 p.m.— Sewing Circle in Crafts Room. 3:00 p.m.—"Computer-Ease" in Library. 4:00 p.m.—Choir Practice in Chapel. 5:00 p.m.— Mass in Chapel. 6:00 p.m.—Country Cookin' in Main Dining Room. 7:00 p.m.—The Good-Book Club in Library. 8:00 p.m.—Yahtzee in Main Lounge (proceeds to go to Catholic Charities).*

Out of curiosity I took the elevator up to Hassan's floor. The hallway was quiet and smelled of stale perfume. I was having flashbacks to visiting my grandma as a boy. Hassan's door knocker was in the form of a crucifix. A short thin gray-haired woman answered. She wore thick black glasses, a plain black skirt and a plain white blouse.

"You're a nun," I said without thinking.

"You're in the wrong place if you got something against nuns."

"Sorry, sister. I'm just surprised. I thought this place was just for lay people. Why aren't you living with other nuns?"

"There're nuns here. There's a short one down the hall. Only eats unleavened bread and soda water. Lord knows how she got so fat. Crosses herself when she gets on the elevator. Like a pulley and steel cables is a newfangled invention. Then there's the ex-Latin teacher. Burns incense before Notre Dame games. Set off the sprinkler system last year in the one against Michigan. *Vene vide torchee.* And, of course, there's the one with Alzheimers downstairs. Keeps going up for the Eucharist at mass. Everyone's too damn polite to say anything. Father Numbnuts had to double his monthly order."

"I guess I meant why don't you live with them in a more organized way?"

"Like in a convent for the Order of Saint Geezers?"

That answered that question.

"I was supposed to," she said, "in the care of younger nuns. But the supply of them has run low. And the ones there are, they don't wants to chip in part of their salary for the care of their elders anymore. So here I am clipping coupons and fighting over Medicaid. Playing solitaire on my computer and waiting for five o'clock so I can start sipping whiskey sours. Contemplating mortality instead of immortality. Let me give you some advice: if you see a statue of the Virgin Mary crying, run to AA, not to church."

Good to remember, I thought.

"You didn't come for my unholy advice," she said.

"I'm looking for a man. He said he lived at this address."

She didn't take the copy of Hassan's license. "What do you want with him?"

"Just some questions."

"You a cop?"

"Just a lawyer."

"Lord, do I hate lawyers."

"Join the club," I mumbled.

She studied me, then the license.

"I've lived here for five years. Never seen him before."

I opened my mouth and she raised a wrinkled hand. "No, I haven't heard of anyone by that name, or seen any mail addressed to him. And, no, I won't call you if I think of anything."

She started to slam the door. I stopped it with my foot, thinking if this was what being an investigator was like I was going to have to start wearing boots.

I said, "You don't happen to drive a Cadillac, do you?"

"Sure, they hand those things out to you when you take your vow of poverty."

With that she finished slamming the door.

"Amen," I said.

Her neighbors were more affable but equally uninformative. I sat back on the bench in front of the building, took out my cell phone and punched in the number on Hassan's employment application. A pay phone behind me rang.

"Garden of Eden, Adam speaking," I said into it, hearing my own voice in the cell phone in my other hand. I retreated to my office in defeat. At 7:00 p.m. Roger Lynch called.

"All six names are clean," he said, "though something funny did come up with Mr. Hassan."

"Don't tell me he's in prison too."

"Worse. He's a woman, and she's dead."

I wanted to give up.

Roger said, "That Social Security number you gave me belonged to forty-five-year-old chain-smoker from Newark named Aliyah Hassan. Died of cancer. No survivors."

"*Aliyah*? But Abdul had a driver's license. Could the DMV have mixed up the first names?"

"He probably changed it after he assumed her identity. Convinced DMV to change gender, that it'd made a mistake. It happens, especially with ethnic names."

"But she's dead."

"Happened only a few months ago, after Mr. Hassan got the license."

"Did he, or she, own a car?"

"Not even a credit card."

I thought for a moment. "Where was Doyle born?"

"That guy in prison? Hold on." Some papers rustled. "Secaucus."

"How far is that from Newark?"

"Twenty minutes. You think there's a connection?"

"Can you check it out? Anything that connects Doyle and Hassan."

"I won't be able to get to it for a few days, and it'll require travel."

"I'm told money is no object."

"In that case I'm hitting the blackjack tables in Atlantic City."

I ignored the fact AC was a long way from Newark. "I don't care if you have tea at the Ritz, as long as you link Doyle to Hassan."

Even though I had all the confidence in Roger, I wasn't optimistic about what he would find. Nor was I optimistic about my upcoming meeting at PEACE. A glutton for punishment, I surfed the nightly TV news programs, searching for an update on the Eugenia Carver story. I couldn't figure out why the stations were replaying the same footage from two nights before...until I found Holly Hickey on Channel One, standing alone in front of Ms. Carver's house, wearing pearls and a frown.

"...questions to which the answers will have to wait until Ms. Carver is located," she said.

Ms. Carver was missing? Of course she was. Why would clearing Mac's good name be easy?

Unlike Holly Hickey I couldn't wait for answers. The next morning, in the privacy of PEACE's offices, I asked Dr. Mukhtar about Abdul Hassan and the improper campaign contribution. He insisted he didn't know any more than what I knew, but he said I was free to talk to his staff.

He escorted me to the office of the associate director, to the office of the deputy associate director, to the office of the legal director—all of whom answered my questions—and then down the corporate ladder...

There was a lot of escorting going on, but not a whole lot of information given.

No one knew anything. Never heard of Conway or Doyle.

Didn't have a close friendship with Hassan. Couldn't even tell me much about him other than he looked to be forty to forty-five years old and had kept to himself since starting work last fall.

"There must be something that stood out about him," I said to the last staff member on my odyssey, Legislative Director Kaseem Jibran. "Did he have any strange friends, odd habits, an accent even?"

"Now that you mention it, he had a sort of nasally voice."

I perked up. "Nasally?"

"Like he'd chop off the ends of his words."

"For example?"

"He'd say, 'I'm going for a walk on the Mall,' but it would come out 'I'm going for a wak on the Mah.' Or he would call Peyton Manning 'Pey'n.'"

Great, that described about only ten million people between Albany and Chicago. Kaseem led me back to the office of Dr. Mukhtar's office, who was hanging up the phone.

"I looked through our records and checked with the bank," said Dr. Mukhtar. "You were right, Abdul never cashed any of his paychecks. I don't get it."

"What about his computer files and e-mails?"

"Nothing about Senator Serling, Riley Conway or Sam Doyle."

"Would it be possible for me to see them?"

"Sorry, we have a confidentiality policy. I'm letting you talk to our staff members only as a favor to the senator. She's been a big supporter."

Confidentiality policy? The woman was in a coma. I felt my blood pressure rise. I said, "I'm sure she'd like to continue to be a big supporter."

Dr. Mukhtar stiffened. "Are you threatening me, Mr. Fisher? I don't believe for a second the senator would turn on us. Even if she did, we have enemies far worse than her."

I felt my face flush. "I'm sorry. I don't have any reason to think she would do that. It's just that I've hit a dead end and I don't know where else to turn."

He leaned back in his chair and studied me. "What's your religious background?"

"Excuse me?"

"If you don't mind."

"I'm just wondering why it's relevant."

"You're a lawyer. You see things in terms of what is legal and what is not legal. I'm a man of God. I see things through a different lens."

I knew what he meant, and I wanted to point out that sometimes the lenses overlap. In college I did my thesis on a comparison of Islamic jurisprudence and Jewish jurisprudence, but I wasn't in the mood for a theological discussion.

"My mother's Jewish," I said.

"So, you're a Jew."

"The jury's still out on that one."

I explained that my father was an Episcopal minister.

Dr. Mukhtar was confused. "Were you circumcised?"

"And baptized."

"Then you are what they call an 'apostate,' one who has renounced Judaism."

My father was too smart for that. He baptized me when I was a baby so I couldn't be said to have freely chosen to reject Judaism.

"I haven't renounced anything, doctor." Yet, at the same time, I had renounced everything.

"You must have chosen at some point. When you were a boy, did you have a confirmation, or a Bar Mitzvah?"

Now he was starting to bother me. "Is that really the crucial fact, doctor? In the Episcopal Church, only the major sacraments of baptism and communion are required, not the minor sacrament of confirmation. And a Jewish boy automatically becomes obligated to observe the commandments of Judaism at the age of thirteen; a Bar Mitzvah isn't necessary."

"Have you observed the commandments of Judaism?"

Only in the way a speeding driver glances at a caution sign. "I think it's fair to say I've equally disappointed both religions."

I wanted to tell Dr. Mukhtar he was still headed down the wrong road. If he wanted to prove I'd taken sides he should figure out if I had *received communion,* when in fact I spat the Body of Christ into my folded hands afterward; or if I had *freely chosen* to be an acolyte, when I climbed into my robe only after a screaming fit; or if I had committed *timely and public* acts of identification with the Jewish people, when I only occasionally attended synagogue. The truth is that, until I graduated from college, I did everything I could to avoid deciding what I was, until I finally gave up trying to be anything at all.

"Forgive me," he said, "I don't mean to pry, but I find this very interesting. Have you ever studied Islam?"

"In college. I liked its view of man as basically good as opposed to Christianity, which starts from the premise that man is a sinner. I also liked the way people atone for their sins. You know, the way all you need is a sincere confession and repentance. In Christianity there's all that carrying the cross stuff. And I liked how Muhammad was just a man, full of faults."

"What is your view of your country's treatment of Muslims?"

"I'm sorry?"

"You are thoughtful. You must have an opinion."

"I don't know. I think the vast majority of Muslims in America condemn terrorism and religious extremism. A couple years ago a group of Islamic religious scholars here issued a religious ruling to that effect, a fatwa, but a lot of Americans don't care about that. All they see are the Middle-Eastern Muslims on TV, burning flags and blowing themselves up. Americans know just enough about the *Koran* and Muhammad to misunderstand them. The fact the

Koran is peppered with quotes inciting violence, and the fact Muhammad was a fighter who killed many people. The problem is not really with the Jihad that all Muslims fight. It's how they fight it. Moderate Muslims view the Jihad as an internal war, a spiritual struggle to submit oneself to Allah, right? Extremist Muslims see the Jihad as an external war, a reason to kill anyone who isn't Muslim."

"So you would agree your country misunderstands Islam, and that is why they mistreat Muslims?"

I smiled, wondering why it was so important to the man to make me say the words he wanted to hear. "I think most Americans probably want to avoid another 9/11 so much they are willing to turn a blind eye as prosecutors and agents harass certain single male Muslims between the ages of eighteen and forty-five, to disrupt any sleeper cells in America."

"What do you yourself want?"

"I just want to find my friend's killer."

"To take an eye for an eye? Why not turn the other cheek?"

I felt my face redden again, just like in the senator's office, with Detective Mills. This investigating stuff was harder than I thought. Finally Dr. Muhktar said, "What information are you really looking for, Mr. Fisher?"

I thought about it, deciding this was probably going to be my best chance at finding out what I wanted, but that I had to pick my question carefully. "Has PEACE taken any controversial stands lately?"

"For instance?"

"Like with regard to the manufacturer of Harappa?"

Now it was Dr. Mukhtar's turn to think for a while. "There has been a rumor. About an American biopharm company."

"*American*?" Was he serious? I could just see the headlines around the world. *US Develops Doomsday Disease.*

Superpower Synthesizes Super Virus. Harappa Hits Home.
It wouldn't matter if the story were true. The rumor alone would send the financial markets into a tailspin and our allies running for cover. "Does the rumor specify which American company?"

"No."

"What's the source?"

Another hesitation. "I'm not at liberty to say. Only that it's a high-ranking intelligence officer from a US ally."

"Did you tell the senator about this rumor?"

"The subject came up when we were lobbying for the pretrial release of some 'suspected terrorists,' American citizens whose only crime is being of Middle-Eastern descent."

I didn't press the matter. I'd all but come out and told him directly that the improper campaign contribution was related to the maker of Harappa. As he was showing me to the door I realized I'd left my blazer upstairs in Kaseem's office. Reluctantly Dr. Mukhtar let me retrieve it unescorted.

Kaseem's door was open, his attention fixed on his laptop. As I went to grab my blazer from the chair of a spare desk I noticed that on the desk sat a computer with a unique screen-saver. The words *Go Chiefs!* floated by in pinkish orange letters in front of a navy blue background. My brain started working again. I put on my blazer and said, "Kansas City fan, huh?"

Kaseem peered over his laptop. "What? Oh, it's not my computer. It was Abdul's."

"He like any other sports teams?"

"I don't know, guess so."

"He ever go to any Wizards or Caps games?"

Kaseem shook his head. "A bunch of us from work went to an Orioles game last fall, though. Abdul was with us."

"Who were they playing?"

"The Blue Jays. I remember because Abdul nearly got in a fight." He stretched his arms, leaned back in his chair and interlaced his fingers behind his head. "The Orioles were down two to one in the eighth and Shannon Stewart was up. Abdul starts shouting, 'Slammin' Shannon!' and 'Shannon the Cannon!' Shit like that. Some guy threw a bag of peanuts at him. We had to, like, smuggle Abdul out of there. I can't blame the guy. Who would root for the Blue Jays in Camden Yards?"

I thanked him. It was a good question.

Chapter 18

Back at my office the garbage was overflowing so I took it out back to the dumpster. When I turned around, Jorge I saw Jorge standing in front of me.

"Finally," he said. "Where you been? I been waiting all day. I knew you have to come back here. I hear you fire you *sirvienta*. She pretty sad. But, hey, that not why I here. I got something for you."

I steadied myself. "Why don't you just leave me a note the next time you're in my apartment?"

"You mad about that? I just stop by to visit. You a hard man to talk to, you know?"

"Is your sister hard to talk to also?"

"She okay. She no listen is her problem."

"That makes you angry."

He smiled. "What you want to talk about her for? The way you always standing up for her, makes me think you in love with her. You in love with my sister, amigo?"

"I'm not your amigo."

"No, you don't got many friends. I been watching you. I seen you with that cop, the one with the skin, and that lady doctor. She sorta pretty. She *Cubano*?"

I forced myself to shrug.

"Also, I seen you with the *viuda* of you dead friend, and that old doctor, the one who real mean looking, like he sucking a *limon*. I been reading about him in the *gaceta*. But that's about it, no one else. You one lonely hombre."

He hit the nail on the head with that one. "What do you want?" I said.

"This here, *documento*." He stepped closer. "Someone left it for me when I get home."

"Yeah?"

"Yeah. It say something, I don't know."

"You want me to read it for you?"

He smiled again. "I want you to eat it for me."

Before I knew it he'd grabbed my arm and he was shoving the paper in my face. I hooked an arm around his neck and we fell to the ground, him on top of me, pinning my arms with his knees, slamming his fists into my face, my *nice cheekbones*. The image of Barry chastising Jorge for his rude manners flickered in my mind, as things started to blur. Jorge grabbed my jaw with his hands and squeezed my mouth open. Then he shoved the paper into it until I could taste my own blood. He didn't stop until the back door to the office swung open. Dr. Marshall stood there blinking at us. His face darkened. Jorge stood up, and brushed off his pants. He wasn't even breathing hard.

"Me and you *abogado* just talking about you. He say he wanna *chinga tu sobrina*, how you say, you niece."

"Get out of here, you punk, before I call the police. The only *chinga*-ing you'll be doing is bent over a sink in Lorton."

Jorge just smiled and turned around, disappearing around

the corner of a building. I was too tired to do anything about him. Back in the office I locked the back door and thanked Dr. Marshall. He just handed me his blazer. It was bright green. When I took a good look at him I saw him dressed like Rodney Dangerfield. Yellow golf shirt, madras slacks, white shoes. If the senator hadn't been in a coma, she'd have died.

I hung up his blazer. "There's valet parking out front," I said. "Will you be dining on the porch this evening?"

"I told my man Maddox to take a couple laps around the block until I call. He would've taken care of that dirtball. You're lucky I found you. When I came in no one was home so I just kept walking. What was that about anyway?"

As I told him he led himself on a tour of the first floor of the brownstone. I followed, imagining the office through his eyes. Small reception area, no receptionist, two offices with views of the alley, small kitchen, small bathroom and fire-proof vault lined with file cabinets. He seemed most comfortable in the conference room, which doubled as a library. He examined the casebooks and treatises along the walls. Then he took a leather case from his pocket, removed a cigar and sat at the head of the table.

"You don't mind," he told me. "Damn hospital rules. Have to go outside with the riffraff now to smoke."

"Those pneumonia patients raise such a fuss."

"You're a real smartass, aren't you?"

I bit my tongue and placed a coffee cup saucer in front of Dr. Marshall. Then I told him what I'd learned since I'd briefed him last: my visit to ARM, his wife's office in Dirksen and my interviews at PEACE. When I finished he was frowning.

"No one followed you, did they?"

"To PEACE? I took the Metro to Union Station, a cab to the Library of Congress, then doubled back by foot." I showed him the photocopy of Hassan's license.

He studied the photo, tapping ash into the saucer. "Never seen him before."

"What about Aliyah Hassan?"

"Who?"

"Never mind. Have you made that list of biopharm companies? The ones that could've made Harappa?"

He snapped his fingers. "I'm not myself these days."

I slid him a pad and pen. "Only the American ones are necessary."

"Why?"

"Dr. Mukhtar said the rumor was an American company did it."

"You didn't tell him about the blackmail scheme, did you?"

"Of course not."

"What did you say? Give me your exact words."

I described my conversation with Dr. Mukhtar, assuring Dr. Marshall I hadn't connected the improper campaign contribution and Harappa any more than necessary. Still, his face hardened.

"I hired you to keep this matter quiet. I didn't know you were going to blab it to the entire Muslim community."

"He has just as much incentive to keep the violation confidential as we do."

"Sure, we're regular allies."

"What about those names?"

"It's not going to be easy. Some of the companies are subsidiaries of foreign-owned conglomerates."

"Do the best you can."

Dr. Marshall jotted down some names, tapped the end of the pen on the table thoughtfully, then added some more. When he was done, there were a dozen of them. Some looked familiar from the news after the anthrax scare, some didn't. *Advanced Biosystems*, *Applied Chemical Sciences*, *Avant Immunotherapeutics*...

"Wait a minute," I said. "Wasn't ACS where Shifflett was working when he lost his family in the World Trade Center?"

"Who?"

I put an asterisk by the company's name then went through the remaining ones. *BioPort, DynPort Vaccine Company, Elusys Therapeutics, GeneSoft, GenPharm, Maxygen, Novavax, Vaxgen* and *Xeric*. I looked at the list again.

"What about that company you owned?" I said.

"Panacea?" He sucked on the cigar, tilted back his head and blew a gray cloud at the ceiling.

"It may be a long shot," I said, "but you are paying me to be thorough."

"I suppose it could've created Harappa, I mean, theoretically. It had the technology and the brainpower, but realistically it couldn't have done it. I would've seen evidence of it. Monkey necropsy reports, vaccine test results, something. Besides I know the people. They're good folks."

"I imagine the same could be said of all the American biopharm companies on the list."

"I imagine it could, Hank."

"So why did you sell it?"

"Vicky made me do it. When she was running for Senate, news came out Panacea had once made biowarfare weapons. The whole thing was a mess."

It was my turn to give him a look.

"Save the sanctimony, Counselor. A bunch of American companies were doing it, besides the US Army at Fort Detrick. Hell, we probably helped end the Cold War. Anyway when the war stopped, we stopped. Simple as that. No one cared until some nutball sent anthrax through the mail. Vicky's numbers plummeted. She told me it was her or the company."

"So you picked her."

"Companies come and go, true love lasts forever. Media ate it up. I'm surprised you don't remember it. It was all over the news."

"I was in law school. I wasn't exactly keeping up on current events. Besides, I don't believe everything I read during an election."

"Quite."

So I left Panacea off the list of names. All I needed was another company to investigate. Exploring the inner workings of a dozen companies could take days, if not weeks. "Wish I could just call the presidents of each company."

"As Vicky's criminal defense attorney? That would be a PR disaster. I know all the presidents and can talk to them."

I felt a load removed from my shoulders. "It would save a lot of time."

"I'll call to see if they've heard about the prospect of a government contract to develop a cure to Harappa. Then I'll ask who they thought could've made it. If a number of presidents point to one company—"

"Then we have a winner."

"Just keep your eye on the ball. Keep Mills away from my wife."

As Dr. Marshall's car pulled away, I opened a window, making a mental note to talk to his driver, hoping Mills hadn't beat me to it. Then I opened another window in the back of the office, to create a draft that would clear the office of cigar smoke. Back at my computer I punched in the biopharm companies Dr. Marshall had given me, surfing the internet until I found the names and titles of their top execs. Then I ran searches in a bunch of databases on Lexis, digging up the vitals of the execs: their birthdates, addresses, Social Security numbers, etc. When I was done I called Roger, who luckily hadn't left yet for Newark. I e-mailed him what I had.

"I should just work out of your office," he said.

"I could use the company. Focus on the presidents. I think

they often oversee the research scientists. If something fishy is going on in R&D, the presidents should know about it."

"Be a few hours, chief. Lotta names here."

While he was working I played corporate spy, searching for questionable campaign contributions by the companies, recent lawsuits against them, congressional testimony mentioning them and recent spikes in their debt or earnings. I even searched for websites that had a beef against the companies, adding *sucks* to the companies' domain names. This led me to a porno site that caught my browser in a trap from which even hitting *Control Alt Delete* failed to free it. I rebooted in shame and buried my face in my hands.

I'd checked out Doyle, ARM, PEACE and the top American biopharm companies, and found nothing. What else could I do? The only other suspects were Senator Serling's political enemies, and I didn't know where to begin investigating them. For the sake of my own sanity I punched in the name of the only company left.

Panacea, Inc. was headquartered in Cazenovia, New York. It had fifty employees, four of whom were corporate officers and the rest of whom were research scientists, lab technicians and other staff. The president, who owned one-hundred percent of the company, was a man who Amelia and Dr. Marshall had mentioned before: Robert White. I clicked on *About Us*.

In 1975 Panacea was a start-up company with a dozen employees who helped pharmaceutical giants develop cures for diseases. Panacea's success led the US government to ask it in 1980 to develop a vaccine for a new Soviet biowarfare agent. During the next decade Panacea won dozens more government contracts from DARPA, the Defense Advanced Research Projects Agency, DTRA, the Defense Threat Reduction Agency and USAMRIID, the United States Army Medical Research Institute of Infectious Diseases. Eventually Panacea became the nation's foremost specialist in *medical countermeasures* to biowarfare.

Currently it was working on a new generation of vaccines that target the common molecular components of multiple biowarfare pathogens. It was also working on immunotherapy, a technique for stimulating the body's immune system to fight pathogens without toxic synthetic chemicals. It anticipated this technique will someday be successful in protecting against AIDS, SARS and the avian flu. Panacea had already made great strides in combating botulinum toxin, encephalitis and bacterial meningitis.

There was nothing on White personally. I clicked on *Personnel* and learned only that the company was looking for a junior research scientist. The position had been open for six months. No wonder. Its criteria filled an entire screen.

I researched the company's finances on Lexis and took a stab at a valuation, comparing Panacea to a dozen public companies similar to it in size, line of business and approximate revenues, several of which were companies Dr. Marshall had named. I estimated Panacea's value to be about a hundred million dollars.

Roger called. I rubbed my eyes and yawned. "Tell me about the management of corporate America's dozen finest."

"Sorry, compadre." Roger listed a handful of convictions for speeding and a few tax evasions.

"Nothing more serious," I said, "like a corporate accounting discrepancy? Those are a dime a dozen these days."

"If you want, I can bribe one of the CFOs to cook the books."

"Nice of you to offer, though." I racked my brain.

"Is there anyone else?" he said. "What about that company the senator's husband owned?"

I gave him the information I had on Panacea's new president, Robert White. I got the feeling we were wasting time. Roger called back a couple hours later as I was drifting off, my head on my desk.

"No dice," he said. "Just some traffic stuff. Couple speeding tickets, a reckless driving conviction. There was one thing, though...the guy changed his name."

"Oh?" I said, feigning interest, wondering how many dead ends I could possibly run into on the same case. Maybe I should change my name too, to *Hank Failure*.

"Few years ago," Roger said, "after he filed for bankruptcy. He'd had a dozen years of credit problems, had just left a job and was out of work. Probably wanted a fresh start. His old name was...let's see, I have it here somewhere. Switzer or Swenson something."

I was too depressed to play the name game.

"You okay, chief?" he said.

"Just tired. Send over what you have. When are you going to Newark?"

"First thing in the morning. Should have a report on Monday."

"Have fun in Atlantic City. Play a few hands for me, and don't forget to double-down on eleven."

"You telling me? Been splitting aces since before you were born."

I got up to stretch my legs and shut the windows. Darkness had fallen and the sidewalk in front of the building was empty. The office upstairs, which belonged to a trade association, was silent. It was a time of day I was all too familiar with. Mac would have gone home and Marita would have arrived, her vacuum whirring, cleaning up one day's mess to prepare for the next. I'd recently let her go with three months' pay, promising to bring her back when the firm was solvent again. Only the week before, Mac and I had been on the top of the world, fresh off a victory that had made the phones ring off the hook. Now it was so quiet I could hear my stomach growl. I remembered I had half a turkey sandwich in the fridge. I headed for the kitchen.

Down the hall, in Mac's office, the floor creaked.

I froze. Dr. Marshall had left a couple hours before, Marita had turned in her key and I hadn't called the building's handyman, Earl. The idea of Jorge being inside the office filled me with terror. I crept ahead and peered inside Mac's office. It was empty except for the furniture, a couple boxes and a few dust bunnies. I grabbed the bowling pin, held it by the neck and did my best imitation of a SWAT team. The closets, the bathroom, the vault, all were empty. I pried the bowling pin from my white knuckles and dropped it back into the box. Apparently hunger was preying on my mind.

When I turned around I was flung back against the wall. My head slammed against a picture, which fell to the floor. Tears sprang to my eyes. My throat was pinned by a hand. The hand belonged to a man. The man was about my height but bigger, with broad shoulders, a short neck and a big head. I tried to pry open his vice-like grip. My eyes adjusted, discerning a rubber Bill Clinton mask, complete with red bulbous nose and blow-dried gray hair. I wanted to laugh but the man's hand tightened, choking the air out of me. As my head exploded in pain, a tear rolled down my cheek.

"One question," I rasped.

He loosened his grip ever so much.

"Can I get Hillary's autograph?"

"Laugh now, before I crush your throat."

I didn't hear a Mexican accent, but I wasn't sure.

"You kill Mac?"

"You lawyers love asking questions."

"What do you want?"

"You know what I want."

"Drop the case?"

"Smart too."

"I can't."

I knew it wasn't in my best interest to draw out the man's demand, but every second I spent with him was a second that might yield a clue.

"Course you can," he said. "All you have to do is call that

Marshall fella and tell him you couldn't find anything. That you're in over your head."

There was definitely no Mexican accent. I had trouble placing the man's age from his voice. Twenty or thirty years older than me maybe. He held my throat with his left hand, his sleeve shortening as he extended his arm.

"Or else?" I said.

He pushed me up until my throat closed and my feet dangled, shoe tips brushing the floor. His receding sleeve revealed a bare wrist and pale forearm, but stopped below the location of the killer's tattoo.

"I-I—" I stammered.

"Yes?"

"I voted for you."

The man affected a southern accent. "I feel your pain."

Then the stars came out to shine. The last feeling I had was embarrassment. It was the second time I'd fainted in a week.

W hen I opened my eyes I was alone and my neck burned. I grabbed the bowling pin and checked the office. Nothing looked broken or missing. I went home, turned on every light in the apartment, checked the locks twice and crawled under the covers.

In the morning I wanted to get out of bed only long enough to return the rest of Senator Serling's retainer. I wasn't a bounty hunter who apprehended lock-picking, truck-stealing, Senator-blackmailing murderers. I was an ex-English teacher with an astigmatism and an embarrassing propensity for fainting. Then again I didn't see what choice I had; some bastard had murdered Mac.

I skipped the shower thing and threw on jeans and a wrinkled Oxford from the laundry pile. Georgetown was oblivious to my fashion faux pas, not to mention the recent attack on my life. Cabbies still stopped in the middle of M Street to pick up fares. Trucks still made illegal left-hand turns on Wisconsin Ave. Tourists still jaywalked through it all. I was grateful to see activity at my office on Mass Ave., secretaries smoking on the stoop, a delivery truck backing up in the alley. Inside it was deathly quiet. Sunlight slanted somberly between the blinds in Mac's office. As I was debating another SWAT Team recon mission, the phone rang.

"Good morning, Mr. Fisher. Agent Wang, FBI."

He pronounced the letters distinctly, like they were the last three needed to win an RV on *Wheel of Fortune*. It made me want to congratulate him, but what I said instead was, "Thank God."

"Excuse me?"

"I said, 'Oh, God.'"

"You've been keeping us on our toes lately too."

"If you mean Eugenia Carver, she's lying."

"We're checking it out. When we're ready to hear your side we'll let you know. Right now I'm more interested in talking to Senator Serling's staff. Problem is they all told me to call you. I told them I'm sure there's some sort of misunderstanding. I'm sure you haven't instructed witnesses in a criminal investigation not to cooperate with the FBI."

"Relax, a police detective already talked them. He took notes."

"Mills? His notes don't interest me. We're looking for something different."

"Why don't you tell me what you're looking for? Then I'll tell you if anyone on the senator's staff has the information you want."

"That would be a good start. Why don't you come on down?"

Although a spare suit hung in my closet the last thing I wanted was to play twenty questions at the FBI. Last time Mac and I were there they made us wait in a room with no windows for over an hour. Even Mac was ready to talk.

"You guys are always so generous with your office space," I said. "How about I return the favor?"

There were some voices in the background, then he returned to the line. "Be there in half an hour."

In twenty-nine minutes Special Agent James Wang showed up with an Assistant US Attorney named Manuel Guerrero. I remembered hearing of the duo before. They were known, at least to the less-politically correct members of the DC bar, by the nickname *Rice & Beans*. They worked together on the Attorney General's Campaign Financing Taskforce and weren't above strong-arming suspects. I unfolded an arm toward the conference room and Wang led the way, but after a few steps we lost Guerrero, who had stopped to look around. He was wide with a bald spot on the back of his head. He wore a shiny gray suit and had a hairy neck and ring-around-the-collar.

"Nice hickey," he said without turning around. "That from your girlfriend?"

I wondered if he knew about my lunch with Amelia.

"Nice digs too," he said, wandering down the hall toward my office. "You gonna keep it, you know, now you're the Lone Ranger?"

I caught up to him and clamped a hand on his shoulder. "Whoa, Tonto."

He turned around. "Is that an Indian crack? Because I'm half Navajo?"

Nothing like small talk to make everyone feel comfortable. My guests declined coffee and took their seats. Guerrero slipped right into a slouch, head cocked to the side, arm hung over the back rail, as if he had to hold onto it or he would slide right out of the chair. Next to him Wang sat erect and so close to the table that the edge jabbed his ribs. He cleared his throat.

"In our investigation into the assassination attempt on Senator Serling, we've obtained reason to believe she may have been involved in some potential wrongdoing. Any thing you'd like to comment on?"

"Can you be a little more specific?" I said.

"As in a possible campaign finance violation."

"Oh, that kind of potential wrongdoing. Why didn't you guys just say so? No comment."

Wang's eyes narrowed. "Let's cut the crap. Dr. Mukhtar told us everything after I explained we weren't after PEACE. He told me all about Hassan, if that's his real name. CTU is looking into it."

"That's FBI talk for counter-terrorism unit, isn't it? I saw that on *24*. I love that show. Want me to be straight with you? Okay, the fact you knew I met with Dr. Mukhtar means you had me tailed. That bothers me, makes me feel like I don't want to help you so much, you know? Though I guess I should be happy that at least you didn't put a nanny cam in my bathroom and tap my phones."

Both men looked at the center of my conference table. I leaned over and grabbed the handset, unfastening the transmitter. Nothing but wires. I remembered Roger telling me the government could tap into conversations anywhere along a phone line.

"Great," I said. "Guess you intercepted that call between me and my mother yesterday about my Father's Day gift. Seeing as how that's a federal offense and all."

Deep down, the real source of my anger was that an FBI agent had probably been parked across the street last night when Slick Willie broke into my office. Wang glanced at Guerrero, who was acting surprised.

"For the record," Wang said, "I was investigating suspected criminal activity, based on probable cause I'd obtained from a MPD detective."

"You were on a witch hunt," I said.

"Evidence of crimes other than those being investigated are fully—"

"You got exactly what you were investigating."

"That's not true. We were simply—"

"It is true."

"No, it's not. We—"

"Then what are you looking for?"

"I—"

"What? Tell me."

Guerrero reached over to put a hand on Wang's arm, but he was too late.

"How much the contribution was for," Wang said, "and when it occurred. Did the senator personally accept it or did someone on her staff accept it? If it was someone on her staff, did she know anything about it?"

When Wang stopped talking, his face was red. Guerrero hung his head. So Dr. Mukhtar hadn't yet told Wang everything. Wang and Guerrero had been baiting me.

"Neither Senator Serling, nor anyone currently on her staff," I said, "has broken any campaign finance laws."

I held my breath, wondering if my use of the word *currently* was too conspicuous. Wang focused all of his superpowers on me for a sign I was lying. My looking away, my shifting my weight in my chair, my breaking down and sobbing. Finally he exchanged a look with Guerrero.

"We don't believe you," Guerrero said.

"Wow, that was amazing. Do you two do birthday parties?"

Guerrero took my business card out of his breast pocket and picked at a piece of lunch between his teeth. "You're a funny guy. Funny guys are real popular in prison."

"Now you're threatening to prosecute me?"

"I'm just telling you, one attorney to another, that lying to the government is not a wise litigation strategy."

"And I'm telling you, one attorney to another, that you're wasting your time. I've spoken to Senator's Serling's husband and everyone currently on her staff."

Again with the *currently* bit. Damn my father for teaching me to tell the truth. But Rice & Beans were too distracted, or too dense, to notice.

"I appreciate that, Hank, but maybe you'd let us talk to the senator's staff ourselves. You know, just to be sure."

"Umm, I don't think so."

"No?"

"Not considering the subject matter of your investigation and your aggressive investigative techniques."

Guerrero and Wang shared a smile. "I'm sowwy," Guerrero said, "awe we pwaying too wuff? Frankly I'd expect a little bit more from the associate of a standup guy like Mac."

"Don't bother bringing Mac into this, Manny. He never liked you. While you're at it, drop the attitude. You're the one who invaded my privacy on a hunch."

Guerrero shrugged. "Guess I'll just have to get a grand jury subpoena."

"You're going to impanel a grand jury over this? So fast? Gee, it's almost as if this investigation is politically motivated. What's going on? Are Bush and Mukasey leaning on your boss to indict Senator Serling? Maybe going to cut her loose if she doesn't fall into line?"

"Martina doesn't take marching orders."

"Then she's doing it as a favor to an old friend?" US Attorney Martina Rowe, a partner in a big Houston law firm before she started their DC office, used to be counsel to Bush when he was a Texas businessman.

"She doesn't play favorites, either."

"Not even for the sake of national security? From what I understand, Senator Serling's the only one who stands between the president and the passing of his new anti-terrorism budget."

Surprisingly Guerrero didn't have a response. I was just gambling, trying to play the political persecution card, but maybe I was onto something. "You tell Martina that if she's going to subpoena the testimony of Senator Serling's staff she better get a court order granting them immunity too."

"Why would they take the Fifth if they have nothing to hide?"

"Your sidekick just asked me if someone on the senator's staff accepted an improper campaign contribution, and you just told me you don't believe me when I say they know nothing. Do you think I'm dumb enough to advise my client to talk under those circumstances?"

"You represent Senator Serling and her staff? Sounds like a conflict of interest."

"No need to disqualify me. I don't represent them. But, to the extent they ask for my advice, I'll give it to them."

"Isn't that obstruction of justice?" Wang said, nudging Guerrero.

"No." I stood. "That's criminal defense."

After I showed Rice & Beans to the door I grabbed my cell phone, carefully scanned the back alley and stepped out the back door.

"We need to talk," I told Dr. Marshall.

"We talked yesterday."

"I thought you wanted me to keep you notified of every development."

"The only thing I want to hear from you is that the government has stopped snooping around my wife's life."

"I got a visit from the Campaign Financing Taskforce."

A siren rose and fell at the other end of the line.

"Hello?" I said.

"I'll be over as soon as I drop off Amelia."

"It isn't safe to talk here."

"What's that supposed to mean?"

"It means this probably isn't the best place for a sensitive conversation."

"Your office is bugged?"

I didn't answer.

"Good work, Counselor."

"I didn't do it."

"The government doesn't just watch someone without reason."

"They're fishing."

"Isn't that reassuring? Is that going to be your closing argument to the jury?"

"Will you give me a chance to explain?"

"You've had your chance." I heard Amelia's voice in the background. He sighed into the transmitter. "Meet me at Amelia's place," he said, then hung up.

Of all the places to be fired.

Chapter 20

Amelia opened the door wearing a pink towel around her head, a pink bathrobe and pink bunny slippers. "You look like hell," she said.

"You look like _Hello Dolly._"

She raised herself on her toes to examine my forehead and caught sight of my eye and the marks on my neck. "What happened? Don't tell me you walked into a door."

"I walked into a door."

"You're not one of those martyr types, are you? The kind who suffers in silence?"

No one had ever accused me of suffering in silence.

"I'm surprised you can even see me," I said. "Last time I looked, your eyes were green, not black, blue and red."

"Been on duty two days straight. Lawrence told me the bad news."

"I'm here to face the music."

"Sorry if I don't watch the show. I have a date with a pillow. Any chance I could get an update later? I have the weekend off."

"How about breakfast at Eastern Market?"

"Best blueberry pancakes in the city. Pick me up tomorrow morning?"

She turned and was gone. In the kitchen Dr. Marshall was scowling at the TV, which was replaying footage of the senator's ambulance pulling up to GW Hospital. I waited for a commercial then described what had happened since I saw him last, starting with my late-night visit from Slick Willie and ending with my visit from Rice & Beans. Dr. Marshall ground his teeth, jaw muscles rippling. "A goddamn grand jury?"

"They'll be bound by a vow of secrecy."

"In this city? Christ, the press will eat it up."

I wondered where I'd messed up. Maybe back at the hospital, when Mills asked me why Mac and I had been visiting the senator, I should've kept quiet. Or maybe I should've told him we'd been there on business. Then I realized Dr. Marshall was staring at me. "Do I even want to know what happened to your neck?"

"No."

"You probably want to go to the police."

"I'm not sure what they could do."

"Not to mention the fact you'd have to tell them about the campaign finance thing."

I'd considered that. Frankly it didn't seem like such a bad idea. The government already thought the senator had done something wrong. Coming clean might take the air out of their tires. Then again, maybe Guerrero wouldn't buy the story about the setup. Maybe admitting receipt of the contribution would just add fuel to the fire.

"We need to stop the bleeding," Dr. Marshall said. "First of all, stop leading the government to clues about the violation. And for God's sake, don't let them get to Conway."

"I'll do what I can, but ultimately that's up him and whatever lawyer he hires."

"Lawyer? He doesn't have any exposure."

I gave him a look.

"Fine," he said, "but why can't you represent us both?"

"I wouldn't be comfortable."

"Oh, if you wouldn't be comfortable—"

"The potential conflict of interest is too strong."

"What conflict?"

Was the man serious? "I may learn it's in his best interest to roll over and buy immunity. If that happens his bargaining chip would be the dirt he has on the senator. I'd have to decide whose case to drop at a critical point in the representation, if not both cases."

"We both know you'd drop him and keep me. Can't we just jump off that bridge when we come to it?"

"It would be taking advantage of him."

"At least get rid of the phony call sheet and resignation letter."

I laughed, then I saw his face. He was serious.

"No," I said.

"I'm not asking."

"Setting aside the illegality of it, I don't let clients tell me how to practice law."

"Then you won't be practicing law for this client."

"Okay." I got up. I'd worked too hard for my license to lose it for a client, much less a client I didn't even like. Not that I had any idea how I was going to catch Mac's killer without Dr. Marshall's help, but I would figure something out.

"Hold on," Dr. Marshall said when I was almost to the door. The color had risen in his cheeks. "Christ, why can't you show that sort of moxie with this Guerrero fellow?"

I came back into the kitchen. "Look, if Conway hires an attorney I trust, we can form a joint defense agreement. I'll bring him up to speed on the case and anything I tell him will be privileged, with the senator holding the privilege. In return, maybe I'll able to persuade Conway to take the Fifth."

"Do you lawyers always have to make things so complicated?"

From my car I called Conway and summarized my meeting with Rice & Beans. When he asked for referrals I gave him the name of Mac's old boss at the US Attorney's Office.

"The guy who represented the president in that business deal thing?" Conway said.

"He's the best white collar criminal defense lawyer in the country, at the best white collar criminal defense firm."

"Sounds like a pal."

"We'd work well together."

"No use waging war on two fronts."

I gave him Aaron Weissman's number. When I got back to my office I researched the various offenses the grand jury would probably investigate and the legal defenses available to Conway and the senator. I wanted to know my stuff when I got a call from the King of Crime.

Penny's kids showed up at the dinner table wearing long faces. First their grandpa had taken Aunt Fran and her new boyfriend to a Washington Nationals game without them, and now they had to pause *Shrek the Third*. They climbed into their chairs and swung their feet impatiently. They answered my questions in nods and grunts until it turned into a game.

Had Clare just finished ballet? Nod. Was she looking forward to summer camp? Nod. Was she going to bait her own hooks? Grunt. Was Tommy done with baseball? Nod. Was he looking forward to swim team? Nod. Did he still need to learn how to do a flip turn? Grunt. What's the sound a gorilla makes? Grunt. Then it came, Clare's giggle. Grunt, grunt, grunt, went Tommy, scratching under his arms. The kids squealed with delight.

After they went back to the den and Penny and I finished loading the dishes, we brought our beers to the porch. Rain poured off the corners of the roof, splattering against the patio.

When my brother had died, my parents were really into moving me through the *five stages of grief*: denial, anger, bargaining, depression and acceptance. I'd humored them but I'd had real trouble getting past depression. This time I didn't even want to get that far. I preferred to stop right at anger and make a right turn onto vengeance, and take that one all the way down to self-destruction. I carefully examined Penny to see if she shared my dysfunction. I looked for any sign she was having trouble coping: anger at Mac, irrational fear about money, inappropriate harshness with the kids. I found none. I didn't even find an inordinate consumption of white wine, which would have been totally acceptable under the circumstances. She was acting perfectly normal, which, of course, was perfectly insane.

"I've decided you're still in the denial phase," I said.

"Oh, yeah. Big time."

I smiled and thought for a moment.

"Let's not talk about it," she said, "okay?"

"Fine."

Penny sipped her beer. "That's the first they've laughed in weeks. Remind me that things get better."

"Things get better," I said, wanting to believe it. "Did you get that claim form I sent?"

"Thanks for speeding it up."

"Just send it in with a copy of the obit and death certificate. A week later you'll get a checkbook in the mail." I removed an envelope from my pocket. "Here's the rest of it. It covers the office equipment and furniture. If you need anything more—"

"If I need anything more I'll go back to work."

I raised my arms in surrender.

"Sorry," she said. "I'm just tired. We're going to be fine."

"That's all I wanted to know. One more thing." I got up and returned from my car carrying two boxes.

"I don't like the look of this." She got up and turned on a light. "Just what I always wanted. Framed diplomas, rock paperweights and a bowling pin." She stopped when she came to a photo: Mac standing with one arm around her and another raising a pint of Guinness. She laughed, her eyes shining.

"I'm sorry," I said.

She shook her head, then went down to the basement, returning with a box of her own. On top of it was another photo: Mac standing with one arm around me and the other raising a pint of Guinness. I put the two photos next to each other.

"Look at how red his cheeks are," she said.

"'An Irish tan,' he used to call it."

Penny closed the box. "Are the police having any luck?"

"They seem more fixated on the senator. They think the hit-and-run was an assassination attempt, but I have some leads."

"Anything promising?"

"I'd better wait before I drag you into it."

She took another sip of beer. "I know punishing the guy won't bring back Mac, but I can't stand the thought of him getting away with this."

Neither could I.

After a moment she said, "He was proud of you."

I knew what she was talking about and she didn't have to say it. Still, I didn't stop her.

"He always said he was just a hack, schmoozing prosecutors and hoodwinking jurors. He said one day you would make a really good criminal defense lawyer. The only thing stopping you was..."

"My lack of experience."

"He said it would come with time."

Time I didn't have.

"Hank, I know you don't think you can do this. I mean, I

know you're probably sitting there thinking, 'Oh, shit, what have I gotten myself into?' But for what it's worth, I know you can do it."

It was nice, what she said, but she was completely wrong. I was in way over my head. I was thinking about telling her about Slick Willie when Tommy came into the porch. "Mom, what's an ogre?"

Clare showed up behind him. "He wants to be like Shrek."

"An ogre is a monster," said Penny.

Tommy turned around. "You mean, like a werewolf?" He threw up his hands and snarled at Clare, who screamed.

It was time for bed.

I helped tuck in the kids, then I picked up the box from Penny and promised to take Tommy and Clare off her hands the next time a Disney movie came out.

Penny put a hand on my shoulder. "Do me a bigger favor."

"Anything."

"Take this with you." She stuffed the bowling pin into the box.

Outside the rain had stopped, although the sky was still rumbling. From the sidewalk I could see the dim glow of a night-light in Clare's bedroom window. A tiny flame to keep away the world's boogeymen.

Chapter 21

The next morning Amelia pulled open her door again—this time wearing a cotton blouse, cropped khakis and unlaced tennis shoes.

"Overslept," she said. "Coffee's in the kitchen. Nice haircut."

She disappeared down the hall. I caught sight of myself in the foyer mirror and resisted the impulse to smooth out the wrinkles in my polo shirt and shorts. I stared at my Docksiders and wondered when the eighties were going to make a comeback. Amelia reappeared with her hair in a barrette and a pale pink sweater over her shoulders. She shoved her wallet and cell phone into a straw handbag then rushed outside, locking the door behind her.

I stood alone in her foyer, admiring the quiet after the storm.

She returned, wearing a sheepish smile. "Hello," she said.

"Hello."

She kissed me on the cheek and took my arm. But she had forgotten something else, this time her sunglasses, which were in her car in the garage.

"Oh, no," I said.

"What's the matter?"

"Your car."

"What about it? That dent?"

"No, it's just that it...it has more testosterone than mine."

She crossed her arms and smirked as I circled the sedan. It was a mid-nineties Chevy Caprice, dark blue, no hub caps, antenna on the trunk.

"It's an old cop car," she said. "Florida Highway Patrol. My dad bought it for me at an auction outside of Fort Myers. Said it was safe. Over two tons, driver's side air bags, awesome brakes."

"V-eight engine, a gazillion horsepower."

"Supposedly it can get up to a hundred and forty, do a quarter mile in something like eighteen seconds."

"You don't know?"

"Sure, I drag race trick cars from *The Fast and the Furious* on M Street all the time. People just step out of the way and wave me on with checkered flags."

"I mean, on your way out to Middleburg, to visit your Uncle, on those back roads."

"You want to spend the night in jail, get your license suspended and pay twenty-five hundred bucks in speeding tickets, you go right ahead."

"You seem to know a little too much about that."

"I work in an emergency room. I see the ones who hit telephone poles."

"Still it'd be worth it. My favorite part is that floodlight on the driver's door."

"It doesn't work."

"But it looks cool. I bet people get out of your way on the highway. Just flash your high beams and they pull over, right?"

"How old are you?"

"I can't help it. You want to trade? My VW runs on a nine-volt battery. It has AM radio and the convertible top still works...most the time."

"Tempting but I think I'll pass."

"You sure? This thing's too middle-age for a cute young doctor."

"I'll grow into it."

"The gas mileage must suck."

"Eighteen miles per gallon."

"See? You're funding terrorism. Killing the environment. Contributing to global warming. Hurricanes and floods and FEMA disasters. I don't know how can you live with yourself."

"You'd rather kill the environment?"

"I hate the environment. Mother Nature kicked me out of the house when I was sixteen. Al Gore won't even talk to me. Dolphins and rain forests and spotted owls—that stuff's for sissies. This car, this car is for ass-kicking private-eye-wannabe lawyers."

"When you find one of those, you let me know."

I ran my hand along the car's sleek hood. "I've got everything nailed down except the ass-kicking part. But with this baby I'd be on my way."

She rolled her eyes and got in my Cabriolet.

Saturday morning traffic was light. No road race, walk-a-thon or march-on-Washington to avoid. Just parents dragging their kids to the next museum. I drove down Constitution Ave. in the cool shade of giant elm trees. Instead of going up Capitol Hill I turned north onto 7th Street.

Amelia's eyebrows wrinkled. "I hate to be a know-it-all, but this isn't the way to Eastern Market."

"It isn't?"

She peered into the back seat and pulled a blanket off a wicker basket. "You're taking me on a picnic." She turned back around. "Now you're turning right on New York Ave., toward Route 50. We're going to Annapolis." She smiled. "You're taking me sailing."

"You're the one who should be a private eye."

"I told you at lunch about my Uncle Harry. Aren't you sweet for remembering?"

"You up for it?"

"Just what the doctor ordered. Lawrence is taking the noon to eight shift."

We talked about how her mom was holding up, how her family took turns sitting with her aunt and how they would talk to her, tell her about their day, share some gossip from back home, even read the newspaper. I wanted to ask Amelia if she'd told her aunt she'd met a dashing young lawyer. Some questions are best left unasked.

Out the window, buildings gave way to houses, which gave way to farms. Cows lifted their heads, chewing methodically. A horse cantered in a ring, shaking off flies and kicking up clouds of dirt. A white clapboard farm house gleamed in the sun. Eventually I started to enjoy it all and stopped looking for Slick Willie in my rearview mirror.

Amelia looked over her shoulder. "There a cop back there or something?"

"Just tailgaters."

I turned on the radio and found NPR, which was covering a story about Harappa. Contemplating a plague of Biblical proportions wasn't the way I'd planned to spend the afternoon. I surfed on.

"Go back," Amelia said.

"...cities in which Harappa has recently appeared include Bangkok, Manila, Taipei and Tokyo," the man on the radio said. "The secretary of defense said transmission of the virus may have been achieved through so-called 'suicide couriers,' terrorists who have intentionally contracted the virus, traveled to the target cities and circulated in densely populated areas. The secretary warned that he has obtained reason to believe an American city may be the terrorists' ultimate target. He announced that a joint task force of agents from the CIA and FBI will be deployed to Asian airports from which airlines fly into the US. The task force will help local authorities screen passengers.

"Meanwhile, on the domestic front, the secretary of homeland security has placed the nation's airports on 'yellow alert,' indicating a significant risk of terrorist attack. The secretary assured Americans that teams of physicians from the Centers for Disease Control and Prevention have been deployed to American airports that receive direct flights from Asian cities. Those airports include Los Angeles, New York and Washington. The secretary said passengers arriving from Asia should expect a slight delay as they are deplaning, since they will be briefly examined for sign of the virus.

"Finally, in his Saturday morning radio address, the president announced that, if his terrorism budget does not pass, he plans to ask Congress for emergency funding to combat the threat of Harappa. Some of the funds would be used to research and develop a vaccine for the mysterious virus. Several leaders of Congress have stated they expect such a request would be granted."

Amelia turned down the volume. "Looks like I'm going to have to take that refresher course on biowarfare after all."

We talked about the biowarfare training she received after the anthrax scare in 2001. She'd learned to identify an intentional release of a biological agent by looking for an unusual clustering of illnesses among people who had attended the same gathering. She'd learned to identify the clinical features of the three dozen most common biowarfare agents. They had names as exotic as they were terrifying. *Tularemia, Brucellosis, Machupo, Q fever.* Not exactly date-talk.

We arrived in Annapolis, had iced tea at the Market House and strolled up and down Main Street. Amelia bought some sunscreen and a straw hat. At the harbor, when she saw I'd chartered a twenty-seven-foot sailboat, she said, "Where are we going, Key West?"

"It was the smallest one they had left."

Our captain was a freckle-faced kid named Hunter. He sucked in his gut and squared his shoulders when he got a look at Amelia. Then he clapped my back patronizingly when he learned that I, unlike Amelia, didn't know how to sail. To entertain Amelia he gave me a lesson on jib sheets, bow plates, fairleads, mainsheets, mainsails, batten pockets, goosenecks and halyards, speaking to me as if English were my second language. I pretended not to mind, although I'd read a book on the rudiments of sailing the night before. I knew what it was like to have a school-boy crush on Amelia.

As we sailed around the Naval Academy Amelia opened the picnic basket. Inside were apples, cheese, French bread, hummus, dried apricots, marinated olives, banana bread and lemonade.

"I'm impressed," she said.

"So am I." I'd gotten the whole basket from Fresh Fields.

When we were done eating, Amelia leaned against my shoulder and we watched the descending sun set a mountain of clouds afire. After we docked and stretched our legs, Amelia looked at her watch.

"We'd better get back," I said.

"Maybe your car won't start."

It wasn't until we were back on Route 50 that I spoke again. "The day's been so nice. I don't want to risk ruining it."

"You're not married, are you?"

"Would that upset you?"

She smirked. "What were you going to say?"

"Dr. Marshall said that, during the campaign, the press learned Panacea had once made biowarfare diseases."

"Boy, was Aunt Vicky mad."

"She didn't know before she married him?"

"When the Department of Defense decides to break a world-wide treaty, it keeps its mouth shut."

"Even hiding it from members of Congress?"

"Especially them."

"So when your aunt found out, she and Dr. Marshall squared off?"

"Almost got divorced. Lawrence would shout that having biowarfare weapons was a deterrent, like having nuclear weapons. My aunt would shout back that biowarfare weapons are worse than nuclear weapons because they're meant only to kill people, and they work in the most inhumane way: fever, diarrhea, ulcers, lesions, bleeding, paralysis."

"You agreed with her."

"If we have to resort to targeting civilians, maybe the war isn't worth fighting."

"So she won?"

"He joked he was sick of the commute, but the sale broke his heart. That company was his life's work."

"Now you sound sympathetic."

"He can be sweet once you get to know him."

I hoped it would never come to that. "Do you know anything about Robert White?"

"You think he might be involved?"

"Your aunt was about to investigate the manufacturer of Harappa."

"And Panacea previously made biowarfare agents."

"I admit, it's weak."

"I met him only once. Lawrence took us all to dinner at Congressional, you know, the country club. He was so proud he'd gotten in. The waiting list is something like five years. My aunt pulled some strings, but White was so unimpressed. All through dinner he went on and on about how Congressional wasn't nearly as good a golf course as Winged Foot, his home club in

New York. Said Winged Foot had something like six major championships, while Congressional had only three. Then he asked the waiter to bring out the chef. We thought he was going to compliment the man, but instead he lectured him about how to not over-cook a filet."

"Classy."

"And not too smart about things pharmaceutical. He thought a peptide was a brand of antacid."

I nodded, embarrassed to ask. "No background in science, huh?"

"Said he would hire people to 'handle the lab work.'"

I was trying to imagine a businessman managing a team of high-tech biopharmacologists, when the last of the daylight faded. I told Amelia she could put her seat back and take a nap. She said she wasn't tired, then closed her eyes. It made me feel, I don't know...nice, having her there asleep next to me. Calming. She didn't awaken until I opened her door on 23rd Street. She got out and stretched. Then she wrapped her arms around my neck and laid her head on my shoulder.

"What a perfect day," she said before lifting her face to mine. Her kiss was unexpected but welcomed.

As I watched her saunter into the hospital I began to worry I was going to have to break more than the law to find Mac's killer.

T his is when I'm supposed to tell you how guilty I felt about thinking of love before the grass had covered Mac's grave. How Mac reminded me of my brother Grady, and how Grady had been teaching me how to drive without permission when an asshole strung out on crystal meth ran a red light in a stolen car and sideswiped Grady's dreams of going to Arizona State and getting his PGA Tour Card. Except I finished talking about that stuff long ago, after people stopped listening. I'm not sure people really want to know what grows in the darkness of a young man's heart.

At the office my phone rang.

"You're there," Aaron Weissman said. "I was going to leave a message. Thanks for the referral."

"Did you take it?"

"He signed the retainer agreement yesterday."

"Did he tell you much about the case?"

"A little. We're going to meet tomorrow afternoon, go over some documents. I thought maybe you and I could get together before then, if you're available."

"How about this afternoon?"

"It's not too much trouble?"

I looked around at my empty office, at the dust collecting on the table tops. "It's not too much trouble."

"Want me to come over there?"

I pictured listening devices in the light fixtures. "Stay where you are," I said.

Pound & Shields was the crown jewel of East Coast law firms. Specializing in litigation and operating out of a single office in Washington, DC, it was a rare species in the jungle of world-wide professional limited liability companies. From the top floors of its own building on Pennsylvania Ave., it overlooked the government buildings where it waged war. It leased the bottom floor of the building to a restaurant called *The Sagamore*, home of the best oyster bar in DC. In the lobby the only sounds were the roar of the Nationals beating the Red Sox coming from behind the security desk and the splash of a two-story fountain. Above the lobby loomed the interior windows of associate offices. Only a couple lights were on. I hoped one of them belonged to Brock Aurelia. If the kid was chained to his desk he couldn't be out chasing Amelia.

Of course she'd been right, back at Tony & Joe's, when she'd accused me of being jealous of Brock. I'd envied him ever since law school, when I learned he'd landed a job at P&S. Working there would have offered me everything that working with Mac would not. Starting pay for first-year associates was a hundred and fifty grand, with a guaranteed bonus of fifteen grand if you exceeded the firm's shallow eighteen-hundred billable-hour requirement. The firm's resources rivaled those of many law schools, a library that occupied an entire floor, a moot court room rigged with video cameras, a gym equipped with showers and a sauna, even a café. Every associate was issued a laptop and enrolled in the firm's litigation training program, which offered manuals, weekly lectures and clinics. None of the firm's three hundred lawyers fought his battles alone.

Aaron had a corner office that overlooked the J. Edgar Hoover Building. His face lit up when he saw me. "You keep getting younger," he said.

"I'm supposed to say that."

"I'm just an old man who needs a new hip. I can only play doubles now. I just stand by the net and hold up my racket." What was left of Aaron's hair was gray, and his shoulders seemed narrower than before, but I was fairly sure he could still kick my butt on the tennis court.

"I'm familiar with that strategy," I said.

He motioned toward a seat. "I'm glad you could come."

"Always nice to see how the other half lives."

"This place is becoming more and more like a hotel. I thought it was bad when they started delivering our lunch. Now they pick up our shoes and dry cleaning. All we have to do is hang them in a bag behind the door. They even have a nap room down the hall."

Never a good sign at a law firm, although I could get used to it. I'd check in at 9:00 a.m. and request a wake-up call for 5:00 p.m.

"Sometimes I wish I were on my own," he said.

I forced a smile. "It has its advantages."

Aaron closed his door, although no one was in the hall. "As I said before, Conway told me a little about the case. I get the sense the senator didn't keep him in the loop about everything."

"Like where the money came from."

"And why."

"She wanted to limit his exposure and keep the news from spreading. It's the main reason her husband kept me on."

"Don't tell me he doesn't want you to talk to me."

"As long as there are some ground rules."

We agreed we would share information to the extent it would benefit our clients, but that the information retained its privileged status. Because written agreements could be obtained by the government through discovery, we kept ours oral. Finally we discussed attorneys fees. Dr. Marshall had agreed the senator would pay Conway's legal fees, unless he were convicted of a felony, in which case he would have to reimburse her.

"One more thing, and I know this is a lot to ask," I said. "Dr. Marshall would like you to limit your staffing."

"On the whole case?"

"At least until there's an indictment. He's concerned about leaks."

Aaron thought about it, then agreed. "Only until Conway becomes a target. Then it's gloves off."

It was the most I could ask for. As I described the facts of the case, Aaron listened with a furrowed brow. When I was done, I gave him a memo of law. I didn't give him the records I'd gotten from Marni Bardoni because the attorney-client privilege might not cover them. When he finished reading the memo he frowned.

"So what we have is a race," he said. "You discover the culprit before the government discovers the violation."

"I know it's a little unconventional."

"Usually time is an asset, not a liability. You stall until the government bumps your guy from a target down to a subject."

"And then from a subject to a witness."

"A witness they hopefully forget about."

I laughed, realizing where Mac had learned that from.

Aaron studied me, apparently evaluating how well Mac had trained me. "I probably don't have to warn you, Hank, about these Guerrero and Wang characters. Guerrero's pushy, and Wang...he's just a machine. Pretty soon, we're going to have a search warrant on our hands."

I reached into my briefcase and handed him a draft of the motion to quash.

Chapter 23

Roger showed up at my office and whistled. "Nice eye," he said.

I explained.

"If you want," Roger said, "I'll take care of it."

I studied him to see if he meant what I thought he meant. Even though he was retired he still looked like a cop. Husky build, steel-gray hair, pock-marked skin, a large bent nose and an I-mean-business moustache. Did I want him to take care of Jorge? Hell yeah. I just didn't want to know about it.

I found a pen and handed Roger a piece of paper with Jorge's home address on it. He put the paper in his pocket and that was that. I wondered if Mac had fully discovered Roger's utility.

He handed me a black pager-sized device that had a short antenna on it. He told me to follow him and watch for a blinking red light. He checked under table tops, behind picture frames and inside phones. He unscrewed light fixtures, electrical wall outlets and smoke detectors. He took apart my photocopier, my fax machine and my computer. Then he closed his briefcase and poured himself a cup of coffee. "Coast is clear," he said.

"Who's gonna put this stuff back together?"

"I just take it apart, compadre."

"How come when you're doing what I want I'm 'chief,' but when you're doing what you want I'm 'compadre'?"

He sipped his coffee. "Can't tell you, compadre."

"Can you at least tell me how they're listening in?"

"I'd have to sweep the rest of the building to be sure. Contact microphones can hear through walls and floors."

I looked at the ceiling. I realized this amateur sleuth thing required flexible morals, but I wasn't up to breaking into other people's offices just yet.

"Stay away from windows and doors," Roger said. "Feds could be camped out nearby with a parabolic dish."

"Those microphones they use at football games?"

"A little more powerful than those."

I peered through my window at a white Ford Econoline van parked across the street. No logos, no plates, no windows on the panels. "Why am I picturing two men in earphones eating Chinese food?"

"Look on the bright side," he said, clapping me on the back. "It's probably cold pizza."

I slumped down behind my desk. "So how'd the card counter do at the blackjack table?"

"Let's just say I'm keeping my 401K."

"You have better luck with Doyle and Hassan?"

He handed me a three-page single-spaced report. "I'll give you the *CliffsNotes* version. Visited Doyle in prison on Saturday and talked to Hassan's neighbors on Sunday. Bottom line, there's a connection."

"You waiting for a drumroll?"

"Doyle and Hassan both worked at the same company in the late seventies. Federated Petroleum."

"The oil company that went bust?"

"Wasn't just an oil company, but an international conglomerate of drillers, distributors and refineries. Was divvied up to its competitors in the early eighties."

"Doyle and Hassan knew each other when they were there?"

"Don't think so. Hassan was in communications, a translator or something. Doyle was a janitor. Says he never heard of Hassan."

"You believe him?"

"Don't know why he'd lie. Can't do any more or less time than he's already doing. Plus I gave him a carton of smokes and a stack of *Maxims.*"

"Soft porn, good work."

"I was on a roll so I decided to do some more digging on that White guy, the one who changed his name. His last few addresses were on the Upper East Side so I knocked on some doors."

I was still dizzy from learning there was a connection between Hassan and Doyle. So this wasn't all just some kooky conspiracy theory.

"I guess the guy was kind of a swinger," said Roger. "Single, no ex-wives, no kids. Always hitting on the ladies in the building, even the married ones. This one woman, a real snob, said she'd never date a man who hadn't gone to grad school. Then I got to thinking, how could a guy without a graduate degree and with a boat load of debt buy and run a high-tech pharmaceutical company? That's where I hit a dead end. I couldn't find out how much he'd paid for it."

"It's a private corporation. Doesn't have to report the amount to the SEC."

"That's what my accountant buddy said. He said it wasn't that big a deal that White didn't have a graduate degree in science or medicine before he bought the company. He said some of the best biotech companies are run by businessmen, like Amgen, whose CEO came from the telecom industry, but he was stumped how White could have come up with more than a fraction of the purchase price. He did a quick-and-dirty valuation of the company, you know, based on the values of comparable companies in the industry. Figured the company was worth about a hundred million. Said White must've hidden some assets from the IRS when declaring bankruptcy."

I sighed. Tax evasion was bad, sure, but it was not among the sort of conduct I was looking for. I was wasting my time.

Undeterred by my obvious lack of interest, Roger tossed a Manila folder onto my desk. "His credit reports, criminal records and some court documents. Got 'em off the internet. The charge on the reckless driving thing is fun reading. Guy's the poster boy for road rage, nearly landed himself in jail. Must've had a good lawyer."

I pushed the file over to the top of my *To Do* pile. To Roger a good lawyer was someone who was connected, able to make problems go away with a phone call, regardless of the law. In other words someone I would never be. What was I doing?

Roger eyed me. "You don't think much of me, do you?" he said.

"What're you talking about? I didn't say that."

"I don't mean professionally. I mean personally, morally. Whatever. My being kicked off the force and your dad being a minister and all."

I still wasn't sure what he was talking about.

"Don't sweat it," he said. "We've gotten along fine so far. It hasn't gotten in the way of our doing business. I just thought it was worth mentioning, you know, bringing out in the open, now that Mac's not around and it's just you and me. All I'm saying, it doesn't bother me if it doesn't bother you."

I left that one alone for a minute. The mention of Mac lent a certain gravity to the subject. I thought about it, more out of respect for Roger than anything else. Although I didn't think I looked down on Roger, apparently he felt I did. So he was kicked off the force? It wasn't for lying or stealing. It was basically for losing his temper. Besides, if anything, my dad would say, "Don't judge him." But did I?

"I'm not saying I agree with you," I said, "but is there some way I act around you that's different from the way Mac did?"

"He was more relaxed. He wouldn't ask the details of what I did, how I got the info he asked for, unless he needed to admit it into evidence, but you could tell from the way he put his feet on his desk that it was 'cause he didn't give a shit. Not 'cause he had his panties in a bunch."

"So I wear panties because I'm nervous at the idea of you picking through the garbage of a disgruntled employee for evidence he'd given a client list to a competitor?"

"Relax. See, you know exactly what's going on. No, I guess the question is, why can't you talk about it? Or do it yourself?"

"Because I'm a lawyer and it's unethical, if not illegal."

"Dirty too. Can't tell you how many ties I've ruined, but it's not illegal, for your information. Garbage can's on the curb, owned by the town, and the stuff inside's been abandoned by the homeowner. He's got no property interest in it, no privacy interest, nothing. You never bothered to learn about that stuff, never had to I guess, until now. Now you got to know the ugly side of the law, because you gotta enter it, and you don't like it."

That one really got me thinking.

"Look," I said, "maybe I have been judging you. You know, unconsciously, but I've always respected you, your work. I'm not perfect, morally, I know that. I'm sorry if I've treated you like I'm better than you."

He smiled. "As I said, kid, don't sweat it." He seemed to mean it. I felt a little better. Then he said, "By the way, you are better than me. Not much, though, and not for long."

Middleburg was an hour west of DC, nestled in a valley between the Blue Ridge and Bull Run Mountains. I turned off of Route 50 onto a narrow road that bent and turned for several miles before disintegrating into dirt. To the left rolled green farms, sprinkled with brown horses, white fences and sprawling mansions. To the right, a string of bushes and poplars eventually gave way to a brick wall. The wall led to a black iron gate, in front of which stood a red mailbox shaped like a barn. I pushed a button on the intercom.

"Hank Fisher to see Dr. Marshall."

"Very good," a voice said.

The gate swung open, revealing a brick driveway that stretched a few hundred yards to a cul-de-sac. On the left stood a two-story four-car garage with curtains in the windows. On the right stood an enormous Dutch colonial with a broad gambrel roof, second-story dormers and flaring eaves over screened-in porches. Not too shabby. Ivy slithered up cut-stone walls around a red door, which opened. The man in the doorway wore a coat and tie. "Good evening, Mr. Fisher."

"Good evening, Mr...? Maddox, is it?"

"Walter Maddox, sir."

"Sorry to pull you out of the limo like that."

"No need to apologize. You were right to do what you did. I was only in the way, sitting there."

Maddox was stout and spoke in the raspy voice of a smoker.

"I've been meaning to ask," I said. "Did you recognize the driver?"

"Didn't even see him, sir. Too shocked at the sight of Dr. Marshall and the senator on the ground. I was fumbling for my cell phone when you opened the door."

"Did anyone else know you were picking Mac and me up that night? Your wife, your kids, a friend?"

"Been widowed for nine years now. My two girls have moved to California. As for friends, Dr. Marshall prefers me to keep my duties confidential."

"How long you been with him?"

"Twenty years next month, sir."

"Congratulations."

"I've had a pretty good run. Especially the past few years."

"After you thawed out from your stint in Syracuse?"

"My toes are still a little numb."

"By the way, have the authorities contacted you? MPD, FBI, US Attorney's Office?"

"No, sir. Should I contact them?"

I hesitated, not wanting to advise a potential witness not to talk to any government investigators.

"The only reason I ask," he said, "is I'm going to be leaving in a few weeks for a rather extended vacation. Visiting my girls. It's an anniversary gift from Dr. Marshall."

"Sounds like fun. I wouldn't worry about it. If they want to talk to you they'll find you."

"Very good, sir."

Maddox led me into Dr. Marshall's study, offered me a drink, then pulled the doors closed on his way out. I looked around the giant room. Crystal chandelier hanging over a red Persian rug. Black leather couch, two armchairs and a cherry wood coffee table on one end. Oak desk and built-in bookcase on the other end. Fireplace in the middle. On the walls hung a plasma TV and a bunch of diplomas and paintings.

The diplomas glimmered in the waning sunlight. Columbia University, BS in Biology and Chemistry, summa cum laude, Harvard Medical School, joint MD-PhD in Biochemistry and Molecular Biology, summa cum laude. And a one-year NSF-NATO Postdoctoral Fellowship at the Université de Paris, Orsay. No wonder there was ivy on the walls.

The paintings were done in oil and were dark and intricate, each of them signed *LDM*, which I assumed were Dr. Marshall's initials. I rechecked the diplomas and saw I was right, Lawrence Dorian Marshall. Each painting depicted small birds in action, scurrying about in gardens, feeding on leaves of clover or exploding into flight from trees. It was a moment before I realized the birds were all the same: tiny and chick-like with black, brown, red and white feathers. Partridges maybe or quail. In fact, when I looked around the room, I saw the exact same birds everywhere, in paintings and photographs, even as statuettes. Then I noticed a shotgun hanging above the fireplace.

On the other side of the room, behind the desk, hung a framed newspaper page from the *Minqua Messenger*, which was yellowing. Its headline read *Farewell to Class of '59*. On the bottom of the page was an article entitled *Marshall Makes Medicine out of Mold Pill*. The story extolled the childhood genius of Lawrence D. Marshall, winner of the Annual Sons of Minqua Science Contest. To the astonishment of local scientists, Lawrence had made great strides in developing a high-yielding hypoallergenic strain of penicillin by exposing mold from a rotting cantaloupe to X-rays at the local hospital. The photo depicted a baby-faced Lawrence in shirt and tie, shaking the hand of a white-haired man from Bristol-Myers Laboratories.

Tucked away in the bottom corner of the page was a smaller article, which suggested a darker side of Dr. Marshall's otherwise Rockwellian home town:

Man and Teen Accused of Car Thefts

A Minqua man and a juvenile have been arrested in connection with a rash of car thefts, police reported yesterday.

Joseph F. Swindler, Sr., 48, of Mill Street, and a 13-year-old boy are charged with stealing a Packard Hawk Coupe from Shady Lane in May and a Ford Thunderbird from Bedford Manor in April, said police Sgt. Elmore Mott. Swindler is being detained at the Westchester County Jail, said a deputy sheriff. The teenager was taken to the Woodfield Cottage Secure Detention Facility. His name is not being released because of his age.

The duo is also suspected in several auto thefts from the parking lots of downtown businesses over the past few months, Mott said. Police expect to charge the two in those cases before they finish their investigation. "We have an eye witness to the latest theft," Mott said, "and the suspects match a description of the individuals who sold several stolen cars to local used car dealers."

One victim, Dr. Abigail Dorian, of Country Club Drive, was leaving work at Mercy Hospital one evening in March when she discovered her Bentley

S1 Convertible was missing. The car was recovered three days ago in a used car lot in Susquehannock. "They painted it yellow," she said. "They should be charged with bad taste too."

The article was continued on another page, which wasn't on the wall.

"Life was simpler back then," Dr. Marshall said, appearing in the doorway holding a drink. "You worked hard, you were rewarded. You broke the rules, you were punished. Today—" He shook his head as if to say *I don't know what Vicky did to deserve this*.

"Sounds like you were quite the prodigy," I said.

"I was in the right place at the right time."

"Where was that? I'd like to be there next time."

"You don't want to hear the story of my life."

I sat on the couch. "I was thinking more of the secret of your success."

He sat in an armchair. "When I finished my postdoc training I had a choice. Enter the world of research, hiding in a private institute or a government-funded lab, or enter the world of business, real life."

"Real money too."

"You bet. Went to work for Bristol-Myers in Syracuse. Back then, pharmaceutical companies created antidotes and vaccines by mass-screening organic compounds for effectiveness in combating microbes and viruses. If they worked we would snip off a carbon atom, tack on a sugar ring, re-test it and presto."

"A new drug."

"Except by the late seventies pharmaceutical companies had pretty much screened all the organic compounds they could find or at least cured all the old diseases. Tuberculosis, pneumonia, polio. The new challenges were things like Alzheimer's, heart disease and cancer. Luckily recent breakthroughs had been made, giving us the tools to meet those challenges."

"What kind of breakthroughs?"

"Recombinant DNA for one. The technique invented by Boyer and Cohen in the mid-seventies, the one that involved splicing genes together on a molecular level to fight bacteria and viruses. The other breakthrough was monoclonal antibodies, the technique invented by Köhler and Milstein that involved mass producing antibodies by combining B-lymphocytes and myeloma cells."

"Cancer cells?"

"They're immortal. Pretty clever, huh? Those two breakthroughs spawned what was called 'biomania,' the creation of dozens of biotech companies. All sounding the same if you ask me. Genentech, Genex, Genetic Systems."

"So you decided to create something different."

"A niche company to develop human pharmaceutics through recombinant DNA techniques and monoclonal antibodies. Except we focused on the first two phases of drug development: the discovery and preclinical phases. Drug synthesis and characterization, biological efficacy work, then animal toxicology and proof-of-principal studies."

I wasn't sure what he was talking about. "What about the other phases?"

"Clinical trials on humans and FDA approval? Too costly and time-consuming. We sold our research to bigger companies and let them do that, keeping a percentage of the profits. No one had ever seen a company like ours before. Were we a biotech company or a pharmaceutical company? Eventually they started calling us a biopharmaceutical company."

"Now there are a dozen companies just like it, all suspects."

"Not any more. When you arrived I was chatting up the president of Xeric, the last biopharm company on the list."

"No luck?"

"Same as the other companies. The government didn't put the Harappa vaccine contract up for bid. So all the company presidents really know about the virus is what's been in the news. No lead on who made it. General consensus is it was engineered by the Soviets during the Cold War using recombinant DNA technology, went on the Russian black market when the Soviet Union collapsed, then was bought by the Iraqis, who re-engineered it. Saddam must've sold it to his buddy Osama before we put them both out of business."

I forced myself to ignore the Saddam-Osama conspiracy theory. "How would the Iraqis have known how to re-engineer the virus?"

"When the Soviet Union collapsed, so did its biological weapons program, Biopreparat. Its scientists needed jobs. Iraq had the money and it already had some scientists. Dr. Germ, Remember her?"

"It had the equipment?"

"Bought on the open market. Industrial fermenters from Japan. Viral reactors from the Czech Republic. Flasks from France. All documented. When asked by weapons inspectors Iraq said the equipment was for cattle feed."

"I thought we didn't find any evidence of WMD."

"They put all the stuff on wheels, in RVs. Mobile bioweapons labs."

"You mean those trailers they found? I thought they were hydrogen plants for weather balloons." Like the fleeting porn career of John Wayne Bobbitt, Iraqi WMDs was one of my internet-research interests.

"That was before they were modified. They were found in Mosul, in the parking lot of a complex that researched chemical weapons and missiles."

"Yeah, missile research and target ranges."

"No, missile research. As in sarin-tipped warheads, which they found, by the way."

"I thought those warheads were empty."

"Not the hundred and fifty millimeter round they found."

"One round left over from the 1991 Gulf War?"

"What about the one-and-a-half tons of enriched uranium they found?"

"For commercial light water reactors?"

"Nuclear power? The country is sitting on a giant oil field."

"So, tell me, did they find any of these modified vehicles?"

"They'd been dismantled."

"Dismantled?"

"Driven into the desert, salvaged by insurgents, I don't know. Iran or Syria probably has them, along with bin Laden."

Or maybe they're in fantasy land, where you live, I felt like saying.

"What about you, Counselor?" Dr. Marshall said. "What have you found?"

I described my meeting with Aaron and my investigation of Doyle, Hassan and White.

"White?" Dr. Marshall said. "I thought we'd agreed Panacea was a dead end."

"Call it a hunch."

"Is that what I'm paying for?"

"You're paying me to ask questions, hard ones, not just ones you like. Frankly I can't believe you're not asking this particular question yourself. I mean, don't you think it's an awful coincidence that your wife is being set up over a biowarfare virus, and that you just happened to own a company that made biowarfare viruses?"

"So you think White is part of this?"

"No, not anymore. I was just starting with him. Now I'm thinking more like a disgruntled employee. Someone with an ax to grind against you, or maybe just someone who needed the money, like because of a gambling problem or a drug addiction."

"A scientist with a gambling problem or drug addiction?"

"Or an expensive girlfriend, whatever."

"Now you're really hot on the trail of the blackmailer."

"Did anyone there have a grudge against you?"

"My former employees who I pushed, critiqued and then abandoned? Are you serious?"

"Have you talked to anyone there since the sale?"

"I told you when we first discussed this, no."

"No one?"

"Golly, gee, now that you ask. I've spoken to the Directors of Ops. We're on each other's Buddy List on AOL. We stay up at night text messaging each other about what we're going to wear to the lab tomorrow."

"If you don't want my help, then why did you hire me?"

"For Christ's sake. I called my old assistant, Barbara, a few months back to tell her to stop forwarding my junk mail. We chatted a few minutes. She said she was overworked and underappreciated, that she and her husband had separated, and her young daughter was taking it hard. Yada yada yada. It was all very heart-wrenching. You happy?"

Junk mail, work and separation. The stream of questions in my mind had run dry.

"I have to say, I hired you to stop the government from catching wind of Vicky's campaign finance violation. Now they're on the verge of learning everything and here you are laying into me about a company I built from the ground up. Damn it, I wish you'd stop acting on hunches and start practicing law."

"The two things are the same to me," I said, feeling a little bit like I was talking to Mac now.

"Well, son, you're going to have to start separating them."

I wasn't his son, but I let that one pass. "I honestly don't know if I can."

"If you can't, Hank, I'll have to find someone who can."

I laughed. Now that he put it that way... "I'll give it a shot."

"It's a jungle out there." Dr. Marshall put a hand on my shoulder. "Use both barrels."

The sun retired behind the Blue Ridge Mountains, dragging a blanket of stars over the valley. The road to Route 50 was bare except for a fox and some road kill. The jaws of despair nibbled at my heart. I hadn't found Sam Doyle or Abdul Hassan. I'd dug up nothing on Riley Conway, Tariq Shaheen, Ahman Mukhtar and Kaseem Jibran. Warren Shifflett was looking more and more like a red herring, unless ex-biopharm salesmen can genetically reengineer viruses in their basement. My only real suspects were the vice-presidents of a dozen biopharm companies.

I was wondering what to do next when something jumped in front of my headlights, a bend in the road, a parked car, a man. I slammed on the brakes, my tires crunching gravel. When the dirt settled, an old man appeared. He was on his knees, peering under a Cadillac Eldorado, one hand on its bumper. I backed up, pulled over and turned off my engine. The Cadillac's hazards tick-tocked, bathing the ground in orange. Its trunk was open, its right rear wheel missing, a manual jack in place. Across the street rose the charred skeleton of a house. The horizon was black. I got out. "Need some help?" I said.

The old man lifted his head, his hair Albert Einstein wild and white. "Lost my spare," he said. He propped himself up with a cane, not rising beyond a crouch. He wore plaid pants, a brown coat, and bifocals.

"Name's Hank."

"Melvin."

I asked for his flashlight then got down on all fours. "No tire," I said, standing up and brushing off my hands. "Down the hill, there's some grass. Did it roll down there?"

"Who?"

Alrighty then. "I'll have a look."

I climbed down the embankment and swept the flashlight's beam back and forth. The grass was thick and wet, soaking my shoes. Eventually I reached an old barn. For the tire to have rolled this far, I realized, it would've had to pick up a lot of speed. I looked back and saw the old man in the grass, shuffling toward me. Just what I wanted to avoid. I waved him off. "I'll find it," I said.

"Maybe it rolled," he said with a gasp, "in there." He pointed his cane toward the barn.

I lifted the flashlight and peered inside the open door. "No horses, no cows, no tires."

Suddenly I was lying on the straw floor. I felt a dull pain at the base of my neck. I wondered if I'd stepped in a hole. I looked to see if I'd torn the knees of another pair of suit pants. The suit had cost five hundred bucks, which I'd thought was a lot, but Mac had told me I dressed like a used car salesman. I cursed and rolled over. The old man stood over me, wearing black gloves and holding a tire iron. So I said, "Please tell me I tripped."

"You tripped."

A car approached, its headlights sweeping over tree tops. I'm not going to lie to you. I cried for help. I cried at the top of my lungs, my voice filling with terror, my head throbbing with each breath. The man just stood there looking down at me. Soon the engine faded, leaving only the sound of my panting.

"Cry all you want, Dorothy. You're not in Kansas anymore."

Chapter 25

"**A**nd you're not the Wizard of Oz," I said flinging a handful of dirt in the man's face.

As he coughed and spat I found my feet and took off toward the front door. If I could just make it to my VW I'd be safe. But my strides were slow and soon I was on the ground again. The man grabbed my feet and dragged me back into the barn, filling my mouth with straw.

"That was dumb, Dorothy," he said. "I was going to only beat you within an inch of your life, but frankly now I'm a little pissed off."

He raised the tire iron and hit me on the side of the head. When I lifted my arms to block the next blow he struck my stomach. While I curled up he struck my back. When I rolled over he struck my stomach again. He paused to take off his coat.

"I feel for you, Dorothy. I really do. I've been there. Fight someone else's war and now you're getting the snot beat out of you. What you've got to understand, you brought this on yourself. I warned you to stay out of it, didn't I?"

I blinked through my tears.

"Cat got your tongue, huh? That's all right, do you some good to listen. That's the problem with you lawyers. All you do is talk. Never fucking listen."

He dug his shoe under me and flipped me onto my back, like I was a horseshoe crab. Then he went back to work. I felt a snap, then another. I pitied my poor ribs. I wondered why he didn't just kill me. He leaned against a stall and mopped up the sweat on his forehead with a sleeve.

"You know what they say," he said between gasps. "The only good lawyer is a dead one."

He regripped the iron in his left hand and spread his legs like a center fielder about to throw home. Then he cocked the iron behind his ear and raised his other arm. That's when I saw it, the mark of a murderer.

When I opened my eyes the man was gone. So was the battery to my cell phone, and my car keys. Probably collecting dew in the tall grass. I climbed the hill to my VW and peered inside the window at the dashboard...10:45 p.m.

I tried to recognize the face in the side-view mirror. Swollen eye, blood-encrusted nose, purple-and-black cheek, a cut running from lip to ear. I spat into a handkerchief and wiped my nose. Then I ran my fingers through my hair, tucked in my shirt and straightened my tie. After a half hour of walking I reached Route 50.

A tractor trailer rolled over a hill, yellow lights glowing, gears shifting. As its engine grew louder and its headlights brighter I stepped into the road. Its air horn blared then its breaks screamed and its tires squealed. A man climbed down out of the cab. I made out a green John Deer cap and a grizzly beard.

"Boy, what in the hell?" the man said.

My knees buckled, the night started to spin and I had the sensation of being dragged by my armpits. There was the twang of country music and a wall of blue-red lights, both of which started to fade. The man slapped my face.

"Don't go dying in my rig. Jesus, my wife would never forgive me. The woman believes in ghosts. Watches that John Edward fella. Thinks she can talk to her granddaddy. Me, I think it's a bunch a hooey. Name's Roy. I suppose I'm gonna have to do all the talkin.'"

Soon we were surrounded by well-lighted suburbs and then we were on the Memorial Bridge. Roy parked on the edge of Washington Circle and helped me up the circular driveway to the emergency room. Next thing I knew, a familiar voice was telling me to lie back. Someone lifted my feet, a voice boomed over a PA system and a light shone in my eyes.

"I've seen this movie before," I said.

"Do you know what day it is?" Amelia said.

"Why? Is it your birthday?"

She took my hand as I rolled down the hall. "We have to stop meeting like this," she said.

Penny showed up in my hospital room wearing a scowl and holding a pot of tall white flowers exploding above dark green leaves.

"I hope that's a peace lily," I said.

"My sister made me bring it," she said. "I was torn between giving you this and a swift kick in the ass. You break three ribs and don't even call?"

"I didn't want to worry you."

"Ha. Good luck trying that one on your mother."

"She knows?"

"Don't give me that martyr crap. I can't believe you. I'd

expect this from someone else. Do you actually think you have the right to keep this sort of thing from me, after everything we've been through? Like the kids and I are just strangers? We're in this thing too, you know. We don't know who's out there, who you're pissing off. What if he decides to get back at you by coming after the kids? Did you ever think of that? They're scared to death as it is, thinking I'm going to leave them next. But, no, that didn't occur to you, because you're too busy playing superhero. Everything's always about you. You don't give a damn about anyone else. You never have. Well, I'll tell you one thing: you should be glad you're lying in that hospital bed, Mac, because if you were standing up I'd knock you on your ass!"

It was then she realized what she'd said. Her face fell. She looked down and shook her head.

I waited a moment until it was safe to speak, then I said, "Welcome to the anger phase. Some people like to move quickly onto the bargaining phase, but I like it here. Lots of energy. Nothing like the depression phase, all sitting around and sighing. Boring."

"What about acceptance?" She wiped her eyes. "Isn't that a phase?"

"Acceptance is for the birds. The way I figure, once you accept someone's death, you have to let them go. Screw that. I'm not letting the person go until I want to, and I don't want to. I want to hold onto my pain, because that's all I have left of the person. I like my pain. I'd miss my pain. My pain is good. Like Captain Kirk said in that *Star Trek* movie."

"You're really messed up, you know that?"

"I'm just here so that you can feel better about yourself."

She laughed. "It's working."

"How did my mom find out, anyway?"

"Some nice young doctor called."

I groaned.

"Anyone you want to tell me about?" she said.

"His girlfriend," said my roommate, pulling back the curtain. "The one who dumped her boyfriend for him. She stops by twice a day with take-out so he won't have to eat the dog food they serve here. They make googly eyes at each other as they plan their summer. Ride bikes along the C&O Canal, then tour the Vineyards in the Plains, then maybe even spend the weekend at Dewey Beach. I can't take any more. It's worse than watching one of those soaps."

"Penny, Mort. Mort, Penny."

"How do," said Mort.

"Pleasure," said Penny.

"Mort's a retired jeweler who's a little testy because he just had half his colon removed. He shares my love of game shows and *privacy*."

"Don't mind me," Mort said, pushing back the curtain. "I'm not here."

Penny sat on the corner of my bed. "The kids wanted to see their Uncle Hank," she said, "but I didn't think you'd want them here."

"Not my finest hour."

"Do I even want to know what happened?"

I told her, lowering my voice.

"Was it the same man who killed Mac?" she said.

I nodded.

"I was afraid of this," she said. "It's my fault."

"Don't take this the wrong way, but I wasn't doing it for you."

"You think Mac would want you to be a hero?"

I didn't say anything.

"He gave you a job," she said, "that's all."

"It was more than a job."

She waited.

"It would sound dumb to talk about," I said. "All I can say is I can't walk away."

"The way things are going, pretty soon you're not going to be able to walk at all."

"What more could happen to me? I've been run over, strangled and pulverized. I'm fricking immortal."

"You didn't say anything about strangling."

"Guy keeps getting the jump on me. For once I'd like to be ready for him. Make him faint for a change."

"Have you overdosed on your meds or are you just insane?"

"Am I out of life lines or can I phone a friend on that one?"

Mort pulled back the curtain. "Use your fifty-fifty. From where I'm sitting, it's a toss up."

Penny turned around.

"Don't mind me," he said, pushing back the curtain. "I'm not here."

Penny lowered her voice. "All I'm saying is Mac's gone. That may seem cold, but it's a fact. I'm trying to accept it, maybe you should too. Catching the guy who killed him isn't going to bring him back."

I fiddled with the tin foil around the plastic pot. The lily wept white petals onto my hands.

Detective Mills came by, pulled up a chair and put up his soft-spike golf shoes on my bed. He wore black slacks, a black Nike cap and a dark red golf shirt.

"Tiger Woods called," I said. "He wants his outfit back."

Mills reached into a Burger King bag, unwrapped a Whopper and shoved half of it in his mouth. Then he sucked on a King-size Coke. "Don't try to look bored," he said. "I know you'd confess to doing Jimmy Hoffa for a fry."

"Make yourself at home."

"The wife would kill me, I put my feet up at home."

"How do you know if you don't try?"

"I'm getting the feeling you don't like my company."

"Why are you here, Calvin? Couldn't get a starting time?"

He shoved a handful of fries in his mouth. "Are we on a first-name basis now? It's my day off. I was hitting balls at Haines Point and I thought, I bet Fisher's ready to talk now."

"Does the MPD's jurisdiction ever end?"

"DC and the Virginia State Police have what you call an understanding. You know, share information. I'm just cutting out the middle man."

"The middle man was here yesterday. I answered all his questions."

"I know, Sergeant Stoltz. Got his report right here. Funny name, Sergeant Stoltz. Know what that reminds me of?"

"You're not going to lecture me on German philosophers again, are you?"

"Wittgenstein was Austrian and no. I'm talking about *Hogan's Heroes*. You know that big fat guy, Sergeant Schultz. What did he used to say? I see nothing, I hear nothing, I know nothing."

"I'm trying to picture him but all I see is Colonel Klink."

"You're saying I remind you of Klink? Nah, there weren't any German brothers, that was their problem. Too much Wonder Bread, not enough pumpernickel."

Mills unfolded a piece of paper, getting a dollop of ketchup on it. He tried to wipe it off with a napkin but only transferred it to his shirt. He removed the top of the Coke container, dipped a corner of the napkin inside and rubbed the stain until it was the size of a golf ball.

"How do you ever catch anybody?" I said.

"Now I know why the missus got me this color." His shoulders sagged, then he stuffed the rest of the fries in his mouth. "Anyway, the reason Stoltz reminds me of that guy from *Hogan's Heroes* is the way he half-assed his job. Like with this report."

"Is this your way of saying Stoltz missed something?"

"Like why the perp didn't take anything."

"The perp. I love police-talk. Makes the guy sound like a purse snatcher."

"Your assailant, whatever. Why didn't he take your wallet if he was trying to mug you?"

"No money in it."

"Or credit cards?"

"Maybe he got a look at the piece-of-shit I drive and figured my credit's no good."

"How about why you were visiting Dr. Marshall? I bet Stoltz didn't even ask that."

"He's my client, and for your information my office isn't secure, thanks to your pals at the FBI."

"Bugged, huh? Well, I don't know anything about that. Those guys don't tell me diddly. Favors are a one-way street with them. All I know is looks like someone doesn't want you to represent the senator."

"You have mustard on your nose."

As Mills fumbled for a napkin Mort cleared his throat. I saw on his TV that *Jeopardy!* had already begun. I found my remote control and turned on mine. Alex Trebek had just finished announcing the categories. I said, "Sorry, Mort."

Mort grunted.

A contestant picked a category called *Commander-in-Chef*, which reminded me of Dr. Marshall's apron. "'I do not like broccoli,' declared this president," Alex said.

"Who is George H. Bush?" Mort blurted.

I held up one finger. "Chalk one up for the man with the catheter."

"These happy legumes were a favorite of the Gipper," Alex informed us.

"What are jelly beans?" Mort shouted. "Hey, you're not even

trying. It's no fun beating you if you're not gonna play."

Tell that to the guy with the tire iron.

Mills finished his Coke with a loud slurp. "Know what else Stoltz forgot to ask? Whether you recognized the perp."

"I told him the guy was wearing some sort of disguise."

"How do you know it was a disguise if you didn't recognize him?"

"How do you know Mickey Mouse wears a costume?"

"The perp was in an animal costume?"

I felt a headache coming on.

"You don't know who he was," Mills said. "Never saw him before. No idea what his motive was. The man didn't say a word to you."

I knew I could always just keep quiet, but that wouldn't stop him. I thought about how, in my office, Slick Willie had alluded to the attack on Mac, and I opened my mouth. Mills waited. He wanted the truth and he wasn't going to leave until he got it. The problem was that telling him the whole truth would compromise my client's confidences and my own investigation. So I twisted the bedspread dramatically in my hands. "He did say something."

Mills took out his tiny notepad and pen.

"He said, 'The only good lawyer is a dead one.'"

I'd noticed from interviewing white collar criminals that the most convincing lie is a half-truth. Of course the white collar criminals I'd interviewed had all been caught, so how good at lying could they be? I started to panic. Could the DC Board on Professional Responsibility discipline me for lying to the police? Then there was Mills himself. If he caught me in a lie, he would do more than sanction me.

Mills stared at me, eyes narrowing. I felt a bead of sweat form on my forehead and hoped Mills wouldn't catch sight of it. His face broke out into a grin. Pretty soon he was busting a gut.

"What's so funny?" Mort said, pulling back the curtain.

Mills told him. Soon Mort was laughing too.

I love a lawyer-joke as much as the next guy, but having two adults, one of whom is sworn to protect you, laugh at the motive of a man who is trying to kill you is not my idea of comedy. Mort apologized and Mills put away his notepad.

"You're telling me an old guy beat you up 'cause you were once his lawyer?" he said. "That he's a disgruntled client?"

I shrugged.

"Now I see why you don't want me to catch him. Your malpractice is his motive. It would come out at trial, probably make the papers. Let me give you a piece of advice, kiddo. You really want to catch this guy? Review your files, make a list of the cases you lost and give it to me. I'll have him behind bars within a week."

"Something to think about."

He shrugged. "It's your ass."

I pretended to turn my attention back to *Jeopardy!*

He got up to leave. "Whatever you do, Fisher, don't keep up this private eye thing. It's bad for your health."

Late one night I woke up to find Penny sitting on the corner of my bed. "You're being discharged tomorrow," she said.

"My health insurance carrier has declared me completely healed. They told me I could have a nurse check up on me at home, as if that's free."

"I'm taking the kids to Cape Cod for the summer. My dad's place."

I had to admit, I was surprised. "When are you leaving?"

"Tomorrow."

"What about school?"

"I pulled the kids out early."

"What's wrong?"

"I don't know."

"What happened?"

After a moment she said, "He was in my house."

"The guy?" I sat up.

"Last night."

I started to get dizzy, feeling the walls close in around me. "Did he hurt you?"

"He left a message on my mirror in red lipstick."

She started to speak and then stopped herself. I didn't really want to know anyway. I told myself to breathe, that I was a fool for turning down Mills' help. "Have you gone to the police?"

"What are they going to do? The man was in my bathroom, Hank. I can't do this anymore. What if he'd done something to my kids?"

"I'll stop."

She stood up and turned around. She stared out into the night, the black window capturing her pale face. Below her a siren shrieked. Finally she turned back and wiped away a tear.

"No, that's what I came to tell you. I don't want you to stop. I want you to get the asshole. Just call me when it's over."

Chapter 26

"W here have you been?" Aaron said.

I sank into the chair behind my desk and said, "Rescuing my car from the Loudoun County pound."

"You might want to meet me at the senator's campaign office."

"Don't tell me."

"Conway has some visitors."

I was already on my feet. "Be there in five minutes."

I arrived right after Aaron. He was shaking hands with one of the agents who would be conducting the search. As the other agent was slipping on her latex gloves she asked Aaron if he was the one from the Sunday morning news programs. I was on the other side of the room, where there were no adoring fans. Next to me stood Agent Wang, with arms folded, legs spread and eyes fixed on the Band-Aid on my cheek. "Mills told me about your trouble changing a tire," he said. "I disagree with his disgruntled-client theory. Know what I think?"

I couldn't wait.

"I think you were attacked by Mac's killer. I think he doesn't want you representing the senator. I think you're afraid."

I'd thought Wang was supposed to be the good cop in the Rice & Beans good-cop-bad-cop routine. Then I remembered how I'd goaded him into telling me the focus of their investigation. Apparently he was still pissed off.

"I am afraid," I said. I was afraid he needed a new mouthwash. I was afraid that, if he stood any closer, Guerrero was going to get jealous. All I said was, "I'm afraid you need a warrant before you can see these files."

He pulled an envelope out of his coat pocket.

Aaron appeared, holding out a hand for the envelope. He said, "Can we a have a moment before you begin?"

As Wang looked at his watch, Aaron asked me to join him in the hall. Conway remained seated on the couch, where he was flipping through an issue of *Golf Digest*.

Unfortunately the warrant looked okay. It was signed the day before by Magistrate Judge Ronald R. Vanderkamp. It contained a specific description of the place to be searched and the things to be seized. It was supported by an affidavit purporting to establish probable cause. I studied the affidavit.

AFFIDAVIT

I, JAMES M. WANG, being duly sworn, depose and say:

(1) I have been a Special Agent of the Federal Bureau of Investigation (FBI) for nine years. The information set forth in this affidavit is the result of my own investigation or has been communicated to me by others.

(2) For the following reasons, I believe probable

cause exists to issue a search warrant for the campaign finance office of US SENATOR VICTORIA E. SERLING Suite 301, 1999 K Street, Washington, DC, 20006, for evidence of violations of Title 2, U.S. Code, Section 434(b) (federal election reporting requirements), Title 2, U.S Code, Section 441b(a) (political campaign contributions), Title 18, U.S. Code, Section 201(b)(2)(A) (bribery), and Title 18, U.S. Code, Section 1001 (false statements).

(3) On April 15 of this year, the president of the non-profit association People for the Education of Arabic Children Everywhere (PEACE), DR. AHMAN T. MUKHTAR, admitted that on February 14, PEACE's assistant legislative director, a man known to him as ABDUL HASSAN, made a $50,000 contribution on behalf of PEACE to SENATOR SERLING's campaign office (as shown in Attachment A).

(4) On February 27 of this year, SENATOR SERLING voted against the Terrorism Reconnaissance and Prosecution Act (TRAP), HR 1492 (imposing stronger immigration restrictions and broader law enforcement powers), which consequently failed to be enacted into law by the United States Senate by one vote (as shown in Attachment B).

(5) A review of SENATOR SERLING's periodic reports filed with the Federal Election Commission for the past six months reports no contribution by PEACE (as shown in Attachment C).

(6) SENATOR SERLING's campaign finance director, E. RILEY CONWAY, has refused to cooperate with the FBI and the Office of United

States Attorney for the District of Columbia.

(7) The man known as ABDUL HASSAN has been unable to be located by the FBI due to the fact that he used an alias on his application for employment at PEACE (as shown in Attachment D).

(8) SENATOR SERLING's Deputy Campaign Finance Director, SAMUEL DOYLE, has also been unable to be located by the FBI.

(9) The above facts are true and correct to the best of my knowledge and belief.

"This will look just great in *The Washington Post*," Aaron said.

"It's under seal," I said, pointing to the notice next to the caption.

Aaron gave me a look.

If you think it's bad now, I wanted to say, *wait until Wang discovers Doyle used an alias. That'll be the final nail in the coffin.* Instead I tried something a little more constructive. "What about calling the judge and moving to quash the warrant and to stay its execution? The affidavit is totally lame."

"Lame, huh? Try that argument on Rubberstamp Vanderkamp. No, we'll have our day in court, after they've seized the stuff and read it."

"Can't we scare them into stopping? Threaten to call Congress and assert legislative privilege or something, or argue separation of powers?"

"How is it a separation-of-powers issue? Congress passed the Campaign Finance Act. The judiciary approved the search warrant. Now the executive branch is executing it. If anything, it's a *cooperation* of powers."

"What about the speech-and-debate clause? Didn't that

congressman from Louisiana cite that clause when the FBI raided his office?"

"Bill Jefferson, and it didn't work. Besides, that search was of his chambers on the Hill, not of his campaign finance office in downtown DC. The FBI has executed search warrants before on offices during campaign finance investigations, like in New Jersey. A few years ago they searched the State Democratic Party Headquarters when investigating Governor McGreevy. Before that they searched the office of the Essex County Executive when he was running for U.S. Senate. And before that, although they didn't search the office of Senator Torricelli, they searched practically everything else, including the home and office of one of his political donors."

"So we just let them go ahead?"

Back in the office the agents had already begun. They'd finished the desks and had moved on to the phones, fax machine and computers. They were labeling all the cables and components, unplugging them and then folding them in bubble wrap and evidence tape, pausing occasionally to take digital photos. Long gone were the days when agents downloaded documents onto a disk or printed them out. Now they realized merely turning on a computer risked overwriting deleted information, and opening a document altered the computer's embedded data about that document, potentially crippling its evidentiary value. I decided Wang was having too much fun.

"I assume you're going to form a Taint Team," I said, "to review the files for privileged communications."

"Why?" Wang asked.

"Who knows what's on those hard drives?"

He turned to Conway. "These things have any communications with lawyers on 'em?"

Conway shrugged. "Maybe some e-mails to my own lawyer."

"We'll keep an eye out," Wang said and gave me a smirk. "Happy, cowboy?"

I turned my attention back to the female agent, who was converging on the file cabinets as the male agent was carrying down the electronic equipment. Who said chivalry was dead? The woman set aside all call sheets, bank account statements and accounting ledgers that documented the receipt of funds from PEACE. She also set aside all phone bills and correspondence documenting communications between Doyle and Hassan. Before she placed the documents into banker's boxes Aaron and I reviewed them to make sure none were beyond the scope of the warrant, then we recorded them in a log. With each document that slipped through my hands I felt the agents get closer to an indictment, closer to me being fired and Mac's killer getting away.

When the male agent returned, he made a final sweep of the office. He knelt down, pulled out a desk drawer and reached into the cavity. Then he pulled out a Manila folder and stood up. "Doyle's personnel file," he said.

Wang crossed the room and extended his hand. "Gotcha."

"Not so fast," I said, snatching the file from the agent's hand.

Jaws dropped and agents put their hands on their pistols. Conway even lowered his magazine.

Aaron stepped it front of me and held out his arms. "Hold on," he said.

Wang resnapped the safety strap on his holster. "This better be good, cowboy."

The search warrant shook as I held it up. "Doyle's personnel file is outside the scope of the warrant."

Wang made a face. "Bullshit."

"Says here it permits a search of 'all call sheets, bank statements, accounting ledgers, spreadsheets, FEC forms or reports, correspondence, voicemail messages, computer equipment and inter-office memoranda to the extent they evidence, or may evidence, receipt of any contributions from PEACE.'"

"Right," Wang said. "It authorizes us to take 'inter-office memoranda.' I put that in there myself."

"But Senator Serling's inter-office memoranda look like this," I said, grabbing off the desk a document entitled *Inter-Office Memorandum.*

Wang dropped his shoulders. "You're killing me, Fisher. I can just call the judge and have him make a ruling that the term inter-office memorandum includes personnel files."

"That's a stretch," Aaron said. "Besides I'm sure Ron would love to get a call from you on the golf course. Thursday evenings are men's league at Army Navy Country Club. He's probably on the practice range right now."

As Wang stared at the phone I said, "You should thank me. I just saved you the embarrassment of losing a suppression hearing."

"What are we doing here, Fisher?" Wang said. "You know we'll just get a warrant with an expanded scope."

"Maybe you will, maybe you won't."

"Oh, I will. If you pull that crap again, you're leaving here in cuffs."

The two agents left carrying the final load of documents and Wang followed them out.

After waiting a moment to make sure they were gone Conway got up and punched my shoulder. "Thanks, cowboy. Remind me never to be in a room again with you and three armed FBI agents. Why didn't you just give them the goddamn thing? It helps us, doesn't it? Shows Doyle was an impostor."

"An impostor or our co-conspirator," Aaron said.

"You heard Wang. They're going to get it anyway."

"But it might take a few days, especially with the weekend coming up."

"What difference does a few days make?"

Although Aaron didn't answer, I knew what he was thinking. *Maybe the difference between an indictment and a no bill, if we can find the man responsible.*

Conway grabbed his blazer. "I have to get back to my day job, soon to be my only job."

I knew how he felt. I still had to break the news about the warrant to Dr. Marshall.

When I reached Middleburg Amelia was waiting in the driveway.

I smiled. "Nice car."

"It's Aunt Vicky's. She lets me use it. I just thought, it's such a sunny day..."

Sure, I thought. Why not? But I just kept staring at it dumbly.

"Uncle Lawrence got it for her last year for an anniversary present. He insisted, said the Sebring she was driving was an 'abomination.' She wanted a Cadillac convertible. An 'XLR,' I think it's called. You know, 'Buy American' and all that. But he insisted on a Jaguar. Said the company's owned by Ford, so what's the difference? Still, he registered it in his name just in case any reporters wanted to make a fuss. I think this one's called an XKR or something. All the names sound the same to me."

It was silver with flowing lines and large steel-rimmed wheels. The top was down. Inside were soft-looking leather seats and glossy walnut trim, and a touch-screen computer on the console. It must have cost more than a year's salary, I decided. All for an anniversary present.

"My parents just give each other gift certificates," I heard myself say.

She laughed with a touch of nervousness. "I heard about the warrant on the news, so I called Lawrence. I thought you'd need some moral support."

"Thanks, but I can handle it."

"Like you handled that guy with a tire iron?"

"Look, I appreciate your concern, but I'm not your patient anymore."

"I wasn't asking your permission, Hank."

I didn't have the energy to argue. Dr. Marshall's study was dark, the blue light of the plasma TV flickering against the walls. When he saw me he spread his arms in mock crucifixion. "What're they going to search next? Her office on the Hill? Our house? My fucking study?"

On the TV screen Holly Hickey stood in front of the Capitol Building. "While we've been unable to obtain a copy of the search warrant," she said, "we have learned it was executed this afternoon on Senator Serling's campaign office on K Street." The camera switched to the entrance of the office building, from which the agents were carrying boxes. "The FBI wouldn't comment on the focus of the search, but sources say it concerned a possible campaign finance violation. When Senator Serling awakens from her coma she'll find a much different political landscape than before she was injured."

Dr. Marshall turned off the TV and Amelia sat down. He approached her, raising his hand. "Amelia—"

"We've been through this before, Lawrence. I'm staying and that's all there is to it."

Dr. Marshall finished his drink, then turned to me and lifted his chin. We faced each other, lawyer and client for one final moment.

"Hank, what can I say? You're fired."

I forced myself to laugh. "Don't beat around the bush, Dr. Marshall."

"You're just not the right man for this particular job, son. Vicky needs someone with more experience, someone with some pull in Washington. Like that Weissman fellow."

"A fellow Harvard grad."

Dr. Marshall smiled condescendingly. "Is that what you think this is about?"

"Look, finding the guy behind this thing is the key to keeping the press from eating your wife alive, and keeping me on the case is the key to finding the guy behind this thing. I'm this close, Lawrence."

"I understand that, Hank. I'd appreciate it if you'd give my new lawyer any information you have about 'the guy.' You can send me the balance of the retainer, that is if there's any left given your outrageous hourly rate. Don't worry about the damage you caused to my limo."

What a guy.

Amelia caught up with me in the driveway. The sky was dark, stars twinkling above.

"For the record," she said, "I didn't know he was going to do that. I thought he was just going to rant and rave like usual."

"Sorry you missed the show. You could've made some popcorn and invited your friends."

"Hey," she said, putting a hand on my shoulder. "Don't be like that. Maybe we could work something out. Maybe I could hire you."

"I don't want any handouts. Your uncle doesn't think I can hack it. That's not going to change if you give me his money."

I regretted the words as soon as they left my mouth.

"First of all," she said, "it's my money. I put myself through med school and I paid for that townhouse. Second I wasn't going to give it to you but hire you with it. And third—"

Amelia's voice had grown so loud that I glanced at the guest house, where I figured Maddox lived. Its lights remained dark.

"Don't worry, he's on vacation," she said. "And third, who cares what Lawrence thinks, or what Maddox thinks for that matter? Isn't it more important what I think? I thought you wanted to help my aunt."

"I thought I was."

I stared at the driveway, each brick evenly spaced and level. Must have cost a small fortune to build. "I'm out of my league here."

"What league?" Amelia asked. "There's no secret club."

"Yes there is, and guys like your Uncle and Brock Aurelia are in it. Middleburg, Congressional Country Club, Georgetown Prep. You just don't see it because you're a lifetime member."

"My father came to Florida on an open boat."

"Your father, the Cuban-aristocrat-turned-judge, who married the sister of a US Senator? My father says mass in a pair of sandals and married a Jew from Poughkeepsie."

I regretted those words too. I liked Poughkeepsie and being Jewish, and I loved my mother.

"What do you want? A medal for being more middle-class than me?"

"Do you really think you're middle-class, Amelia?"

I got in my old VW. When the engine finally started I turned the car around, feeling the weight of her stare. At the end of the driveway I stopped and looked in my rearview mirror, but she was gone. I couldn't blame her. There's only so much crap a person can take.

Chapter 27

When my brother Grady died I inherited all his stuff. I kept it in a footlocker under my bed. Every night before falling asleep I would pluck out one of his golf biographies. Bobby Jones, Sam Snead, Arnold Palmer. All of the players had lived, or were still living, full lives. They only reminded me of how many holes short Grady's golf game had been cut.

So I moved on to his books about golf architects. Donald Ross, designer of the Inverness Club in Toledo. Allistair MacKenzie, designer of Ohio State University's course in Columbus. And A.W. Tillinghast, designer of Lakewood Country Club in Westlake. I knew Grady had liked to read about the design of Ohio courses he'd played, but the courses meant nothing to me.

I decided to turn to books with more practical value. *How to Play Your Best Golf All the Time* by Tommy Armour. *Five Lessons: the Modern Fundamentals of Golf* by Ben Hogan. And *Golf My Way* by Jack Nicklaus. Every now and then I would find an underlined word, like a coded message from the Great Beyond. Then I would see Grady's calloused finger turn the page. He couldn't afford a golf glove when he started playing at age eight, and he figured he didn't need one when he started winning tournaments at age twelve. The image gave me nightmares.

One weekend I decided to see how well the books worked. I dug out Grady's golf clubs, a set of Walter Hagen forged irons, three MacGregor persimmon woods and a Spalding Cash-In putter, which he'd used to win the Ohio Junior Golf Championship. He must have used up all their magic. I couldn't hit the woods because the shafts were too long. I couldn't hit the irons because the shafts were too stiff. I lost the wedge in the hay on a public course. When I couldn't find the wedge, I got so mad I threw the putter into a pond. When I was fishing out my putter, I slipped and fell in.

My wedge was later returned to me in the pro shop, but I decided I needed to adopt one of Grady's more therapeutic hobbies, like model airplanes. Since the time he'd learned our grandfather had been a pilot with the Flying Tigers, Brady had been in love with World War II model airplanes. He'd preferred allied aircraft with nice names, like *Liberator*, *Peacemaker*, *Guardsman*, *Sentinel* and *Vigilant*. I'd preferred allied aircraft with nasty names, like *Destroyer*, *Devastator*, *Mauler* and *Vildebeest. Demon*, *Hellcat*, *Helldiver* and *Fireball*. Even the TBF Avenger, the Navy torpedo bomber that Bush senior bailed out of in World War II. But I liked the enemy planes the best. Kawasakis, Messerschmitts, Focke-Wulfs.

I would spend long hours in the basement, ignoring my mother's orders to take out the garbage and getting dizzy off epoxy glue and acrylic paint. When I was done with each one I would throw away the rubber-band powered prop and screw onto the firewall a gas-powered aluminum motor. I could send a piece of balsa wood and tissue paper high over the walls of Cleveland

Stadium. One time a guy stopped, rolled down his window and shouted, "Hey, kid, you could hurt someone that way," and my heart leapt at the possibility.

When my mood was particularly sour I would fasten on the prop backwards to increase the torque, and then I would straighten the flaps and tail. The plane would jump out of my hands and climb straight up, growing smaller until it was a dot in the sky, where it would hang for a moment, then turn and roar back into view, like a missile from outer space, growing larger and louder until you wanted to dive for cover. It would crash into a field or parking lot, leaving behind a pile of sticks and shreds, a charred wing next to a smoldering motor. Like in a Viking funeral.

I would whistle the theme from Star Wars as I pieced them back together. Reinforcing the struts with long match sticks and nylon thread, using razor blades and nail files to keep the edges straight and smooth, and gluing on an extra layer of tissue paper to balance the weight. After a half dozen reconstructive surgeries, so many parts had been replaced that the planes had grown new identities.

My flying days ended one Sunday morning when I decided to launch a Mitsubishi Zero in the most forbidden of territories. As I was waiting for the parishioners to leave my father's church I picked a piece of glue off my finger. A strip of skin came off, drawing a bead of blood. When I picked up the plane I left a crimson mark on it. Squeezing my finger I produced enough red ink to fill one side of the hull. Then I touched a straightened paper clip from the battery to the spark plug and turned back the throttle until the sputter and hiss of the motor tightened to a fine high-pitched whine. I hooked the spring around the prop and wound it backwards one full turn, then I took aim and let go. The plane climbed dutifully. Then, as if knowing its fate, it dipped a wing and circled before making its final, fatal turn toward the steeple, showing the world its name.

Spirit of St. Grady

F or the next three days CNN told me about the spread of Harappa. CSPAN told me what to think about it. PBS taught me about the vast right-wing conspiracy. Fox News taught me about the vast left-wing conspiracy. The Golf Channel improved my putting. The Food Channel improved my nachos. Comedy Central made me laugh. The Women's Entertainment Network made me cry. And *Law and Order* made me wish I was a prosecutor. Or a police detective. Or a criminal. Anything but what I was.

At some point, I decided human contact was completely overrated. I stopped answering Mrs. Baumgartener's knocks at the door, I turned off the ringer on my phone and I started watching only TV programs that minimized the appearance of people: The Weather Channel, The Discovery Channel and Animal Planet. I even pared down my talk with the pizza guy. He would say, *Hey*. I would say, *Hey*. He would hand me the pizza. I would hand him the money. He would shove the change in his pocket. I would shove a slice in my mouth. Swiss watchmakers could have used us to calibrate their instruments.

By the third day Pizza Guy and I had dispensed even with saying *hey*. The box was hotter than usual. When I peeked under the lid it emitted a cloud of steam, fogging my glasses. I didn't want to start a conversation, but I appreciated the hustle.

"Nineteen minutes," I said. "Impressive."

Pizza Guy glanced over his shoulder, like I was talking to someone else. Then he said, "Could've been faster. Parking sucks here."

"I'd give you the guest pass in my kitchen drawer but that would require some effort."

"You didn't order the works this time. You okay, dude?"

I didn't want to admit that pizza three times a day was getting to me. It was as if Pizza Guy could read my mind.

"You have to mix things up," he said. "Throw in some wings and cheese sticks."

"You kidding?" I said, stuffing a slice in my mouth. "Those things will kill you."

As I wrote a check he peered over my shoulder. My blinds were drawn. My mail was strewn about on the floor. My TV cast eerie shadows against the walls. Who knew what was hidden in my freezer? "Boo," I said.

Pizza Guy jumped.

"Tell your boss this check probably won't bounce," I said.

"You gonna keep missing work?"

"I wouldn't say I'm missing it," I said, stealing a line from a slacker movie.

Pizza Guy laughed, then made a fist of indolent solidarity. "Hey, I respect what you're doing here. I only took this job 'cause my parents started charging me rent."

Pizza Guy's encouragement aside I felt a bit weary of solitary confinement. So the next morning I caved in and turned on the news.

There was Aaron Weissman, standing before a bouquet of

microphones in a Senate conference room. Beside him stood Dr. Marshall, hands joined and head-bowed. On the other side stood Marni Bardoni. Beside Marni stood a square-jawed guy in a dark blue suit. I couldn't believe it. Of all the associates at P&S that Aaron could've picked to help him on the case, he picked Brock Aurelia. I tried to push out of my mind the thought of him working with Amelia. Aaron introduced himself as the senator's new legal counsel, admitted an investigation was pending, and explained that he was getting up to speed on the case.

"Why the change in counsel?" Holly Hickey said.

"You'd have to ask Dr. Marshall that," Aaron said. "But I believe it was just a change in defense strategy."

"Are you saying he's unhappy with the senator's former counsel?"

"Certainly not. I know Mr. Fisher. He's a very skilled attorney."

Whoever said it, was right. There are liars, damn liars and then there are lawyers.

The next news story was about Harappa. Congress had granted the president's request for emergency funding to combat the virus abroad, before it arrived in the US. A large part of the funds would be used to discover the virus' manufacturer, the key to finding the al-Qaeda operatives responsible. The rest of the funds would be used to research and develop a vaccine. Because national security was at stake and only one company could provide the services needed, DOD had granted what was known as a *sole-source* government contract to Panacea, Inc. There was no need for the company to bid. All it had to do was sign on the dotted line and the government would pay it hundreds of millions of dollars. Panacea's president, Robert White, was shown exiting the White House. He was stout and broad-shouldered, with a thick neck supporting a balding head, his skin darkened by the sun, probably from lying beside some swimming pool in Vegas. He wore an impeccably tailored suit and a large gold wristwatch, which glinted as he put his hand on a limo door that had been opened for him. Even uneducated government contractors made more money than me.

"What did the president say?" a reporter shouted.

White stopped and turned around. "Terror is a disease and Panacea is the cure."

Someone laughed. White didn't even smile. He was dead serious, his small dark eyes fixed on the camera. It was spooky how black-and-white the world was to some people. To me, everything had faded into various shades of gray.

Someone knocked at the door, making me jump. I looked through the peephole, half-expecting to see Slick Willie holding a tire iron.

It was worse.

"I know you're home," Amelia said. "I can hear your TV. I brought Café Asia. See, you can tell from the grease at the bottom of the bag."

I pulled open the door. "That better not just be soy sauce."

She looked at my pajama bottoms and T-shirt. "Having a sleepover, are we?"

"Why? Are you interested?"

"Nice try."

"I'd kiss you on the cheek but I ran out of toothpaste yesterday. Had to dip into the baking soda in the back of the fridge."

She pushed the bag to my chest. "Then chicken curry breath should be an improvement."

I followed her to the kitchen. "What would you like to drink? I have water, ice water and, if you want a treat, hot tap water."

"I see you've resorted to a more crude form of pain relief."

"What, that pyramid of empty cans? It's just Miller Lite. That stuff doesn't even count."

I got two beers from the fridge. She shrugged and took one. In the living room she swept the comforter and pillow off the couch, found the remote and switched to a soap. We ate in silence, watching a melodrama unfold about a love triangle between a professional golfer, a doctor-turned-spy and the head of an international diamond-smuggling cartel, which, given recent events, seemed entirely plausible. When the show broke for a commercial Amelia put down her fork, leaned back and looked around from the dirty dishes on the kitchen table, to the mail and bedding strewn across the floor, to the putter and golf balls in the corner. "So this is where lawyers go on vacation," she said.

"Not much of a view but, once you visit, you never want to leave."

"So this is it for you?"

"The end of the line."

"Do not pass go?"

"Do not collect two hundred dollars."

"Seriously?"

"I'm thinking of a career change. There are children all across this country who don't know the difference between 'that' and 'which,' between 'anxious' and 'eager,' between a colon and a semi-colon. It's a national crisis, like poverty and drugs. They need me."

"You shouldn't take what Lawrence said personally. He didn't even want to hire Mac."

"He was just looking out for your aunt's best interests."

"He was being an ass."

"Yes, but an ass who was technically right. I spent too much time investigating and too little time lawyering."

"Don't second-guess yourself."

"I let down Penny and kids."

"You haven't let anyone down. Why can't you find Mac's killer on your own?"

"Like I have access to the execs of America's top biopharm companies. I can't even talk to your aunt's staff anymore."

"Then why don't you just go to the police, talk to Mills?"

"What would I say? I can't disclose the campaign finance violation without breaching the attorney-client privilege."

"Isn't that over now that you've been fired?"

"Like a venereal disease, it survives the end of the relationship."

"What do you know about venereal diseases?"

"Why are you asking?"

"Can't you disclose things if you know a crime is going to be committed?"

"Only if I know the client is going to hurt someone. Not if I think someone else is going to commit a crime."

"There's got to be another way."

"Face it, I screwed up."

"You didn't screw up."

"Then I was a smashing success."

"You're right, you screwed up. You're the worst lawyer in DC. Hell, you're the worst lawyer in America. The killer beat you up because you were on the wrong trail."

"I'm glad you understand." I knew what she was getting at: I'd made the killer nervous. But I wasn't to be reasoned with.

"I'm just wondering," she said, "how did you expect all of this to go?"

I didn't know. Then I said something without thinking. "I saw what's-his-name on TV."

Amelia had no idea what I was talking about.

"Brock," I said, unable to stop myself.

She was looking at me like I was crazy now, which irked me even more.

"Brock Aurelia, your ex-boyfriend, remember him? He's working on the case now. I've been replaced by a robot. You're probably going to be working long hours with him. Staying up late, changing into something more comfortable, falling asleep on each other's shoulder."

She didn't get mad. She just said, "I thought you'd let that one go."

"Hey, it's gone. I'm just waving goodbye to it. *Y'all come back now, ya hear?*"

I picked at the rice hardening on my plate. She stood and stared at me. I wondered how I must look to her: a failed teacher, a failed lawyer, a failed boyfriend. "I'm not here because I'm afraid, you know."

"I know," she said, picking up her purse. "You're just living it up on vacation."

Chapter 29

My answering machine beeped and my dad's voice filled the room.

I picked up the phone. "Don't tell me, Dad. A nice young woman named Amelia called."

"I'm glad she did. I was looking for an excuse to be nosy. I didn't want to crowd you at the funeral."

"Sometimes the soul needs room to breathe."

"Bingo."

"You're not going to ask if I'm going to church, are you?"

"No, I know the answer to that one. I was going to start off with some small talk, like how you've been filling your days lately. Then maybe move onto something more ministerial, like if you're involved in any charities."

"This isn't going to be a pitch for ECS, is it?" My dad's solution to most of life's problems was Episcopal Community Services.

"Boys Club, United Way, Red Cross," he said. "It doesn't

matter which one you choose. It could be the Salvation Army, Habitat for Humanity, Make a Wish, Big Brother—"

"Okay, okay."

"Well?"

I thought about it. "Can you read the list again?"

"The bar association at least?"

"I did some pro bono lately."

"How did it make you feel?"

"Tired."

"The pro bono work, not this conversation."

"Inadequate. Embarrassed. At one point, afraid."

"What happened?"

"I ducked when I should have covered."

"You were hurt?"

"Just my ego."

"Did it make you feel good at least, helping someone else?"

"I don't know, I haven't had time to think about it, I guess."

My father was quiet, thinking...or waiting. I cleared my throat.

"Is that tic back?" he asked.

"No, Dad."

After my brother Grady died I started to experience "spasmodic muscular contractions," as my mother called them. Eye-blinking, nose-twitching, neck-flexing. I had 'em all. Not the best way to fit in at school. My mother brought me to a doctor who asked me some questions and concluded it wasn't Tourette's. *So what's the matter with him?* my mother asked. *He's retarded,* the doctor said. My mother didn't laugh but I did. *Think less, talk more,* he said to me on my way out of his office. Eventually the ticks went away but I still occasionally got the urge to blurt out *Bullshit!* in the courtroom. According to Mac this was perfectly normal considering the quality of some of our opposing counsel.

"Listen," I said, "I know mom's worried about me."

"She's not the only one. Why don't you come home for a while? On my nickel."

"Dad."

"We could hang out, pretend we're a family. The last time was, what? Four years ago?"

"I couldn't make it last Christmas."

"Or Thanksgiving."

"I had to work."

"And the three years before that it was law school."

"I had to study. What's your point?" I heard the edge in my own voice, but my father was made of Teflon.

"A good minister doesn't have a point," he said. "He just asks questions."

"I forgot. Socrates."

"He was a good teacher."

"The man drank hemlock. Besides, why does everything have to be a lesson?"

"That's a good question."

"Oh, God."

My father was taken aback only a moment by my invocation of the Lord during our conversation. "Have you considered a career change?" he said. "Going back to teaching English?"

"Why are you and Mom so stuck on that? Wanting me to teach a bunch of hormone-enraged kids how to write topic sentences?"

"Your mother just likes having you back in Cleveland."

"And you?"

"I guess I'm just curious about why you ever left home, took off for law school like that. You had a pretty good deal here. Great job, loving family, lots of friends. It's like you were in self-destruct mode. Was it because of that girl, the one who said you were dull?"

"Uninspired. Graduates of Yale don't use monosyllabic words."

"So it was her?"

"Not really."

"Good, she didn't know the first thing about C.S. Lewis."

"Is that the worst thing you can say about someone?"

"She was a phony."

"That's better. Now say something about her teeth."

"She wasn't ready to get married."

"And I was?"

"Are you now?"

"You're starting to sound like Mom."

"What about teaching law?"

"I'm not smart enough to teach law."

"There are some people who would find that statement funny."

"Maybe I should be a comedian."

"Why is representing this senator so important to you?"

"I don't care about her."

"It's a means to an ends."

"Was."

"That's right. Amelia said you're not on the case anymore."

I was still trying to imagine what a conversation would be like between Amelia and my father. *You understand he's a heathen,* he would say. *Yes, I prefer Vikings, but there were none of them left,* she would say, or something equally flip. No, now she would say nothing but *Good riddance.*

"I needed more time to pursue my other interests."

"The senator's husband fired you because you were just representing her so you could find clues about Mac."

"Did Amelia say that?"

"Isn't it the truth?"

I didn't answer, trying to freeze him out. It was no use; my father was the king of silence. We could go on like this for days. The phone company would shut off my service before he uttered a word.

"Look," I said, "I know what you're going to say, that catching Mac's killer isn't worth losing my life over."

"That's true, but I'm more concerned with a deeper issue: why catching him is so important to you."

"You're wondering if I'm doing this because of Grady, out of guilt."

"I told you, I'm just asking. But now that you mention it, do you feel guilty about Grady?"

"No, not anymore," I lied.

"Good, you shouldn't."

We shared a moment of silence in honor of fallen comrades.

Then I said, "I guess I'm doing it because I owe a lot to Mac."

"He told me once he was lucky to have you."

"When? That time you guys came for my birthday? He was drunk."

"Why do you feel a need to make a joke of everything?"

I let out my breath. "It wasn't the job so much, it was what he meant to me. He was the person I wanted to be. If I let someone take that away..."

"Then you won't know who you are anymore?"

"The way you say it, it sounds stupid."

"No, just like you're confused. Let me ask you something. Do you believe in God?"

"Now you really sound like Mom."

"Well?"

"I guess."

"Do you pray?"

"I try to listen."

"That's good. What do you hear?"

"Nothing, that's the problem."

"Nothing, or nothing you want to hear?"

"He, or it, doesn't say anything. Just kind of hums along on a great ontological superhighway."

"You've been reading Paul Tillich again."

"The heretic."

"I'll never understand why someone would choose to follow a person who doesn't give them hope."

"Maybe the people he appeals to aren't looking for hope."

He ignored that one, or maybe he couldn't answer it. "Why would anyone want God to be impersonal?" he said. "The 'Power of Being'?"

His sarcastic tone got to me. "You can be so myopic, Dad. You may not like the face Tillich put on God, but he believed God was a person's ultimate concern. What's wrong with that? It's not like his views were antithetical to Christianity. He believed sin was one's estrangement from oneself, and that Jesus was the bearer of the New Being, the conqueror of man's estrangement, anxiety and guilt. I wish people could get past their know-it-all judgments about other people's faith, and just deal with it."

I'd momentarily forgotten I was talking to a minister who had married a Jew. There was silence again. Then my father said, "It's nice to hear you get passionate about something."

"It's the Power of Being boiling over."

"You'd make a lousy minister. Maybe a good theologian, though."

"When I'm done being a law professor."

"When you're done being a law professor."

I felt my blood pressure return to normal. "Dad?"

"Yes?"

"You're a lousy Socrates."

"That's okay," he said. "I was aiming for the big J.C."

Chapter 30

T he conversation with my dad got me thinking. The simple fact was I didn't do anything when Grady was dying. Didn't pull him out of the car, didn't give him CPR or even tie a tourniquet. I just watched him. A doctor later told me I'd probably been in shock, and that I was not to move him, but I knew better. I had promised myself to be different the next time. That was probably why I jumped in the limo after Mac had been run over. The problem was courage wasn't all there was to being a hero. You also needed a cool head...which was something I sorely lacked, evidently. Not that it mattered anymore. I felt helpless again, like my limbs were made of lead, like a weight was on my chest, like I couldn't move, or, even if I could, what was the use?

So I did what most guys do when facing unemployment, eternal loneliness and emotional ruin, cracked a beer and flipped on ESPN. After what seemed like nine innings of baseball scores, a segment came on about the upcoming NCAA Division I men's lacrosse championship. As usual two powerhouses were facing off in the finals: the Syracuse University Orange and the University of Virginia Cavaliers. As a warm up for the big name ESPN showed highlights of the semi-finals, including the shoot-out between the Orange and the Princeton Tigers.

Together the rivals had taken more than a hundred shots. At the end of regulation play the score was tied at sixteen. One minute into sudden death overtime, an Orange attackman made a behind-the-back shot that bounced off the goalpost before finding the net. His teammates rushed the field, their sticks high, their jerseys melding into a sea of bright orange and navy blue. So what was new? I reached for the remote then stopped.

Bright orange and navy blue.

I remembered the *Go Chiefs!* screen-saver at PEACE. Its colors were orange and navy blue. At the time I'd figured Hassan had been a fan of the Kansas City Chiefs football team, but the Chiefs' colors were red and gold. Why would you take the time to design a screen-saver for your favorite sports team but use the wrong colors? I went to my computer, logged onto the internet and punched the words *Chiefs* and *team* into a search engine. I got a half-dozen good hits.

At the top of the list was the Kansas City Chiefs football team in Missouri, but its colors were dark red and gold. Below that was the Peoria Chiefs minor league baseball team in Illinois, but its colors were navy blue and red. Below that was the Spokane Chiefs minor league Hockey Club in Washington, but its colors were light blue and red.

Then came a slew of high school teams. The Piscataway Chiefs high school girls' basketball team in New Jersey, Navy blue and gold. The Lakeland Lady Chiefs high school softball team in Pennsylvania, light blue and red. And the Thunderbird Chiefs high school baseball team in Arizona, light blue and red.

Finally I found what I was looking for, the Syracuse SkyChiefs minor league baseball team in central New York, formerly known as the *Chiefs*. The team emblem was a flying growling baseball bat. As the farm team for the Toronto Blue Jays, the SkyChiefs' colors were orange and navy blue. I found the phone number of the main office.

"SkyChiefs," a man said.

"Got a quick question. I grew up in Syracuse and used to be a Chiefs fan. What's up with the new name?"

"They wanted something that wouldn't offend the local Native Americans. Something 'politically correct.'"

"When did this happen?"

"Back in ninety-seven when we moved from MacArthur Stadium to the new P&C Stadium. Now it's called Alliance Bank Stadium. Anyway, we figured the timing was right."

"Has the name caught on? You know, among long-time fans?"

"Lots of people still just call 'em the 'Chiefs.'"

"Where is the new stadium?"

"Still near Carousel Mall."

He had a nasally voice, the word coming out *mah*.

Well, there you had it. An honest-to-goodness clue.

As soon as I started hatching my plan the thought occurred to me that I was, in fact, insane. Why hadn't I immediately picked up the phone and called Guerrero and Wang? Sure there was that pesky attorney-client privilege thing, and the strong possibility the two jerks wouldn't believe me, or that even if they did believe me they would be totally inept at helping me. The question was, would they be any more inept than I would be, by myself? This was a pretty crafty set of criminals I was dealing with, who were experienced at doing very bad things not just at the national level but the international level. I didn't even have a passport. Shouldn't I do what people are supposed to do under the circumstances? I mean, wasn't that what the criminal justice system was for?

The problem was sometimes the criminal justice system didn't work so well. It didn't always catch the bad guy. Or even if it caught him it didn't convict him. Indeed for a few years now, I, along with Mac, had made a living relying on this very fact. On a few occasions I'd even heaved a giant wrench into the system's finely tuned engine. The belching and smoke that resulted never bothered me much because, I'd reasoned, the law allowed me to fight the system. That was due process, and, as a whole, it was more important than the particular *result* of that process, right? Besides, I had always thought, the wrongdoers were just white collar criminals; they didn't really hurt people, but why did that not make me feel better now? Maybe it was because, at some point during the past few days, I had come to understand that even white collar criminals had victims. Employees, stockholders, consumers. Wives, husbands, children. It made me realize my ex-clients were no better than common street thugs, troublemakers and rule-breakers, causing pain and ruin for others.

What was worse, now I was one of those victims and I wanted justice. The question was did I want to shop at a store that I knew sold shoddy merchandise, or did I just want to go out and take what I wanted? In other words did I really believe in the noble concept of due process, even if I knew the process might result in Mack's killer getting away? Or was I ready to break the law to ensure the result, and by doing so risk going to jail? What I was contemplating was an important decision for anyone to make, much less a lawyer. It was definitely a decision that was not to be made lightly. So I reached for the thing that had answered all of my major questions in life so far, the oracle of modern times, the plastic prophet, the floating fortuneteller.

"Oh, Magic 8-Ball," I said, shaking the oversized sphere, "should I call Rice & Beans?" I turned the black-and-white ball over and peered into its window.

Concentrate and ask again, it said.

"Oh, Magic 8-Ball," I said, shaking the ball harder, "can I catch Mac's killer all by myself?"

Don't count on it, it said.

I decided this answer was too ambiguous. I tried one final time. "Oh, Magic 8-Ball, can I do this alone?"

My sources say no, it said.

Stupid Magic 8-Ball. I picked up the phone.

"How can I help?" Amelia said when I told her about White. "I feel a sick day coming on."

"Find me the name, address and Social Security number of a young research scientist who graduated from Georgetown Med School."

"Is that all?"

"No, I'd prefer it if he looked like me too."

Amelia thought about it for a moment. "Well, I did go out with this guy in med school. Loved to talk about autopsies, especially when I was eating. What was his name? Paul, Patrick, Peter—"

"Sounds like you two were close."

"Peter something. Rhymed with Aunt Vicky's name. Gerling. 'Hurling Gerling,' they called him."

"He threw up when he drank?"

"He threw himself at me when he drank."

The resemblance was already apparent.

"I think he got a job at NIH. I'll find his number and try to set up a lunch date."

"I like everything except the date part."

"You have nothing to worry about except his charm, intellect and rugged good looks."

Amelia called back in a few minutes. "He's still on the market."

"What a surprise. What else do you need?"

"Your résumé, a certified copy of your med school transcript and an academic catalog."

"Should I even ask where this is headed?"

I told her my plan.

"Isn't that dangerous?" she said.

"Is there a safe way to catch a murderer?"

"I'm just saying be careful."

"How soon can you get back to me?"

"I think I still have a med school catalog. I can write my résumé tonight. I don't have a certified copy of my transcript, and the registrar's office is probably closed, but I can get one tomorrow morning. What else? I've got to get ready for my big date tomorrow."

"Amelia?"

"Yes?"

"Don't tell your uncle about any of this."

"He wouldn't want us to investigate the company he dedicated his life to?"

"We might not find anything."

"As long as you come visit me when I'm in prison."

As soon as I'm paroled.

"Ever hear about the boy who cried wolf?" Roger said the next morning, after he had double-checked my light fixtures and wall outlets.

"Ever hear about the US Attorney who had a hard-on for the target of his investigation?"

"Isn't that his job?"

"Can you come by again this afternoon? I'll explain everything."

"Can't make it 'til after five. Boss is under the strange impression we have clients other than you."

"Tell him to send me a bill. I might even pay some of it."

"What happened to Daddy Warbucks?"

I told him.

"So let me get this straight," he said. "I get paid only if you crack the case and Senator Serling is so overcome with gratitude that she breaks out her checkbook?"

"Do I actually have to answer that?"

Roger chewed on a toothpick. "What the hell."

After he left, Amelia showed up wearing a short black skirt and no stockings. "My face is up here," she said. Her hair was styled and on her ears diamonds glimmered.

I grinned. "You clean up nice."

She handed me her transcript. "Got to run."

"Eating in the corporate cafeteria, I hope."

"Cozy Italian restaurant."

"Don't have too much fun."

"Aren't you sweet? I think you really mean that."

Using everything I could find on biopharm companies from the internet, I created the profile of a small company in Munich, Germany. Bauer Biochemica GmbH. *Ich bin ein bullshitter*. When I was done, Amelia returned wearing an exhausted look and holding a pan covered by tin foil. "Cavatelli," she said. "Lost my appetite after the Marburg monkey story."

I paused out of respect for our sacrificed primate-cousins, then got a fork.

She took off her suit jacket, unstrapped her sandals and fell down on my couch. "You owe me, big time. Boy, does the brilliant young doctor love to talk about himself."

I took a look at the snug blue T-shirt she wore under her jacket and had no trouble imagining why.

"Stop smiling," she said. "I've had root canals less painful than that."

She told me how he'd droned on about what diseases he was trying to cure, delving into the daily details. "I finally got his Social Security number. Told him how different he looked from the photo on his driver's license when he pulled out his wallet." She handed me a cocktail napkin bearing the number.

"I thought you were going Dutch," I said.

"He insisted. It's a power trip for some guys."

A problem I never had, due to my financial position.

"What now, Dr. Gerling?" she said.

"Now we create the ideal biopharm research scientist."

First we used Amelia's résumé to write Dr. Gerling's résumé, which featured a recent stint at Bauer Biochemica. Der Doktor's telephone number just so happened to be the same as Doyle's number at the office. Luckily I'd written down the senator's system-wide voicemail passcode when Marni Bardoni showed it to me. I just hoped the FBI had already seized the office's voicemail tapes. Next we came up with Dr. Gerling's transcript, which included extensive coursework in epidemiology and biopharmacology. I got up to stretch. When I returned, Roger was lying on my couch.

"I keep telling myself to lock that front door," I said.

"It was locked," he said.

When he noticed Amelia he stood up. "Hank didn't tell me he had company," he said.

"I'm just his co-conspirator," she said. When she introduced herself, Roger smiled.

"The name of my favorite B movie star," he said.

"Never met anyone who'd heard of her," she said.

"Amelia Fuentes? Are you kidding? *Curse of the Vampires* is one of my favorite movies."

"*Curse of the Vampires*?" I asked.

"Eddie Garcia, Linda Rivera, directed by Gerry de Leon, 1970. Young man returns to his family mansion to find that his father has locked his mother in a basement, claiming she's a vampire. The young man investigates and is bitten. He in turn passes the curse along to his fiancée, the lovely Amelia Fuentes. The bites continue until the mansion burns in the final scene."

"Thank you, Siskel & Ebert."

Amelia said, "It was the sequel to something, right?"

"*The Blood Drinkers* also known as *The Vampire People*. 1966. Vampire decides to do a heart transplant on his girlfriend. I didn't like that one as much. Poorly constructed and not as complex."

"I had no idea you were such a dork," I told him.

Roger shrugged. "When I was in 'Nam, the movies were big in the Philippines. That's where they were made. I was recovering from surgery at Clark Air Force Base. Best time of my life. I knew I was going home. I'll spare you a look at my scar. What do you have for me?"

I handed him a copy of Amelia's certified transcript, along with some notes on yellow stickers. I said, "Seems Dr. Gerling's transcript has a few errors on it: wrong name, Social Security Number, home address and phone number. Could you have it revised?"

"I have a guy," he said. "Owes me a favor from an immigration thing."

"You let him off the hook?"

"He didn't know anything. Government would've thrown the book at him: 9/11 and all that."

"Plus it doesn't hurt to have a counterfeiter in your pocket."

"He wasn't trying to help terrorists, just make a buck. He was hanging out at the DMV, looking for illegal Mexicans who were denied a driver's license."

There was an awkward silence.

"Don't look at me," Amelia said. "I made my license myself."

"Can he do college transcripts?" I said.

"I've seen him do C-notes. Course I had to seize the plates."

"Still a cop at heart. How long to do a driver's license?"

"Don't tell me, Dr. Gerling lost his wallet too. I assume the home address is the same as on the résumé. Got an extra passport photo?"

I handed him one.

Roger whistled. "Dr. Gerling sure is ugly."

"How soon can your guy have them done?"

"I don't know, tomorrow maybe. You two aren't planning a little B and E, are you?"

"How did you guess?"

"I have a criminal mind."

After Roger left, Amelia went out to her car and came back with a backpack. She spread out a half-dozen textbooks on my coffee table then began a crash course in biopharmaceutical research. We covered subjects like human physiology, pathology and virology. Required reading included chapters about the biotech industry and Russia's abandoned biowarfare program. When we were done, it was dark out.

Amelia yawned. "You're a quick study," she said.

"My mother made me take AP biology and chemistry in high school."

She put her head down. "Renaissance man."

"Hardly, I hated every minute. My mind isn't built that way. Protons, neutrons and electrons. Atoms, molecules and covalent bonds. I would've gone crazy studying that stuff for six years. How'd you do it?"

Amelia's only response was a soft snore. I put up her feet, covered her with my Case Western sweatshirt then went to Mac's couch.

I awoke to the smell of coffee. The sun was streaming through the windows. Amelia had pulled down a UVA baseball cap over her head and folded up the cuffs of my Case Western sweatshirt. I said, "I didn't know a Cavalier would be caught dead in a Spartans sweatshirt."

"This Cavalier wouldn't be caught dead with bed-head and wrinkled clothes."

"The good old walk of shame."

Her voice lapsed into a gentle drawl. "Southern girls don't do the walk of shame. They are driven home and given a proper proposal of marriage."

"How many proposals did you get?"

"Boys didn't appreciate me in college."

"Come on."

"I was forty pounds heavier and wore a pair of huge Drew Carey glasses."

Look at that. We had something in common.

Roger arrived. "You two look like my kids during finals," he said.

"Pull up a bagel," I said.

"Just stopped by to show you my guy's handiwork."

We compared the transcript and driver's license to the originals.

"What did I tell you?" Roger said. "Right down to the raised seal. All the talent's wasted on criminals."

His phone beeped and he was off. I pulled a second chair up to my computer and together Amelia and I wrote a cover letter to Panacea's human resources director, Adara Karafilopulos. Amelia and I explained how I'd recently returned to America from Germany to marry my college sweetheart, who had just been admitted to SUNY Upstate Medical University in Syracuse. When we were done we walked up the street to a Kwic Copy. We'd decided faxing the cover letter, résumé and transcript to Panacea would save time.

As we waited for the fax to go through, Amelia drummed her fingers on the counter. "Why are we going to all this trouble for a lousy interview?" she said. "I know you don't want to get Lawrence mixed up in all of this, but wouldn't it be quicker just to let him pull a few strings? I could tell him it's for a friend."

I shook my head. "It would leave a trail for them to trace to us later," I said. "Plus, it would be like asking him to betray his former company."

Reluctantly she agreed.

That afternoon I used a payphone to return Ms. Karafilopulos' phone call.

She whistled. "Impressive credentials."

"I'm surprised the position is still open."

"We've been looking for the right person. When can you come in?"

"How about tomorrow?"

She laughed. "Ready to go, huh?"

"I already have a ticket. I'm taking a long weekend with my fiancé. She just finished her first year of med school at Upstate."

We scheduled the interview for noon so some of the scientists could take me to lunch afterward. Before Adara hung up she asked for my Social Security number. "The Director of Security makes me run background checks on everyone. We're a BSL four lab, you know."

I was trying to forget. Biosafety Level 4 meant the lab employed the highest possible contaminant measures. I was walking into a real live hot zone.

Amelia pulled up to National Airport, kissed me goodbye and touched the scar on my cheek. "We're not such a bad team. Don't ruin it by getting yourself killed."

"Who said anything about getting killed? I'm going for a job interview. I'll be out of there before they can say *you're hired.*"

I kissed her goodbye then took my place in the line through security. I took out the *Washington Post*. The front page headline read *Race for a Cure*. A man infected with Harappa had flown from Tokyo to LA. The plane was isolated and boarded by LA County Health Department workers. Its passengers were taken by bus to a CDC Quarantine Station, where triage doctors were currently evaluating each patient and deciding how to treat them. Meanwhile the Department of Defense was pushing Panacea to discover a vaccine, for which the FDA had promised fast-track approval. Under the story was a photo of a scientist wearing a white spacesuit and rubber gloves while reaching through a glass shield to pour the contents of a beaker into a test tube.

A feeling of panic and doubt seemed to fill the article. This was a government that couldn't get water to the people of New Orleans after Hurricane Katrina. Was there a Mike Brown working somewhere in the CDC, ready to drop the ball at a critical moment?

During the flight I took out Amelia's notes about Panacea, which included a hand-drawn map. Lawrence had given her the grand tour when he was dating her aunt. He'd flown them up one weekend to take them to see the vineyards around the nearby Finger Lakes. Panacea was a fortress, she said.

Its campus was surrounded by security cameras, motion detectors and a ten-foot-high brick wall. At the entrance stood a security booth manned by an armed guard with an attack dog. In the lobby of each building sat another armed guard. The interior stairwells were locked and could be opened only by staring into what Amelia called an *eye-thingy* and what Roger explained was a retina-recognition test.

Even germs couldn't get into the buildings. All seams, joints and doors were sealed. Air was pumped in and out through a double-HEPA filtration system. The labs were surrounded by buffer corridors to shield them from earthquakes, tornados and bombs. Even if you could get into the labs you couldn't get out without passing through several airlocks, a fumigation chamber and, if it was your lucky day, a disinfectant dunk tank.

When I landed at Hancock Airport in Syracuse a light rain started to patter against the windows. In the airport was a small shop called *Copy Cat*. Behind the front desk sat a young woman wearing black lipstick, white face powder, multiple lip rings, a studded dog collar and a nametag that read *Envy*. I handed her a single page bearing a yellow sticker showing a name, fax number and phone number. She read the page then looked at me like I was crazy.

"Send it in one hour sharp," I said. "No cover page."

"What, are you, like, a spy or something?"

I glanced both ways and leaned in close. "Of course, if I told you I'd have to kill you."

Envy cracked her gum. "You look more like an insurance salesman."

"Thank you."

"Two dollars."

I'd run out of fifties so I handed her a five. "Keep it." Enough to get her to do exactly what I asked but not enough to make her remember me, I hoped.

She eyed me suspiciously. "I've already got a boyfriend, you know."

"I'm sure he doesn't appreciate you. Remember, one hour. No sooner, no later."

I rented a car and grabbed a roadmap. Cazenovia was twenty miles east of Syracuse, past a half-dozen quaint towns and villages, on the other side of a round blue lake. Panacea, Inc. was a few miles outside of the village perched on a green grassy hill. The front sign read *Ready for the Defense*. It reminded me of what Mac used to say before trial. The judge would say *Are counsel ready?* And the prosecutor would say *Ready for the Government, your honor*. And Mac would say, *Ready for the defense, your honor*. So what was I at the moment, someone who was still defending a person who was otherwise helpless, or someone who was now doing something altogether different? The guard at the security booth made me feel like it was the latter. He wore green army fatigues, a black beret and dark sunglasses, even though the sky was gray.

I lowered my window halfway. "Peter Gerling to see Adara, the HR director." I was too nervous to pronounce the woman's last name.

The guard ran his finger down a clipboard. "Driver's license." As the man studied Dr. Gerling's doctored license, a Doberman poked his head out of the booth, ears pricking, tail erect. He fixed his black eyes on me and snarled.

The guard handed the license back to me. "DC, huh?"

I nodded.

"You're early," he said.

"Tail wind."

"You look nervous."

"Job interview."

The Doberman curled his lips and growled.

"Nice doggie," I said.

The dog lunged at me, jaw snapping, slobber flying.

I pried my white knuckles from the steering wheel and wiped my face, as the guard struggled to haul back the dog. Finally he punched a button, lifting the parking gate arm.

"Parking lot is straight ahead. Park in one of the guest spaces, proceed directly to the stone building and sign in at the front desk. No pocket knives, pepper sprays or camera phones. And Dr. Gerling?"

"Yes?"

"Try not to upset the dogs."

In my rear view mirror I noticed the guard wore a police officer's utility belt complete with pistol, baton and handcuffs, just in case I didn't do as I was told. I drove slowly onto the property of Panacea, Inc., trying to not to think about what crimes I was committing.

The company parking lot was filled with BMWs, Saabs and Volvos. Near the lot stood three buildings that formed a triangle. One was a three-story black building with exterior air ducts and no windows. Another was a two-story stone office building. The third was a one-story glass-and-concrete building, which Amelia had told me held a dining hall, a maintenance garage and a kennel. In the center of the triangle lay a man-made duck pond ringed by a footpath, some picnic tables and a smattering of trees.

I turned off my engine and looked at my watch. Envy would be sending my fax to White about now. The fax was on Department of Defense letterhead. It was signed by a Deputy Director of DARPA, the Defense Advanced Researched Projects Agency. It said,

Mr. White,

The Director has assigned me to help facilitate the FDA approval process of the Harappa vaccine. I would like to meet with you personally at your earliest convenience. I am in Syracuse today on an unrelated matter, but will not be able to make it out to Cazenovia due to an early return flight to Virginia. If you are available, could you please meet with me at the Defense Department's Office in the Federal Building in Syracuse at 12:30 p.m.?

After a few minutes White left the stone building and walked through a giant puddle in the parking lot. I slid down in my seat, behind my roadmap. He looked just like he had on TV: medium-height, bald, with broad shoulders pressing snugly against a slick suit. He got into a canary-yellow Porsche and drove by me, engine purring.

I called Amelia. "The ferret has found the nest. Duck number one has flown. Over."

"What did I tell you about the commando talk?" Amelia said. "I'll make the phone call as soon as I get back to your air-conditioned office. This humidity is ruining my hair."

"Amelia."

"I'm just kidding. I'm having trouble hearing with the sound of traffic in the background."

She had recalled the name of the president's assistant, Barbara Gluck, and the name of her ten-year-old daughter, Samantha. With Roger's help, Amelia had learned the name of the nurse at

Samantha's elementary school. The plan was for Amelia to call Barbara and, impersonating a substitute nurse, tell her Samantha had a fever and needed to be picked up. If Barbara had any medical questions, Amelia would answer them. If Barbara asked to speak to Samantha, Amelia would say Samantha was napping. The school was located in a suburb closer to the city. The drawback with this plan was that, as soon as Barbara realized the real nurse hadn't called she would probably alert Panacea that something suspicious was happening. But that still gave me about thirty minutes: five to get in, twenty to work, and five to get out.

In a little while Barbara left the stone building, put up a bright pink umbrella and carefully walked around the giant puddle in the parking lot. She got into a sky-blue Plymouth Voyager and drove away.

I got out and jogged across the parking lot. At the front desk I brushed the rain off my suit jacket and introduced myself. The security guard leaned back in his chair, running his fingers over his brush cut. "Didn't want to go through with it, huh?" he said.

"Excuse me?" My heart began to thump.

"Come in through the rain. First thing you do when you come to the 'Cuse is buy an umbrella."

I steadied myself. "I was waiting for it to let up."

"I've been waiting for that for fifty years."

A moment later a tiny woman appeared and introduced herself as Adara. I apologized for being early and followed her down a hall, glad to be free of her cumbersome last name. Along the way we passed a plate-glass window. Behind it lay a lab.

The lab was lined on two sides with stainless steel counters spiked with gas valves and long-necked faucets. On one counter sat a binocular microscope, a row of petri dishes, a round-bottom flask and a Bunsen burner. On the other counter sat a steel box, something that looked like a ham radio and an old computer with a giant hard drive. Against the third wall hung a fume hood and ventilator over a cart, some stools and a dishwasher. From the ceiling hung a maze of exposed pipes holding coiled yellow hoses, which Amelia had said provided filtered air to workers in an emergency.

"They don't make hot boxes like that one anymore," Adara said.

I assumed she was referring to a giant glass house attached to the other side of the plate-glass window. Next to the glass house stood two mannequins in biocontainment suits, complete with bubble helmets, rubber gloves and rubber boots. One of the mannequins was reaching through two holes in a glass wall into an additional pair of rubber gloves, to pour the contents of a beaker into a test tube, while the other mannequin stood behind writing something on a clipboard. Just like the photo from the *Post*.

"Used to be part of our main lab," Adara said. "It was mothballed when we built the new facility. The mannequins were DARPA's idea. Said they'd give reporters something to look at."

She led me to the elevator, which delivered us to a long hall, at the end of which was her office. She handed me a ten-page employment application to send in later, then started making small talk. She mentioned Panacea was getting ready to announce it had just developed an experimental vaccine to Harappa.

"Sorry," she said. "I'm also the company's PR director."

"That's okay. I'm interested. The company has developed a vaccine so soon?"

"We're just finishing up the last test."

"I thought you just got the contract."

"We've been working round the clock, and we do have the best people in the country."

As she explained who I would be meeting, her phone rang. I glanced at my watch. I had about twenty minutes until Barbara Gluck returned.

Adara hung up. "Looks like Dr. DeVoe is running late. He went to the wake of a former employee. So sad."

I politely asked what happened, though I was more concerned with the delay in the interview schedule, the imminent return of Gluck and White, and how to implement Plan B, which involved, among other things, the improbable act of pulling a fire alarm, crawling through the ceiling to White's office and strolling out of the building in a gas mask among an influx of fireman, hopefully undetected. Reluctantly, I tuned back into what Adara was saying, something about how one of the company's retirees, Dr. Hubbard, had gotten sick last week, had gone to the hospital, had seemed to get better, and then had taken a sudden turn for the worse. *Sudden turn for the worse*? I stopped worrying about the time. "What do the doctors think it was?"

"They're not sure. Maybe a rare strain of bacterial meningitis."

"Like the kind you work with here?"

"Yeah, that's the funny thing. He retired last year and hasn't been back to the building since then."

As the wheels began turning in my head, Adara took out my résumé and ran her eyes over it. "So, summa cum laude, Georgetown Med School, very nice. You know, we interviewed someone from your class a few years back. A Cuban girl, the niece of one of our former president, what was her name?"

The wheels stopped turning. "Fuentes?" I prompted.

"That's it...Amelia...sweet girl. Didn't work out. She wanted to be an ER doctor."

A million questions ran through my mind. Before I could ask any of them, Adara's eyes were back on my résumé. "So," she said, "what part of Munich did you live in while you working at Bauer Biochemica? I was on the Munich study group in college."

My mouth went dry. I remembered Munich is the capital of Bavaria. "I lived a few blocks from the capitol building."

"You mean the *Landtag*?"

I didn't know if that was the name of the capitol building or an apartment building. "I lived in an apartment building called *The American*. It's where the company puts up their foreign employees. It's only a few years old."

"Oh," she said, apparently disappointed my German experience wasn't more authentic. "Your German must be great. Tell me how mine is. *Wo gibt es hier in der Stadt eine tolle Diskothek?*"

I stared at her. Next time I pretend to have worked in a foreign country, remind me to pick one whose language I speak. There's not a lot of Latin being spoken on the streets of Europe these days. I thought I'd heard the German word for disco. "You probably asked that a lot over there."

She laughed.

I would have loved to keep flirting with disaster, but it was show time. I stood up and asked where the men's room was. She laughed at my abruptness and walked me down the hall. I went inside then turned around. When she disappeared around a corner I walked down the hall in the other direction. A sign in the antechamber of the corner office read *The Bug Stops Here*. I removed from my pocket a pair of latex gloves, shut Barbara Gluck's door and drew the blinds on the window to the hallway. Due to the small talk in Adara's office I had less than fifteen minutes.

The success of my whole plan hinged on two *tiny* conditions. The first was whether Barbara had left her computer on in her hurry to leave work. I saw the glow of her screen and let out my breath. The second condition was whether the company's personnel files were on its computer system. Of course the files would be in hard copy form in Adara's office since she was the human resources director, but I couldn't think of a way to get in there without her around. No, I was betting that a high-tech company like Panacea stored its personnel records also on its computer system, electronic versions of documents that had been generated by performance-reviewing executives, and scanned-in images of documents received as hard copies from employees or former employees. I searched furiously through the computer's dozens of disc drives. I didn't find any drives labeled *Human Resources* or *Personnel*. Finally I found a drive labeled *Karafilopulos*, and I let out another sigh. I was on a roll.

I skipped over the drive's files that appeared to involve subjects like employee recruitment, selection, salary, income tax, accidents, vacation, parental leave, health, pension and retirement. Instead I focused on files that appeared to involve employee reviews or terminations. What exactly was I looking for? I wasn't sure. I wanted anything that involved controversy: notices of warning or discipline, grievances about failures to promote based on gender or race, claims of wrongful discharges, legal proceedings, etc. There was nothing. I couldn't believe it. What, the place was a fucking utopia? Everyone just *loved* working there? That was impossible. Maybe the files were in another drive, like one labeled *Legal*. But there was no such drive on the company's system. No duh, I realized, maybe it was on the computers of the company's law firm, a firm that would be filing a civil action against me in short order if I didn't get moving. I checked my watch. Time was up. I went back to the window and parted the blinds to see if the coast was clear for me to return to Adara's office.

It wasn't.

Marching down the hall, heading straight for me, was Robert White himself. I let out an audible gasp and retreated to his office, where I crawled into his closet and pulled the door shut.

In no time I heard his shoes brush against the carpet. He was in the room. I could hear the *swish-swish* of fabric between his legs. He seemed to be moving quickly, like he was all worked up about something. Maybe he was onto me, his senses alive with suspicion. He'd seen me through the blinds, or had seen my footprints on the carpet, or had heard me breathing. I sucked in my breath and held it. Suddenly the noises on the other side of the door stopped. Shit, now he'd definitely heard me. Even if he hadn't, surely he could hear me now, my heart thundering away in my chest, my blood coursing through my ears. Any second now he was going to open the door and find me. The thought of escape flickered through my mind: the image of me flinging the door open, pushing him down and making a break for it. Then I imagined the Doberman leaping upon me as I tried to scale the company's ten-foot-high brick wall, the security guard jamming my face into the ground as he locked my wrists together behind my back, the company's employees watching, clicking away on their camera phones, e-mailing photos of me to friends who would post them on the internet. I could see the caption. *Criminal Lawyer Needs Criminal Lawyer.* The image kept me frozen in place, my knees bolted squarely to the floor. Sweat broke out on my forehead and a drop rolled down my face.

There I was, sitting in a dark closet holding my breath, like a complete idiot. What's more, I was absolutely and inexcusably vulnerable. For the first time in my life the law was no protection to me. What was I doing? Someone kills your friend, you let the law work for you. That's what the police are for. You don't forge a driver's license and a letter from a government agency and use the interstate telephone lines to submit them to a government contractor in order to trick it. You don't enter their property to fake a job interview, infiltrate their computer system and steal documents. You certainly don't break into the office of the company's CEO, a man who had every right to call the police and have you thrown in jail. Was that what he was deciding to do right now?

Gently I turned and leaned in closer to the door, placing my ear practically against it, careful not to loudly crinkle my starched shirt as I moved. Slowly there emerged from the silence the faint sound of labored breathing. Not mine.

Christ, I realized, the man was standing on the other side of the closet door.

Chapter 33

I bowed my head and silently said my prayers, feeling like a hypocrite. *Dear, God, sorry I've blown you off for the past ten years but can I ask a teeny favor?* Or maybe something with a little more zip. *Father in heaven, hear my prayer: when White opens the door let him just see air.* Or maybe something more direct. *God is good, God is great, please stop the Doberman's teeth with a metal plate.* Oh, who was I kidding? I was a goner. I closed my eyes and winced, bracing myself for the end of life as a free man.

The closet door didn't open. There was no phone call to security, no alarm, no attack dog. Instead a key rattled, a drawer opened, then it closed, then the key rattled again and the office door slammed shut.

I pushed the closet door open and crawled to my feet. The latex gloves had clung to my sweaty palms and my legs had fallen asleep. I limped over to where I had heard the jiggle of a key. I couldn't help but wonder why the man had returned to the office.

Beside the bookshelf was a gym bag containing some sweaty clothes, smelly sneakers and a spiral notebook. The notebook's worn pages recorded White's workouts. Exercises he'd performed, numbers of sets and repetitions, and amounts of weight. The man could bench press two of me. Another reason to hate overpaid CEOs with too much time on their hands. There was no key wedged between the pages of the notebook or located anywhere in the gym bag.

I moved on to the bookshelf, whose top shelf held popular books about business. *Barbarians at the Gate, Den of Thieves, The Predators' Ball, Liar's Poker, The Takeover Game* and *The Complete Arbitrage Deskbook.* Their pages were highlighted and dog-eared. The bottom shelf held textbooks on more academic subjects. Accounting, business ethics, calculus, etc. Their spines were unbroken. Big surprise, but what was I doing criticizing the man's literary tastes? I checked quickly but could see no key hidden on top of the books, between them or inside of them.

I looked above the bookshelf, where there hung a painting of a tiny bird with short red-brown feathers, a white patch under its throat and a white mask over its eyes. What was the deal? Did every rich guy in the world hunt quail? I ran my fingers behind the painting. No key was taped there.

I saw, standing next to the bookshelf, a brass statuette portraying the famous image of the Marines raising the flag on Iwo Jima. I was about to raise the white flag of surrender. I hopelessly checked the pile of rubble at the Marines' feet but it wasn't hiding a tiny brass key. I started to turn away then stopped. I carefully tilted the heavy statuette over. Underneath was a tiny silver key. *Semper Fortunatus.* Always lucky. I brought the key over to White's desk and plopped down in his soft leather chair, totally exhausted from the day's criminal activities. No wonder burglars slept all day. Sure enough, the key fit nicely inside the lock on the desk's large side drawer, and for a second I could enjoy a modicum of success.

Then I saw what was in the drawer: dozens of open Redweld folders. They would take forever to go through and I was already well behind schedule. Adara was no doubt scouring the building for me. Barbara was no doubt pulling into the parking lot at this very moment. Fortunately the folders were neatly labeled and alphabetically arranged. *Agreements*, *Banking*, *Bankruptcy*, *Club*, *Credit Cards*. Amazing. This White guy was both a packrat and a neat freak. I flipped ahead to a folder labeled *Status Reports*. It was filled with Manila files containing memos and correspondence regarding various vaccination projects the company was working on. Each of the folders was full, except one, which was labeled *Harappa Vaccine, FDA Approval*. So that was what he had come back to the office to get. I was such an idiot. What was I doing here? I mean, what was I expecting to find? A folder labeled *Disgruntled Employees*? Oh, sure, that would be right there, between the files labeled *Debt Consolidation* and *Federated Petroleum/Globex*. I started to close the drawer then did a double take.

Federated Petroleum/Globex.

I opened the folder and started reading. Inside was a letter of resignation and a bunch of names and nine-digit numbers. A creepy feeling came over me. I removed the folder's contents, slipped into Barbara's office, photocopied the pages, returned the originals to the folder in the drawer and put the folded copies inside my coat pocket.

Down the hall Adara was talking to a man in a lab coat. He went into the men's room and I knew I didn't have much time. I took out my cell phone and prayed for good reception. "Ms. Karafilopulos, please," I said. "It's an emergency."

Over the loudspeaker in the ceiling, the receptionist paged Adara. Reluctantly she left her post outside the men's room.

I opened Barbara Gluck's door, put the latex gloves back in my pocket and walked down the hall, passing Dr. Lab Coat as he left the men's room. I didn't look back. Adara was still on the phone when I reached her office.

"Hello?" she was saying into her phone, her voice emanating from my pants pocket.

I reached into my pocket and turned off my cell phone.

Adara hung up. "There you are. I was starting to get worried."

"Sorry." I put a hand on my stomach. "Not feeling too well. Must've picked up something on the flight."

"Oh, my. Would you like someone to take a look at you?"

"No, thanks. Probably just the flu. I'm sorry to do this but can I reschedule?"

"Sure." Her expression fell. "I mean, if you really need to."

We set something up for Monday and she walked me down to the lobby.

Outside it had stopped raining. No blue minivan. No yellow Porsche. As I was passing under the parking gate, Barbara Gluck pulled in. She sure looked mad.

I took out my cell phone and changed my location from Syracuse to Newark. Then I called directory assistance for the number of the public library in Minqua, New York.

Chapter 34

T hat evening, at the Newark airport, I returned my rental car and checked my voicemail. There were three messages from Amelia, each one sounding more urgent than the last. During the flight I organized the documents I'd collected, carefully piecing them together. When the plane landed I was overcome with guilt and called Amelia back. "I'm not in jail."

"I thought you might be dead. Why haven't you called? Where are you?"

"Layover in Newark. How's your aunt?"

"How's my aunt? You go on an interstate crime spree and you ask how my aunt is?"

"If you don't want to tell me..."

"She's fine. The pressure in her brain is back to normal. They're going to cut the pentobarbital in the morning. Are you going to be here?"

"I don't know. I have some business to wrap up."

"What's wrong with you? Why are you being so mysterious? What did you find?"

"Nothing."

"Nothing?"

"Went through White's entire office. Address book, phone bills, e-mails. Guy's clean."

"Slow down," she said. "Give me the play by play."

I did, telling her everything except the part about finding the key to White's desk drawer...and everything after it.

"So that's it?"

"We can still investigate Shifflett. It's a longshot, but he did go to college near Syracuse."

"We were so close."

"We'll find the guy. You didn't mention anything to your uncle about my little adventure, did you?"

"Are you crazy?"

Probably, but I was just making sure.

"When are you coming in? I thought maybe we could have dinner."

"Can I take a rain check? This sleuthing stuff is wearing me out."

"Sure."

I knew she didn't mean it. It takes a liar to know one.

When I got home I called Marshall. He picked up on the tenth ring.

"Fisher?" he grumbled. "What the devil is it?"

"We need to talk."

"It can't wait? What's wrong?"

"I know who the blackmailer is."

He waited. "Well?"

"I can't tell you."

"Excuse me?"

"For your own safety."

He let out a snide laugh. "I'd be worrying about my own safety right now, if I were you."

"The man is a cold-blooded murderer. If he found out you knew, you wouldn't be safe."

"So what're you going to do?"

"Get a good night's sleep then go to the police. I just thought you should know before the press does."

Another pause. "Maybe I should go with you."

"I know you don't want to be dragged into this."

He didn't deny it. "Well, then, assuming you have indeed found the man responsible, I suppose I should thank you."

"I suppose you should." But he didn't. "One more thing."

"Yes, I'll pay your expenses, even though your representation has technically ended."

"No, don't tell anyone about this."

"I know, for my own safety."

"No, mine. I didn't risk my life today to be whacked before I make it to the police tomorrow."

"It's in the vault."

When I hung up I took the bowling pin trophy down from my bookshelf, peeled the blue ribbon off its chest and wrapped my hand around its neck. Then I turned off the lights, unlocked my front door and took my post behind it.

Y ou have a lot of time to second-guess yourself when you're standing alone in the dark in the middle of the night holding a bowling pin.

Why hadn't I picked Warren Shifflett to investigate? He was a member of a perfectly good hate-group that despised Senator Serling. He owned the type of car used in the hit-and-run. And he had access to biowarfare agents at Applied Chemical Sciences, Inc. He could've hired a classmate from his alma mater in central New York to play Abdul Hassan, a student from the DC-area to play Sam Doyle, and some muscle to give Senator Serling a good scare as he sat in the Manassas Police Department, making a stolen vehicle report. And what about the Eden Gardens connection, home of both Hassan and the woman who owned the stolen plates? Hell, I'd even forgotten about Jorge, the disgruntled fighter who had threatened to kill me.

The digital display on my VCR read 12:00 a.m. I should've gone to Mills when I spotted the Cherokee in Manassas. As I started toward my bedroom there was a knock at my door.

I froze. I regripped the bowling pin and looked through the peephole. It was a black woman with a scarf around her head. I opened the door.

"Thank God," the woman said.

"Mrs. Carver?"

Eugenia Carver started to go down and I caught her in my arms, as if the witness to Mac's innocence had been dropped from heaven into my hands, but this wasn't a gift from God. Her skin was clammy and her breath was short.

"They're killing me," she said.

"Who?"

"The men with the money."

Then her eyes rolled back and her body began to jerk.

As one of the EMTs fastened Mrs. Carver to a gurney, the other examined my throat with a gloved hand. After I convinced him I felt fine, he joined his partner. "Don't want to freak you out," he said, "but don't be surprised if you get a visit from the CDC."

"The Centers for Disease Control?"

"Woman's got a fever of a hundred and four, chills and red spots all over her body. I'm not sure but if I had to guess, it looks like septicemia."

"Is that bad?"

"It ain't good."

Mrs. Baumgartener popped her head out her door. "Was something wrong with my cookies?"

"No, Mrs. B. I'll explain everything in the morning."

I locked my door, turned off my light and went to my bedroom window. How had Mrs. Carver gotten so sick? Why had she come to me? And was the CDC really going to show up? I could just see my neighbors standing outside in their pajamas as men in moon suits erected a white tent around our building. They were still getting over the onslaught of reports a few days earlier. My landlord would have an eviction letter in my mailbox before the sun came up. I brushed my teeth, wondering if I should pack my shaving kit since I was probably going to spend the night in some hospital. There was a knock at the door, one of Virginia's finest come to interrogate me before I too went into convulsions.

"Just a minute," I called out down the hall. I took out a duffel bag and threw in the shaving kit and a change of clothes. The cop knocked again.

"I'm coming."

I turned off the lights, braced myself for a blizzard of infuriating questions then opened the door. There was no man in blue, no men in moon suits, not even a reporter. Just a guy in a leather jacket. He looked lost, an unfolded road map in his hands. I waited for him to say something.

"Can I help you?" I said.

He smiled and a shiver ran down my spine. I grabbed the door but he jammed his foot in the way. We stood there a moment, each pushing. I felt his hot breath on my face. The barrel of a silencer stuck out under his chin.

"Special delivery," he said.

The door slammed into my head and knocked me back. Just like that the man was standing over me, a shaft of light spilling into the room from the hallway. He stepped inside and closed the door, leaving us in darkness. I heard his hand on the wall, fumbling for the light switch. I knew I didn't have much time. I found the bowling pin, twisted around until my tender ribs ached then let loose. There was a pop, followed by a groan.

"You're going to regret that, Dorothy."

But I'd already crawled to my knees and cocked the pin over my head. I swung it down with all my might in the direction of the voice. This time there was a thud and then silence.

I found the lights. The man was lying on the floor, face down. I grabbed his collar, pulled up his head and gave it another whack, just in case. Then I rolled him over and kicked his gun across the rug. His eyes were closed and he was dead still. I quickly checked the peephole. Mrs. Baumgartener was in the hall again, staring at my door with a worried look. I had to explain the noise somehow or she was going to come calling. I laughed loudly then turned on my stereo. Mrs. Baumgartener hated loud music. She retreated to her apartment.

I leaned over the man again and rolled up the sleeve of his left arm. There it was, on the underside of his forearm: a globe and anchor. The Marine Corps emblem. Then I noticed there was something funny about his face. I swiped my hand over his head, pulling off the world's worst toupee. Then I ran my fingers over his nose, peeling off a layer of something that felt like greasy Silly Putty. Staring back at me was the face of the man driving the Cherokee, the face of the man driving the Cadillac, the face of the man driving the canary-yellow Porsche.

Robert White.

I buried my shoe in his belly to make sure he was alive. His grunted and rolled over. So I kicked him again...and again, and again, and again. So this was what it felt like. It wasn't barbaric at all. It was a completely reasonable thing to do to a mother-fucking-son-of-a-bitch-asshole who had killed your best friend. When I finally got tired, I caught my breath then calmly put on my latex gloves, picked up his Beretta and emptied his pockets. Lock-picking kit, car keys, cell phone. I checked his recent calls, pulled his arms behind his back and joined his wrists with a pair of handcuffs, a gift from Roger. Then I slapped his face, hauled him to his feet and led him to his rental car.

"What are you doing?" he finally said, sitting up in the passenger seat.

I held out his cell phone and jabbed the Beretta in his ribs.

"You killed me, you need to talk and you're coming over," I said. "Or I go to the police with everything I found in your house. Or worse, I put a bullet in your head and dump you in the Lorton landfill."

"You're crazy."

"That's right. Deranged. Demented. Diseased. Who knows what I'll do?"

"You don't have the balls. You drive a fucking Rabbit."

"It's a Cabriolet." I shot the seat between his thighs.

"Jesus Christ!" he yelped. He jumped and hit his head on the roof.

I put the barrel of the pistol to his head until he lowered himself back into his seat. Then I pushed *Redial* and held the phone to his ear.

I pressed the Beretta into the small of White's back, nudging him toward Marshall's front door in the darkness. In his hand, hanging loosely at his side, White limply held an unloaded Glock. Another gift from Roger.

Marshall must have heard the car because the front light came on, bathing the stone sidewalk and manicured lawn in golden light. Then the front door swung open, revealing Marshall standing in bare feet and plaid pajamas.

"Before you say anything," White said, "this isn't what it seems."

Marshall just ignored him, his suspicious eyes having already found me. He said, "So that's what this is about."

"Contract renegotiation," I said over White's shoulder.

"You're his agent?"

"I get ten percent."

"I would've demanded fifteen."

"I'm new at this."

"What?" White said, looking back at me. "No, no. That's not what's going on at all."

Marshall ignored him again. "I appreciate the entrepreneurial spirit, you two, I really do. Employees are worth what their employer is willing to pay, and you have been valuable to me, but, under the circumstances, I'm afraid I'm going to have to impose a salary cap." He brought a shotgun from behind the door.

White stopped dead in his tracks. "Whoa. What're you doing? That isn't necessary." I jammed the Beretta into his back, causing him to stumble forward in such a violent manner that the shotgun did, in fact, appear necessary. Marshall brought the shotgun up to his hip, and leveled both barrels at us. I began to have second thoughts about my little plan. I remembered Roger telling me that a deer-slug from a shotgun could easily clear through two human bodies. I could feel my heart thundering in my chest again.

"Christ, would you just hold on a second, Larry?" White said. "Look, don't do anything stupid. I told you, this isn't what it seems. He's *making* me do this. He's got a gun to my head. The kid's a psycho."

"Did he make you do this the last time you blackmailed me?"

"What, that? No, that was stupid, I admit. This is different."

"I'll say it is." He raised the shotgun to his shoulder. "This time I have some leverage."

"No, no, stop. You don't understand."

"*I* don't understand? *You* don't understand. I've taken certain precautions since our last contract renegotiation. Anything happens to me now and the police will look in my safe-deposit box, connect you to Eugenia Carver and Don Hubbard. Then it's bye-bye, Bob. So put down the gun, before I lose my patience."

"What, this? I can't drop it. He stuck it to my hand with

something, Super-Glue, I think. But it's not even loaded. I can't pop out the magazine to show you because he glued that too. He even glued the safety shut. It's totally harmless. See, I'm not even pointing it at you. I'd try to rip it away from my skin, but he'll go ape shit again. He blew out my window on the way over here."

"Super Glue, huh?"

"Look, just trust me on this, okay? I'm not here for more money. I'm not here to fight. I'm not going to hurt you."

"That makes one of us," Marshall said, and fired.

Luckily I'd seen Marshall's index finger start to curl around the trigger, and crouched down. The shot knocked White back into my forehead, sending me onto my ass, and White on top of me. I pushed White off of me, rolled over and got onto my knees, the shotgun blast still ringing in my ears. I hid my gun in the back of my waistband, and ran my hands over my clothes for any rips or blood. White had staggered off in front of me. I saw Marshall's finger move again, and I wasn't sure if he was aiming at White or me, so I fell onto my belly and covered my head with my hands just before the next shot rang out. It didn't seem as loud as the first, probably because I was deaf by now. I looked up and saw White was down for good now. He rolled onto his back and gasped, his chest rising and falling, rising and falling, rising and falling. Then suddenly it stopped. He lay still, shirt soaked black, bloody skin glistening eerily in the lamplight, eyes open, one hand on his chest. I could hear some birds squawk overhead. His soul would be leaving his body now, and going where? Up, down, somewhere else? I didn't know. All I knew was that, as the son of a minister, I should have felt something for the man at that moment. Sympathy, pity, maybe even remorse. But I would be lying if I said I did.

I got to my feet and showed Marshall my gun.

"You're out of ammo," I said.

"I was planning on reloading before you grabbed his gun. I didn't know you brought your own."

"He was telling the truth. His wasn't even loaded, and there was a small dose of Super Glue involved."

"You set him up?" Marshall snickered, not sounding like himself. Or maybe he was sounding like himself. Maybe this was the real Marshall.

"What do you want? Money? No, not money. You're not that simple. This is about something more than that. This is personal. Revenge. You get the guy who killed your friend. But it's not all over yet. So, what now? Going to make a citizen's arrest?"

"Tell me why, first."

"You want a confession, like in the movies?"

"I want to hear you say it."

"All right. I'm a businessman. I work hard for a living and I don't do it for free. I busted my ass my whole life, learning my profession, building a company. I'd landed my biggest government contract yet. Worth hundreds of millions. Then the Soviet Union fell and the government terminated my contract. Said they were doing it 'for the convenience of the parties.' Hell, it wasn't for my convenience."

"They must have paid your costs."

"Peanuts. I'd built a new facility to do the job, bought new equipment, hired new scientists. Company lawyer said we could sue, but I'd seen what happened to government contractors who tried that."

"So you sold Harappa to al-Qaeda?"

"A Saudi businessman called me out of the blue, said he'd heard about my company's 'unfortunate business deal' with DOD. Wanted to know if he could hire me to perform under the original contract. What would you have done? Tell him to go pound sand? Call DOD and ask for their permission? 'Excuse me, I'd like to sell a high-tech biowarfare weapon to some men in turbans.'"

"You're not even sorry."

He shrugged. "You'd think I'd feel a twinge of guilt but I have to be honest. I don't. The government screwed me and I screwed it. What can I say? That's what it gets for doing business with the private sector. I didn't ask to be paid in purple hearts or silver stars but dollars. If it had paid me, all this could have been avoided."

"How'd you have anything left to sell?"

"You mean why didn't DOD seize what I made? The contract was classified, national security. Only a few assholes at DARPA even knew it existed. When the contracting agent showed up, he brought a couple of military types who he hadn't bothered to fully brief."

"No one except the agent knew what they were looking for?"

"Even he didn't know where to look for it. Just took what I gave him. All the important stuff was in my head anyway."

"Why didn't they recognize the virus when it showed up in Asia?"

"My strain was less lethal than that one. A mutation of Ebola combined with smallpox. It would put people in a coma for a few days then leave them temporarily blind. Tying up enemy transportation, hospitals and governments, while sparing civilians' lives. The perfect weapon. Someone must've re-engineered it. Figured out how to weaponize it."

"No one at Panacea knew what you'd done?"

"There was some turnover after the deal fell through. The ones that stayed got over it. What do they care if the government screws us? It's not like it was their money. The only one who started to get suspicious when the virus showed up was Don Hubbard. Gave me call in the middle of the night. Sounded like he was going to do something stupid."

"So White took care of him."

"That's what he was there for."

"You conspired with him to murder Hubbard."

"You lawyers always make things sound so bad."

I motioned toward White. "How would you make *that* sound?"

"That? That's just the sound of evolution. He couldn't mutate fast enough was his problem."

"What did you have on him?"

"Do you really think that bum had enough money to buy Panacea?"

"The whole thing was a sham?"

"No, he bought it, just with my money. I lent it to him, taking his stake in the company as collateral. It's all in some papers in my safe-deposit box."

I ignored whether such a contract was even enforceable, considering that it probably violated some law. I said, "What about Amelia?"

"What do you mean?"

"How did she fit into all of this?"

Marshall looked at me like I was crazy. I got the sinking feeling I'd made a huge mistake.

His eyes flashed a look of understanding. "Son, you're not as bright as I thought."

"You're not looking too smart either right now."

"Do you think I planned all of this? That I wanted Swindler to come crashing into us like that? Crazy sonofabitch was just supposed to spook Vicky. He was the one responsible for Mac's death, and I took care of him for you."

"You're a hero."

"Well, I don't want to be immodest, but I've always thought of myself as a man of action."

"Like the way you took care of Carver and Hubbard."

"I told you, Swindler did that."

"With your virus."

"You're not one of those guys who blames science, are you?" He pumped the shotgun's action bar, ejecting the two empty cartridges. "Don't mind this. I'm just cleaning up here. All this smoke is killing my sinuses. Listen, it sounds like I'm going to need a good lawyer, someone who doesn't give up, knows how to fight. You interested?" He reached into his bathrobe pocket and pulled out two orange cartridges. "Oh, I admit I doubted you at first. I hadn't seen your potential yet, your guts. A man like you...I'll pay whatever you want, double your hourly rate, triple it even. We can skip over the part about you being here, you know, to keep things from getting messy." He slid the cartridges into the shotgun's receiver and pumped the action bar again. "What do you say?"

I raised my pistol.

"What are you doing?" he said, keeping the shotgun lowered but slipping his finger from outside the trigger guard. "You wouldn't *shoot* someone, an old man, Amelia's uncle, a *client*."

I thought of the senator. I thought of Amelia. I thought of Mac. I said, "You're fired."

A high school counselor once told me, *Remember Hank, there's a difference between letting someone die and killing him.* At the time it made sense to me in my head, but I didn't feel it in my heart.

I mean, I *knew* that the person who had actually killed my brother Grady was the strung-out kid who had run that red light. He was the one everyone blamed and he was the one who was prosecuted. But let me ask you, what if *you* were the one who had caused your brother to be in that car at that intersection at that particular time, and *you* were the one who had been behind the wheel and had not seen the other driver coming, and *you* were the one who had remained uninjured and conscious after the accident, and *you* were the one who had realized your brother had severed his femoral artery causing him to gush blood, and *you* were the one who had learned to tie tourniquets in the Boy Scouts; but, for whatever inconceivable reason, you had simply *failed* to do anything? Would you blame yourself as if you had killed him? The end result was the same whether you had killed him or let him die, right?

Well, regardless of how you feel about it now sitting there in a comfortable chair in a library or an airport or on a beach, the fact is *I* had always blamed myself for Grady's death. The first few years after his funeral I'd buried my feelings of guilt, covering them with school or hobbies. Then, in college, when studying philosophy and religion, I'd been told the distinction between letting someone die and killing him was illusory, the result of a simple misunderstanding of what some theologians called the *pertinent moral principles*. This had caused my feelings of guilt to fester again, manifesting themselves as an unconscious urge toward unhappiness, leading me to later tank several stable relationships and quit a comfortable job as a teacher.

In law school, in torts class, I'd studied the various laws that didn't recognize a difference between letting someone die and killing him, like the state laws holding property owners responsible for failing to warn unsuspecting visitors of hidden dangers on their property. Or the few state laws imposing on bystanders a duty to assist a victim of a wrongful act if they can do so without danger to themselves. Or the more common state laws providing that, in assisted suicide cases, no meaningful distinction exists between a physician's allowing a patient to die and killing him. My feelings of guilt were unearthed and given definition and shape. They were finally given an identity. I tried to avoid the feelings through work, through defending those accused of crimes, defending myself. Seeing Mac bleed to death on Capitol Hill made me face my feelings, which had blossomed into a field of poisonous life-choking weeds, from which it seemed I would never escape. All that changed on that night with Marshall.

That night with Marshall I saw the light of my soul flicker and I refused to let it go out. I met the eternal footman and decided he wasn't such a bad guy. In short, I am here to tell you that, to me, there is a *world* of difference between letting someone die and killing him. I *wanted* to harm Marshall. I *intended* him harm and I *caused* him harm. It was a *decision*, which I do not regret, and for which I stand ready to be judged.

Chapter 37

I surfaced from a deep sleep at noon the next day and turned on the TV.

"The woman who accused Senator Serling's lawyer of jury tampering died last night," the news anchor said. "On April twelfth, Eugenia Carver told our own Holly Hickey that she'd accepted a bribe from now-deceased lawyer John MacPherson as a juror in a trial. The next day, investigators tried to interview Ms. Carver but she'd disappeared. She didn't reappear until last night, when she was admitted to Fairfax Hospital, suffering from a high fever, seizures and a skin rash. As doctors treated her, she reportedly told a nurse that John MacPherson hadn't bribed her, that she had been paid to say that by two men, and the men who had paid her were the ones who had poisoned her. Before a police officer could get their names, she lost consciousness and suffered a fatal stroke. Doctors have identified the cause of death as an extremely virulent strain of bacterial meningitis, accompanied by an acute case of septicemia, a form of blood poisoning. Investigators don't know how she contracted the diseases. Ms. Carver has no survivors, which has further baffled investigators, since she'd told Holly Hickey that she accepted the bribe from Mr. MacPherson to help her sick granddaughter. We now go to Holly, live in Middleburg, on a related story."

Holly Hickey stood beside a red mailbox shaped like a barn. Behind an iron gate, in a cul-de-sac, sat a half-dozen police cars, their red lights spinning.

The words *Double Homicide* flashed across the screen.

Holly Hickey lifted a microphone to her crimson mouth.

"Two men are dead this morning under mysterious circumstances. They were found shot to death in this Middleburg home of Senator Victoria Serling. An anonymous neighbor heard gunfire at two a.m. and called the police, who found the men in front of the home. Police are in the process of making a positive identification of the men. They've traced a shotgun found at the scene to the senator's husband, Dr. Lawrence Marshall, and a handgun found at the scene to Robert White of Cazenovia, New York, a suburb of Syracuse. They've also traced a rental car found near Dr. Marshall's home to Mr. White. Mr. White is the president of a biopharmaceutical company, Panacea, Inc. located in Cazenovia. Dr. Marshall is the former president of Panacea."

The anchorwoman said, "Holly, are you saying that the victims are Senator Serling's husband and this man Robert White?"

"The police aren't saying anything until the bodies have been identified and the families have been notified, but they did say they located Panacea's corporate jet at National Airport. The pilot told investigators he'd flown White to Washington late last night and the two were supposed to return to Syracuse this morning. He didn't know why White was visiting Washington, and investigators have not yet been able to locate anyone else who can answer that question. Apparently no one else was present at Marshall's home. Marshall's wife, Senator Serling, is in the hospital. Marshall's chauffeur, Walter Maddox, is visiting his family in California."

"Do the police have any idea what happened?"

"No one is saying on the record but, according to a confidential source within the Middleburg Police Department, both men sustained fatal gunshot wounds to the chest. One possible theory is White came to Marshall's home with a handgun, and Marshall tried to defend himself with a shotgun."

"Why would White fly from Syracuse with a gun to visit Marshall in the middle of the night?"

"Investigators aren't sure why these two men would even be talking. As you might recall, Marshall sold Panacea to White in early 2002. The understanding at the time was that Marshall sold the company at the insistence of his wife, then a Senatorial candidate. The reason was Panacea had at one time manufactured biowarfare agents, an unpopular line of business to Virginia voters, especially after the anthrax scare that had recently occurred."

"What about the fact Panacea is developing a vaccine for Harappa, a biowarfare agent that first appeared just before the attack on Senator Serling, who sits on the Select Committee on Terrorism?"

"That's a coincidence that has peaked the interest of investigators, especially in light of the fact that yesterday Panacea reported it has already developed an experimental vaccine to Harappa. The Middleburg Police Department, the Loudoun County Sheriff's Office and the Virginia State Police all emphasize they are unwilling to speculate about the two dead men, whose identities haven't even been confirmed."

"Sounds like the police are being careful. Do they know if Senator Serling knew anything about this?"

"The police haven't questioned the senator yet. It's unclear how she would have known anything about the men's meeting. She was awakened from her coma at about eight a.m. That would be five hours after the estimated time of the homicides. After demanding an expedited release she was driven to the Virginia Medical Examiner's Office in Fairfax to identify what is believed to be the body of her husband."

"As a matter of fact, Holly, I understand the senator is preparing to leave the Medical Examiner's Office right now. We go live to Fairfax."

The camera cut to a red brick building, whose parking lot was packed with TV news vans. A dozen men emerged from the building, wearing sunglasses and ear pieces. The men parted a sea of reporters, making way for Aaron and Amelia.

Then Senator Serling stepped into the sunlight and squinted. Cameras clicked and the shouting started. *Did the attack on you have anything to do with Harappa? Why would White want to kill your husband? Is it true Panacea created Harappa?* The men with the sunglasses escorted the senator and her companions to a black car with mirrored widows, which raced away.

I called Amelia.

"Oh, Hank."

"I'm sorry."

"It doesn't make sense."

"What are the police telling you?"

"They think maybe it was blackmail. Lawrence had half a million dollars in cash in a suitcase. Maybe White was the one."

"How's your aunt?"

"Hold on, she wants to talk to you."

Senator Serling said, "Mr. Fisher?"

"Hank."

"I understand you took a little trip yesterday."

"Where are you headed?"

"Amelia's house."

"Mind if I meet you there in an hour? I have to swing by my office first."

"Hank, yesterday my husband and I were on our way to meet my lawyer about a campaign finance violation. This morning I wake up to find a month has gone by, both my husband and lawyer are dead and I'm about to be indicted. I'm afraid I'm going to have to demand a meeting."

"How do you know that this Swindler person was the one who ran us down?" said Senator Serling.

She'd aged ten years since the night of Mac's death. Her blouse hung loose on her thin shoulders, her skin stretched taught over her pronounced cheekbones, and her shoulder-length blonde hair was gray at the roots. Amelia sat close by, her cheery yellow sweater set clashing with her reddened mascara-smudged eyes.

"I don't get it," Amelia said. "I thought you didn't find anything."

I avoided her stare and started from the beginning, laying a stack of Manila folders on the coffee table. It was my first real trial, except I had three judges.

Exhibit 1 was a copy of the *Minqua Messenger* newspaper article on the wall of Marshall's office, which I'd gotten from the Minqua Public Library. The first page indicated that among the cars Joseph F. Swindler Sr., had stolen in Marshall's hometown in 1959 was the car of one Dr. Abigail *Dorian* who appeared to be a relative of Marshall, since his middle name was Dorian. The second page said the thirteen-year-old boy who had been stealing cars with Joseph F. Swindler, Sr., had lived with Swindler, suggesting the boy was Swindler's son, although it was difficult to be sure since the boy's name had not been released due to his age.

Exhibit 2 was a copy of Joseph F. Swindler, Jr.'s criminal records as an adult, which Roger had gotten for me several weeks before. The records showed Swindler had been charged with a series of violent crimes, everything from assault to reckless driving. Each time the charges were either dismissed upon Swindler's completion of some community service or counseling, or he pled guilty to a lesser offense and avoided jail time.

Amelia fumed. Senator Serling was confused. "So this guy's a bad apple. What does he have to do with Doyle and Hassan?"

I handed her Exhibit 3. It began with copy of Swindler's credit reports, which Roger had also gotten for me. The reports showed some undergrad student loans, which he'd had some trouble paying, and then two long periods of employment, first with Federated Petroleum and then with Globex. The next page of the exhibit was a letter of resignation from Swindler to the president of Globex. The letter said Swindler strongly denied any allegations of theft or fraud, and that he was quitting his position as vice-president of personnel in order to pursue *other business opportunities*. The exhibit ended with the spreadsheets I had found in Swindler's office drawer at Panacea. They contained the names and Social Security numbers of hundreds of employees, including a Doyle and a Hassan.

Everyone was speechless.

"Once he had the identities," I said, "he found someone from Syracuse to play Hassan, and someone from DC to play Doyle."

Aaron frowned at the documents. "How did you get these, Hank?"

I didn't respond.

"From Swindler's files," Amelia said.

"He just gave them to you?" Aaron said to me.

"No," Amelia said, "he took them...from Swindler's office."

The senator furrowed her brow. "Why would this Swindler person have something against *me*?"

This was where things were going to get tricky. "He wanted you to stop anyone from investigating Panacea, which had made a biowarfare agent that was the predecessor of Harappa."

This last little tidbit didn't phase her. Obviously she understood Panacea had, at one time, been a prolific creator of biowarfare agents. Instead she said, "Why would *he* care about Panacea?"

I handed her Exhibit 4, which was a file of legal records, again, courtesy of Roger, showing how Joseph F. Swindler, Jr., had changed his name to Robert Joseph White shortly before he purchased Panacea.

While she was still reeling from this I handed her Exhibit 5, which began with a copy of a Syracuse newspaper article reporting that, in the past week, a retired Panacea executive had died under mysterious circumstances. Dr. Ronald Hubbard, the company's former vice-president of government contracts, had somehow come down with an extremely virulent strain of bacterial meningitis.

"Like the foreperson in the Bustamonte trial?" said Aaron. "Eugenia Carver?"

I nodded. "It's one of the diseases Panacea is working with. They talk about it on their website." I handed the senator the rest of Exhibit 5, a copy of the page from Panacea's website and a copy of a newspaper article reporting Ms. Carver had also died from bacterial meningitis.

"Hold on," said the senator. "*When* did Panacea supposedly make Harappa? They haven't had a government contract do to that sort of thing since Lawrence was there. You're saying he was in cahoots with this White person?" She looked at Aaron and tried a joke. "Frankly I can imagine why he changed his name from Swindler. Not the best name for a businessman."

Aaron didn't laugh, and neither did anyone else.

"Especially a businessman who had grown up with your husband." I handed her Exhibit 6. It began with two Minqua High

School yearbook photos showing Swindler was a freshman when Marshall was a senior. The exhibit ended with bankruptcy documents I had gotten from a federal court records database on the internet right before the meeting. They showed Swindler had filed for bankruptcy only a few months before buying Panacea.

"This is absurd." The senator stood.

Aaron put his hand on her forearm. "Victoria, Hank has put himself at risk to get this information. *Great* risk to both his safety and his career. The least we can do is hear him out."

The senator sat back down. "No one has ever accused me of running from the truth. So Swindler had some financial problems, and maybe he didn't have the background necessary to run a pharmaceutical company. Maybe Lawrence's judgment was clouded since he was doing business with an old friend. That doesn't mean they somehow conspired with each other after the sale."

Her voice was thin, as if even she doubted what she was saying.

"In fact," I stated, "Lawrence denied ever speaking to the new owner of Panacea."

"That's right. Said it wouldn't look good to have him still involved with the company, given its history."

I handed her my last exhibit, a piece of paper with a phone number written on it. "This is White's cell phone number. I'm pretty sure the account is listed under his old name, Joe Swindler. At least that's the name he uses in his voice-mail greeting, when you call the number. When the police check the *Call History* feature on the phone they're going to see dozens of calls to and from Marshall over the past few weeks. I'm guessing they'll find a lot more when they subpoena the phone company's records."

"So the man called Lawrence for advice? You can't prove they were planning something illegal."

There it was. The juror had all the evidence before her and still wasn't willing to convict. Wasn't even *able* to convict, probably. There was nothing else I could do. I stood up and started for the door, then paused. Now I was the one acting like Columbo.

"You know all those paintings Lawrence has of birds?" I said. "And the little statues everywhere?"

"Quail," the senator said, gazing out Amelia's large bay window. She sighed. "He loved them. Spent his whole life collecting them."

"They're bobwhites," I said. "That's how Swindler came up with the name."

The senator turned to me and stared, her cheeks draining of color. Then she leaned forward and buried her face in her hands. Amelia stood up and put a hand on her aunt's shoulder.

"I'm sorry," I said to Amelia.

"Are you?" she said.

"Amelia, please."

"All you care about is the bad guy's dead."

"The guy who sold Harappa to al-Qaeda helped murder Eugenia Carver, Don Hubbard and my best friend, and committed high treason against the United States."

"He was also her husband and my uncle. He should be in jail awaiting trial, not lying in a freezer in some morgue."

"Amelia," said the senator.

Amelia lost control of her voice. "He lied to me, Aunt Vicky. I asked him if he'd learned anything when he went to Panacea and he said no."

"But I couldn't...I couldn't—"

"You couldn't what? Trust me? Because you thought I was part of some evil scheme with Lawrence? Everything out of your mouth was a lie...helping my aunt, stopping an epidemic, not involving my uncle. All lies. Well, you know what? I'm done listening to them." She squared her shoulders and lifted her chin, like her aunt. I couldn't believe it. She was waiting for me to show myself out, to leave her life forever. Like it was as easy as walking through a door.

At various points during the following weeks I talked to the MPD, the FBI, the CDC, the US Attorney's Office, three District Attorneys' offices and once, when I was too demoralized to care to Holly Hickey. I hated myself in the morning. When the questions finally stopped coming I started piecing my life back together. Paying bills, doing laundry, grocery shopping. I even dusted off my running shoes. Anything to keep a step ahead of thoughts of despair about Amelia.

She'd been right. I'd lied to her to find out if she'd been leaking information to White. I'd used her and then betrayed her. The fact I'd realized afterward I loved her wouldn't mean anything to her. I had to move on. Not one of my stronger suits, but there it was.

So one Saturday night I picked up two pizzas, a half-gallon of ice cream, a two-liter bottle of root beer and a six-pack of beer. The MacPhersons had returned from Cape Cod, their front lawn already littered with bikes. In the back yard a boy rounded

second base, arms windmilling. As I walked up the driveway a
tennis ball flew over the roof, bounced off the Blazer and rolled to
my feet. Tommy stepped between some bushes, face tan, nose
peeling, lacrosse stick over his shoulder. Buster followed, jaw
flapping, string of drool trailing. Slobber from the tennis ball dripped
between my thumb and index finger.

"This isn't the home run ball, is it?"

"Sorry, Uncle Hank. We have to take turns playing with
Buster or he, like, totally freaks out when there's a hit."

I tossed the ball to Tommy, who cradled away the slobber
then launched it back over the roof. Buster dove into the bushes
and Tommy was gone. Clare took his place on a mini mountain
bike. Black and pink with a matching water bottle. Under her
helmet sprouted chestnut bangs.

"You on Buster duty too?" I said.

"Baseball is so immature. What kind of ice cream did
you get?"

"I know you used to like double chocolate fudge, but I thought
you might be too sophisticated for that now."

Her eyes widened.

"So I just got— What did I get?" I said. "Oh, yeah, double
chocolate fudge."

"What kind of pizza?"

"One anchovies and liver, the other goat cheese and
pineapple."

"Hank!" She lurched for the boxes, flinging them open. "One
plain, one supreme."

I shrugged.

"When are you going to grow up?" she said, sliding onto her
seat and peddling unsteadily around the side of the house.

It was a good question.

The kitchen table was set under an open window dressed
with white curtains ballooning in the breeze. Penny stood at the

sink, washing a head of lettuce. She put the pizzas in the oven, got two beers from the fridge and took a seat across from me.

Through the window came the pop of the bat, the cries of teammates and the low yelps of Buster. I remembered those warm summer nights as a boy in Cleveland, playing kick-the-can or ghost-in-the-graveyard with Grady and the kids on the block after darkness had fallen, waiting for our parents to call us in.

As we sipped our beers Penny told me how she'd decided to take a part-time job at Fran's stationery store in Alexandria to get out of the house. Her dad had agreed to babysit after school. He was selling his house in Boston and helping Penny convert her basement into a bedroom. Widow and widower making a go of it.

"All in all," she said, "things could be worse."

I told her the same story about Dr. Marshall and Bob White that I'd told Senator Serling. Penny listened quietly. When I was done she said, "Are you sure Dr. Marshall and this White guy were the ones?"

I nodded.

"I know what I said before about how catching the guys responsible won't bring back Mac," she said, "but I can't help feeling glad they're dead. You probably think that's horrible."

"I think you deserve to feel any way you want."

The sun was disappearing behind a row of oaks. On TV a news program called *Order in the Court!* started. The program's host introduced his guest, a local law professor.

"First case on the docket," said the host. "Panacea pandemonium! The verdict is in, say federal investigators. The people of Panacea knew nothing of past-president Lawrence Marshall's manufacture of biowarfare agent Harappa. In an act of amends, Panacea has given the government the antidote to the ailment for free. Shipments of the serum have arrived in Asia, dropping the death toll of the disease."

Footage showed a woman in a white lab coat inserting a syringe into the arm of a copper-skinned boy who lay motionless in an old man's arms. The boy stirred, then opened his big brown eyes, turning his gaunt face toward the camera.

The host turned to the law professor. "Now that the taint has been taken from the company and its financial future again appears viable, one problem persists: to whom should control of the company revert?"

"If White paid even a few hundred thousand dollars to Marshall," the professor said, "a court might find that constituted adequate consideration. In that case, White would have been the legal owner of the company and, because he had no heirs, his interest would revert to New York State, which would probably sell the company."

"What if White didn't pay Marshall anything? What if the sale was a fraud?"

"I don't see how Marshall could've defrauded White if White was in on the scam. Let's assume it was the federal government Marshall and White were intending to defraud. The court would probably find Marshall retained ownership, especially if no money changed hands. From what I understand, Marshall had no last will and testament and no living blood relatives, which would mean ownership of the company would go to his wife."

"I believe the selfless Senator Serling has already said that, if that were the case, she would forsake her good fortune, sell the company and give the proceeds to a fund for the victims of Harappa."

"That would certainly be her choice and probably a smart one, politically."

The host slammed down a gavel. "Sustained! Senator Serling saves her skin."

Outside it was dark. Penny stepped onto the deck and called her kids to dinner.

"Next case on the docket, US Attorney Rowe eats crow!" The host looked at the professor. "What? I'm not above a good rhyme."

Footage showed US Attorney Martina Rowe standing in front of a blue curtain on which hung the emblem of the Department of Justice. To her left her stood the DOJ flag, Assistant US Attorney Guerrero and Agent Wang. To her right stood the American flag, Aaron and Senator Serling.

Rowe stepped up to a podium. "Several weeks ago my office obtained probable cause to believe Senator Serling was involved in a campaign finance violation. As a result we launched an investigation of her campaign finance office. Last week certain facts materialized shedding new light on events. Over the weekend I met with Aaron Weissman, counsel for the senator. Mr. Weissman presented evidence exculpating the senator and inculpating her husband, Dr. Lawrence Marshall, and Panacea President Robert White. In light of this evidence I have decided to end my office's investigation of the senator. At this point I'll take any questions."

"Senator," Holly Hickey said, "did you have any idea your husband's sale of Panacea to White was a sham?"

Rowe allowed the senator to step up to the podium. "As you might recall," Senator Serling said, "I was the one who insisted Lawrence sell Panacea. I had no idea the sale was a sham. I regret trusting him and I apologize to the people of Virginia. I apologize to the people of the world for not knowing what he was doing. I was a fool."

"Did al-Qaeda buy Harappa from your husband?"

"With my help federal investigators were able to find a record of a wire transfer from a French bank during the months following the cancellation of a US government contract with Panacea. That wire transfer led to the identification of a Saudi businessman suspected of purchasing, from my husband, a virus that was essentially the predecessor of Harappa. After interrogating that man, investigators were able to identify and locate the al-Qaeda operatives who developed and released Harappa. Some of those operatives were recently arrested in Pakistan."

"How did you figure out what your husband and White were doing?"

"One of my attorneys, Hank Fisher, discovered the conspiracy. Mr. Fisher risked his own safety to do so. I owe him a great deal."

"Has the president contacted you about becoming the new CIA director?"

"I'm just happy to be with what's left of my family."

She extended an arm and the camera pulled back to show standing off to the side, a brown-haired woman about her own age, who looked like her sister, and then there she was, beautiful as ever. Amelia. An ember of hope began to glow in the depths of my heart. Then it darkened when I saw who stood beside her. Good ol' Brock Aurelia. The guy loved cameras.

The deck door slid shut and the kids stomped into the kitchen.

Tommy threw down his baseball glove. "The game wasn't over."

Clare took off her biking helmet. "We're not even hungry."

"It's not fair."

I finished my beer and turned off the TV.

Maybe things would return to normal after all.

In time I stopped searching the sidewalks for Amelia's forgiving face. I stopped waiting for the phone to ring. I stopped lying awake, thinking, remembering, hoping. I focused on work.

Senator Serling had solved my financial problems by paying for my efforts after Marshall had fired me, and for giving me a nationally televised endorsement. Clients came to me in droves.

They came by phone, by e-mail, by foot. They came telling stories of surprise visits from government investigators, stories of subpoenas, stories of threats of prosecution. They came demanding they were innocent, or admitting they were guilty but able to pay me a lot of money to get them off. I turned them all away. Fed up with the memories of how work used to be, and daunted by the task of living up to Mac's standards, I pointed them in the direction of Aaron.

Instead I called Earl, the office building's handyman, who showed up one fine summer morning with a tool belt hanging low on his waist. We stood outside, staring at the sign Mac had once made me polish.

"He was some guy," Earl said.

"With shoes too big to fill," I said.

"They say on TV you're a hero."

"They don't know what they're talking about."

"You saved all those people."

"Who are you going to believe, Earl, them or me?"

"So what you're saying is you're not a hero? You're a loser? A coward?"

"I believe the right word is 'schmuck.'"

"All right then. Welcome to the club."

He took out his power drill and I went inside to finish writing letters to Mac's clients. After a while there was a knock on my door. "What's the damage?" I said without looking up.

"Are you talking to the guy mooning everyone on Mass Ave?" Amelia said.

I stood.

She wore a white cotton sun dress and white sandals. Dark crescents hung under her eyes. "I just came to say I'm sorry."

"I'm sorry too. I was wrong. Can you give me another chance?"

"We'll see. After a brief probation period."

Then she dropped her purse on my desk and came to me. Her kiss was full of the most wonderful contradictions: eager yet patient, passionate yet tender, brief yet lingering. My heart finally stopped asking questions, except for one. "What about what's-his-name?"

"Brock? He proposed again and I told him 'no' again. Then I told him about you. He didn't take that so well."

"The kid's always been jealous of me."

She laughed and asked me if I'd had lunch yet. She said she hadn't eaten in days. I told her we'd have to fix that. As she was getting her purse she noticed a letter from the Office of Bar Counsel on my desk. "Don't tell me you're in trouble again."

I explained that Dr. Marshall had e-mailed a midnight complaint to the OBC in case White failed, and the OBC had decided to look into the matter once it learned the FBI had placed me at Panacea the day before the murders. "Plus there's a latent print on the shotgun."

"Yours?" Amelia raised an eyebrow. Then she smiled. "Sounds like you need an alibi for the night of the murders. Maybe someone to explain how she let you handle the gun a couple weeks ago."

"You'd do that for me? It was your uncle."

"Step-uncle. Besides, you're more a victim than a criminal. He was the criminal. He had to be stopped. What're they going to do to you?"

"I don't think the Madison County DA's Office will prosecute. Panacea wants to put the whole mess behind it. As for DOJ, it's sick of being slammed by Congress for gunning for your aunt."

"What about the Bar Counsel people?"

"They'll petition the Board on Professional Responsibility for a hearing."

"But you stopped a world-wide epidemic."

I shrugged. "I broke the rules."

"It's so unfair. Can you win?"

"Aaron thinks they'll suspend my license for a while. He agreed to represent me for free."

"What will you do?"

"He told me to take a long vacation and then come to work for Pound & Shields. He'll let me do research until I get reinstated."

"That's great. Then she noticed the look on my face. "Isn't it?"

"I thought maybe I'd try something different for a while."

"You're not going to write a novel, are you?"

As I was giving her a dirty look, Earl came in. "All set, boss."

I took Amelia's hand and led her down the hall. Outside a giant maple whispered, its yellow-green leaves waving hello. Beside my front door hung a new sign, made of bronze like the other one but smaller. Around it you could see an inch of dark stone that had not been bleached by the sun.

"Fisher & Lynch?" Amelia said.

"Roger gave me top billing," I said.

"He's a lawyer?"

"I teach him what the law is. He teaches me how people break it. Together we're DC's newest white collar crime investigation firm."

"There's a market for that sort of thing?"

"Are you kidding? With accounting firms like Arthur Andersen? Companies like Enron, WorldCom and Tyco? Executives like Ken Lay, Bernie Ebbers and Dennis Kozlowski? Jeff Skilling, Andy Fastow, Martha Stewart—"

"All right, already. So good to know business is booming."

"Aaron's already got a job for us."

I told her about the secretary who had helped two men steal company blueprints for precision tools needed to repair a fighter jet engine. The men had later sold the blueprints to a competitor.

When I'd told my father I'd be helping Roger with the law he'd said, "What do you know? You are going to be a law professor, after all." My mother had said, "You're going to be a what? Nobody likes a snoop, dear. It's only one step above being a pawnbroker."

What Amelia said was, "Basically, you two are going to play Hardy Boys for a while until you get your head together again."

"Are you upset?"

"Why?" She slipped an arm around me. "I'm going to have my own little Parker Stevenson."

Earl offered me the invoice and a pen.

I know what you're thinking. How could I give up a promising career at Pound & Shields revering the law for a sketchy one bending it? Searching the personal assets of an accountant who has committed one too many bookkeeping errors. Retrieving company data from the laptop of a worker who has quit to join a competitor. Installing hidden cameras in the home of a business partner who was just busted for possession of prescription painkillers. The truth is that before my recent adventures I'd never broken the law. And it didn't look like I was very good at getting away with it. But I was always willing to learn.

~End~

About the Author

Mike Langan writes novels that draw on his experience as a former litigator in Washington, D.C., and Syracuse, N.Y. He received his J.D. from George Mason University School of Law, where he was notes editor of the *Law Review*. Before becoming a lawyer, Mike received his M.F.A. in creative writing from George Mason University, where he was a graduate fellow, and his B.A. in philosophy from Colgate University, from which he graduated *cum laude*. He has published several short stories and legal articles, and has taught college courses in both English and law. He lives with his wife and two daughters in the Syracuse area. *Ready for the Defense* is his second novel.